Katherine Mansfield – The Short Stories
Volume 3

The short story is often viewed as an inferior relation to the Novel. But it is an art in itself. To take a story and distil its essence into fewer pages while keeping character and plot rounded and driven is not an easy task. Many try and many fail.

In this series we look at short stories from many of our most accomplished writers. Miniature masterpieces with a lot to say. In this volume we examine some of the short stories of Katherine Mansfield.

She was born on 14th October 1888 into a prominent family in Wellington, New Zealand the middle child of five.

A gifted Cellist, at one point she thought she might take it up professionally. However she had a gift for writing that was slowly developing and her first writings were published in school magazines

At 19 Katherine left for Great Britain and met the modernist writers D.H. Lawrence and Virginia Woolf with whom she became close friends.

She travelled to Europe before returning to New Zealand in 1906 she began to write the short stories that she would later become famous for. Her stories often focus on moments of disruption and frequently open rather abruptly.

By 1908 she had returned to London and to a rather more bohemian lifestyle. A passionate affair resulted in her becoming pregnant but married off instead to an older man who she left the same evening with the marriage unconsummated. She was then to miscarry and be cut out of her mothers' will (allegedly because of her lesbianism).

In 1911 she was to start a relationship with John Middleton Murry a magazine editor and although it was volatile it enabled her to write some of her best stories.

During the First World War Mansfield contracted extrapulmonary tuberculosis, which rendered any return or visit to New Zealand impossible and led to her death at the tender age of 34 on January 9th 1923 in Fontainebleau, France

Index Of Contents

BANK HOLIDAY

A stout man with a pink face wears dingy white flannel trousers, a blue coat with a pink handkerchief showing, and a straw hat much too small for him, perched at the back of his head. He plays the guitar. A little chap in white canvas shoes, his face hidden under a felt hat like a broken wing, breathes into a flute; and a tall thin fellow, with bursting over-ripe button boots, draws ribbons— long, twisted, streaming ribbons—of tune out of a fiddle. They stand, unsmiling, but not serious, in the broad sunlight opposite the fruit-shop; the pink spider of a hand beats the guitar, the little squat hand, with a brass-and-turquoise ring, forces the reluctant flute, and the fiddler's arm tries to saw the fiddle in two.

A crowd collects, eating oranges and bananas, tearing off the skins, dividing, sharing. One young girl has even a basket of strawberries, but she does not eat them. "Aren't they dear!" She stares at the tiny pointed fruits as if she were afraid of them. The Australian soldier laughs. "Here, go on, there's not more than a mouthful." But he doesn't want her to eat them, either. He likes to watch her little frightened face, and her puzzled eyes lifted to his: "Aren't they a price!" He pushes out his chest and grins. Old fat women in velvet bodices—old dusty pin-cushions—lean old hags like worn umbrellas with a quivering bonnet on top; young women, in muslins, with hats that might have grown on hedges, and high pointed shoes; men in khaki, sailors, shabby clerks, young Jews in fine cloth suits with padded shoulders and wide trousers, "hospital boys" in blue—the sun discovers them—the loud, bold music holds them together in one big knot for a moment. The young ones are larking, pushing each other on and off the pavement, dodging, nudging; the old ones are talking: "So I said to 'im, if you wants the doctor to yourself, fetch 'im, says I."

"An' by the time they was cooked there wasn't so much as you could put in the palm of me 'and!"

The only ones who are quiet are the ragged children. They stand, as close up to the musicians as they can get, their hands behind their backs, their eyes big. Occasionally a leg hops, an arm wags. A tiny staggerer, overcome, turns round twice, sits down solemn, and then gets up again.

"Ain't it lovely?" whispers a small girl behind her hand.

And the music breaks into bright pieces, and joins together again, and again breaks, and is dissolved, and the crowd scatters, moving slowly up the hill.

At the corner of the road the stalls begin.

"Ticklers! Tuppence a tickler! 'Ool 'ave a tickler? Tickle 'em up, boys." Little soft brooms on wire handles. They are eagerly bought by the soldiers.

"Buy a golliwog! Tuppence a golliwog!"

"Buy a jumping donkey! All alive-oh!"

"Su-perior chewing gum. Buy something to do, boys."

"Buy a rose. Give 'er a rose, boy. Roses, lady?"

"Fevvers! Fevvers!" They are hard to resist. Lovely, streaming feathers, emerald green, scarlet, bright blue, canary yellow. Even the babies wear feathers threaded through their bonnets.

And an old woman in a three-cornered paper hat cries as if it were her final parting advice, the only way of saving yourself or of bringing him to his senses: "Buy a three-cornered 'at, my dear, an' put it on!"

It is a flying day, half sun, half wind. When the sun goes in a shadow flies over; when it comes out again it is fiery. The men and women feel it burning their backs, their breasts and their arms; they feel their bodies expanding, coming alive...so that they make large embracing gestures, lift up their arms, for nothing, swoop down on a girl, blurt into laughter.

Lemonade! A whole tank of it stands on a table covered with a cloth; and lemons like blunted fishes blob in the yellow water. It looks solid, like a jelly, in the thick glasses. Why can't they drink it without spilling it? Everybody spills it, and before the glass is handed back the last drops are thrown in a ring.

Round the ice-cream cart, with its striped awning and bright brass cover, the children cluster. Little tongues lick, lick round the cream trumpets, round the squares. The cover is lifted, the wooden spoon plunges in; one shuts one's eyes to feel it, silently scrunching.

"Let these little birds tell you your future!" She stands beside the cage, a shrivelled ageless Italian, clasping and unclasping her dark claws. Her face, a treasure of delicate carving, is tied in a green-and-gold scarf. And inside their prison the love-birds flutter towards the papers in the seed-tray.

"You have great strength of character. You will marry a red-haired man and have three children. Beware of a blonde woman." Look out! Look out! A motor-car driven by a fat chauffeur comes rushing down the hill. Inside there a blonde woman, pouting, leaning forward—rushing through your life—beware! beware!

"Ladies and gentlemen, I am an auctioneer by profession, and if what I tell you is not the truth I am liable to have my licence taken away from me and a heavy imprisonment." He holds the licence across his chest; the sweat pours down his face into his paper collar; his eyes look glazed. When he takes off his hat there is a deep pucker of angry flesh on his forehead. Nobody buys a watch.

Look out again! A huge barouche comes swinging down the hill with two old, old babies inside. She holds up a lace parasol; he sucks the knob of his cane, and the fat old bodies roll together as the cradle rocks, and the steaming horse leaves a trail of manure as it ambles down the hill.

Under a tree, Professor Leonard, in cap and gown, stands beside his banner. He is here "for one day," from the London, Paris and Brussels Exhibition, to tell your fortune from your face. And he stands, smiling encouragement, like a clumsy dentist. When the big men, romping and swearing a moment before, hand across their sixpence, and stand before him, they are suddenly serious, dumb, timid, almost blushing as the Professor's quick hand notches the printed card. They are like little children caught playing in a forbidden garden by the owner, stepping from behind a tree.

The top of the hill is reached. How hot it is! How fine it is! The public-house is open, and the crowd presses in. The mother sits on the pavement edge with her baby, and the father brings her out a glass of dark, brownish stuff, and then savagely elbows his way in again. A reek of beer floats from the public-house, and a loud clatter and rattle of voices.

The wind has dropped, and the sun burns more fiercely than ever. Outside the two swing-doors there is a thick mass of children like flies at the mouth of a sweet-jar.

And up, up the hill come the people, with ticklers and golliwogs, and roses and feathers. Up, up they thrust into the light and heat, shouting, laughing, squealing, as though they were being pushed by something, far below, and by the sun, far ahead of them—drawn up into the full, bright, dazzling radiance to...what?

THE LADY'S MAID

Eleven o'clock. A knock at the door... I hope I haven't disturbed you, madam. You weren't asleep—were you? But I've just given my lady her tea, and there was such a nice cup over, I thought, perhaps...

...Not at all, madam. I always make a cup of tea last thing. She drinks it in bed after her prayers to warm her up. I put the kettle on when she kneels down and I say to it, "Now you needn't be in too much of a hurry to say your prayers." But it's always boiling before my lady is half through. You see, madam, we know such a lot of people, and they've all got to be prayed for—every one. My lady keeps a list of the names in a little red book. Oh dear! whenever some one new has been to see us and my lady says afterwards, "Ellen, give me my little red book," I feel quite wild, I do. "There's another," I think, "keeping her out of her bed in all weathers." And she won't have a cushion, you know, madam; she kneels on the hard carpet. It fidgets me something dreadful to see her, knowing her as I do. I've tried to cheat her; I've spread out the eiderdown. But the first time I did it—oh, she gave me such a look—holy it was, madam. "Did our Lord have an eiderdown, Ellen?" she said. But—I was younger at the time—I felt inclined to say, "No, but our Lord wasn't your age, and he didn't know what it was to have your lumbago." Wicked—wasn't it? But she's too good, you know, madam. When I tucked her up just now and seen—saw her lying back, her hands outside and her head on the pillow—so pretty—I couldn't help thinking, "Now you look just like your dear mother when I laid her out!"

...Yes, madam, it was all left to me. Oh, she did look sweet. I did her hair, soft-like, round her forehead, all in dainty curls, and just to one side of her neck I put a bunch of most beautiful purple pansies. Those pansies made a picture of her, madam! I shall never forget them. I thought tonight, when I looked at my lady, "Now, if only the pansies was there no one could tell the difference."

...Only the last year, madam. Only after she'd got a little—well—feeble as you might say. Of course, she was never dangerous; she was the sweetest old lady. But how it took her was—she thought she'd lost something. She couldn't keep still, she couldn't settle. All day long she'd be up and down, up and down; you'd meet her everywhere,—on the stairs, in the porch, making for the kitchen. And she'd look up at you, and she'd say—just like a child, "I've lost it, I've lost it." "Come along," I'd say, "come along, and I'll lay out your patience for you." But she'd catch me by the hand—I was a favourite of hers—and whisper, "Find it for me, Ellen. Find it for me." Sad, wasn't it?

...No, she never recovered, madam. She had a stroke at the end. Last words she ever said was—very slow, "Look in—the—Look—in—" And then she was gone.

...No, madam, I can't say I noticed it. Perhaps some girls. But you see, it's like this, I've got nobody but my lady. My mother died of consumption when I was four, and I lived with my grandfather, who kept a hair-dresser's shop. I used to spend all my time in the shop under a table dressing my doll's hair—copying the assistants, I suppose. They were ever so kind to me. Used to make me little wigs, all colours, the latest fashions and all. And there I'd sit all day, quiet as quiet—the customers never knew. Only now and again I'd take my peep from under the table-cloth.

... But one day I managed to get a pair of scissors and—would you believe it, madam? I cut off all my hair; snipped it off all in bits, like the little monkey I was. Grandfather was furious! He caught hold of the tongs—I shall never forget it—grabbed me by the hand and shut my fingers in them. "That'll teach you!" he said. It was a fearful burn. I've got the mark of it today.

...Well, you see, madam, he'd taken such pride in my hair. He used to sit me up on the counter, before the customers came, and do it something beautiful—big, soft curls and waved over the top. I remember the assistants standing round, and me ever so solemn with the penny grandfather gave me to hold while it was being done... But he always took the penny back afterwards. Poor grandfather! Wild, he was, at the fright I'd made of myself. But he frightened me that time. Do you know what I did, madam? I ran away. Yes, I did, round the corners, in and out, I don't know how far I didn't run. Oh, dear, I must have looked a sight, with my hand rolled up in my pinny and my hair sticking out. People must have laughed when they saw me...

...No, madam, grandfather never got over it. He couldn't bear the sight of me after. Couldn't eat his dinner, even, if I was there. So my aunt took me. She was a cripple, an upholstress. Tiny! She had to stand on the sofas when she wanted to cut out the backs. And it was helping her I met my lady...

...Not so very, madam. I was thirteen, turned. And I don't remember ever feeling—well—a child, as you might say. You see there was my uniform, and one thing and another. My lady put me into collars and cuffs from the first. Oh yes—once I did! That was—funny! It was like this. My lady had her two little nieces staying with her—we were at Sheldon at the time—and there was a fair on the common.

"Now, Ellen," she said, "I want you to take the two young ladies for a ride on the donkeys." Off we went; solemn little loves they were; each had a hand. But when we came to the donkeys they were too shy to go on. So we stood and watched instead. Beautiful those donkeys were! They were the first I'd seen out of a cart—for pleasure as you might say. They were a lovely silver-grey, with little red saddles and blue bridles and bells jing-a-jingling on their ears. And quite big girls—older than me, even—were riding them, ever so gay. Not at all common, I don't mean, madam, just enjoying themselves. And I don't know what it was, but the way the little feet went, and the eyes—so gentle—and the soft ears—made me want to go on a donkey more than anything in the world!

...Of course, I couldn't. I had my young ladies. And what would I have looked like perched up there in my uniform? But all the rest of the day it was donkeys—donkeys on the brain with me. I felt I should have burst if I didn't tell some one; and who was there to tell? But when I went to bed—I was sleeping in Mrs. James's bedroom, our cook that was, at the time—as soon as the lights was out, there they were, my donkeys, jingling along, with their neat little feet and sad eyes... Well, madam, would you believe it, I waited for a long time and pretended to be asleep, and then suddenly I sat up and called out as loud as I could, "I do want to go on a donkey. I do want a donkey-ride!" You see, I had to say it, and I thought they wouldn't laugh at me if they knew I was only dreaming. Artful—wasn't it? Just what a silly child would think...

...No, madam, never now. Of course, I did think of it at one time. But it wasn't to be. He had a little flower-shop just down the road and across from where we was living. Funny—wasn't it? And me such a one for flowers. We were having a lot of company at the time, and I was in and out of the shop more often than not, as the saying is. And Harry and I (his name was Harry) got to quarrelling about how things ought to be arranged—and that began it. Flowers! you wouldn't believe it, madam, the flowers he used to bring me. He'd stop at nothing. It was lilies-of-the-valley more than once, and I'm not exaggerating! Well, of course, we were going to be married and live over the shop, and it was all going to be just so, and I was to have the window to arrange... Oh, how I've done that window of a Saturday! Not really, of course, madam, just dreaming, as you might say. I've done it for Christmas—motto in holly, and all—and I've had my Easter lilies with a gorgeous star all daffodils in the middle. I've hung—well, that's enough of that. The day came he was to call for me to choose the furniture. Shall I ever forget it? It was a Tuesday. My lady wasn't quite herself that afternoon. Not that she'd said anything, of course; she never does or will. But I knew by the way that she kept wrapping herself up and asking me if it was cold—and her little nose looked...pinched. I didn't like leaving her; I knew I'd be worrying all the time. At last I asked her if she'd rather I put it off. "Oh no, Ellen," she said, "you mustn't mind about me. You mustn't disappoint your young man." And so cheerful, you know, madam, never thinking about herself. It made me feel worse than ever. I began to wonder...then she dropped her handkerchief and began to stoop down to pick it up herself—a thing she never did. "Whatever are you doing!" I cried, running to stop her. "Well," she said, smiling, you know, madam, "I shall have to begin to practise." Oh, it was all I could do not to burst out crying. I went over to the dressing-table and made believe to rub up the silver, and I couldn't keep myself in, and I asked her if she'd rather I...didn't get married. "No, Ellen," she said—that was her voice, madam, like I'm giving you—"No, Ellen, not for the wide world!" But while she said it, madam—I was looking in her glass; of course, she didn't know I could see her—she put her little hand on her heart just like her dear mother used to, and lifted her eyes... Oh, madam!

When Harry came I had his letters all ready, and the ring and a ducky little brooch he'd given me—a silver bird it was, with a chain in its beak, and on the end of the chain a heart with a dagger. Quite the thing! I opened the door to him. I never gave him time for a word. "There you are," I said. "Take them all back," I said, "it's all over. I'm not going to marry you," I said, "I can't leave my lady." White! he turned as white as a woman. I had to slam the door, and there I stood, all of a tremble, till I knew he had gone. When I opened the door—believe me or not, madam—that man was gone! I ran out into the road just as I was, in my apron and my house-shoes, and there I stayed in the middle of the road...staring. People must have laughed if they saw me...

...Goodness gracious!—What's that? It's the clock striking! And here I've been keeping you awake. Oh, madam, you ought to have stopped me... Can I tuck in your feet? I always tuck in my lady's feet, every night, just the same. And she says, "Good night, Ellen. Sleep sound and wake early!" I don't know what I should do if she didn't say that, now.

...Oh dear, I sometimes think...whatever should I do if anything were to... But, there, thinking's no good to any one—is it, madam? Thinking won't help. Not that I do it often. And if ever I do I pull myself up sharp, "Now, then, Ellen. At it again—you silly girl! If you can't find anything better to do than to start thinking!..."

THE DOLL'S HOUSE

When dear old Mrs. Hay went back to town after staying with the Burnells she sent the children a doll's house. It was so big that the carter and Pat carried it into the courtyard, and there it stayed, propped up on two wooden boxes beside the feed-room door. No harm could come of it; it was summer. And perhaps the smell of paint would have gone off by the time it had to be taken in. For, really, the smell of paint coming from that doll's house ("Sweet of old Mrs. Hay, of course; most sweet and generous!")—but the smell of paint was quite enough to make any one seriously ill, in Aunt Beryl's opinion. Even before the sacking was taken off. And when it was...

There stood the doll's house, a dark, oily, spinach green, picked out with bright yellow. Its two solid little chimneys, glued on to the roof, were painted red and white, and the door, gleaming with yellow varnish, was like a little slab of toffee. Four windows, real windows, were divided into panes by a broad streak of green. There was actually a tiny porch, too, painted yellow, with big lumps of congealed paint hanging along the edge.

But perfect, perfect little house! Who could possibly mind the smell? It was part of the joy, part of the newness.

"Open it quickly, some one!"

The hook at the side was stuck fast. Pat pried it open with his pen-knife, and the whole house-front swung back, and—there you were, gazing at one and the same moment into the drawing-room and dining-room, the kitchen and two bedrooms. That is the way for a house to open! Why don't all houses open like that? How much more exciting than peering through the slit of a door into a mean little hall with a hat-stand and two umbrellas! That is—isn't it?—what you long to know about a house when you put your hand on the knocker. Perhaps it is the way God opens houses at dead of night when He is taking a quiet turn with an angel....

"Oh-oh!" The Burnell children sounded as though they were in despair. It was too marvellous; it was too much for them. They had never seen anything like it in their lives. All the rooms were papered. There were pictures on the walls, painted on the paper, with gold frames complete. Red carpet covered all the floors except the kitchen; red plush chairs in the drawing-room, green in the dining-room; tables, beds with real bedclothes, a cradle, a stove, a dresser with tiny plates and one big jug. But what Kezia liked more than anything, what she liked frightfully, was the lamp. It stood in the middle of the dining-room table, an exquisite little amber lamp with a white globe. It was even filled all ready for lighting, though, of course, you couldn't light it. But there was something inside that looked like oil, and that moved when you shook it.

The father and mother dolls, who sprawled very stiff as though they had fainted in the drawing-room, and their two little children asleep upstairs, were really too big for the doll's house. They didn't look as though they belonged. But the lamp was perfect. It seemed to smile to Kezia, to say, "I live here." The lamp was real.

The Burnell children could hardly walk to school fast enough the next morning. They burned to tell everybody, to describe, to-well-to boast about their doll's house before the school-bell rang.

"I'm to tell," said Isabel, "because I'm the eldest. And you two can join in after. But I'm to tell first."

There was nothing to answer. Isabel was bossy, but she was always right, and Lottie and Kezia knew too well the powers that went with being eldest. They brushed through the thick buttercups at the road edge and said nothing.

"And I'm to choose who's to come and see it first. Mother said I might."

For it had been arranged that while the doll's house stood in the courtyard they might ask the girls at school, two at a time, to come and look. Not to stay to tea, of course, or to come traipsing through the house. But just to stand quietly in the courtyard while Isabel pointed out the beauties, and Lottie and Kezia looked pleased....

But hurry as they might, by the time they had reached the tarred palings of the boys' playground the bell had begun to jangle. They only just had time to whip off their hats and fall into line before the roll was called. Never mind. Isabel tried to make up for it by looking very important and mysterious and by whispering behind her hand to the girls near her, "Got something to tell you at playtime."

Playtime came and Isabel was surrounded. The girls of her class nearly fought to put their arms round her, to walk away with her, to beam flatteringly, to be her special friend. She held quite a court under the huge pine trees at the side of the playground. Nudging, giggling together, the little girls pressed up close. And the only two who stayed outside the ring were the two who were always outside, the little Kelveys. They knew better than to come anywhere near the Burnells.

For the fact was, the school the Burnell children went to was not at all the kind of place their parents would have chosen if there had been any choice. But there was none. It was the only school for miles. And the consequence was all the children in the neighborhood, the judge's little girls, the doctor's daughters, the store-keeper's children, the milkman's, were forced to mix together. Not to speak of there being an equal number of rude, rough little boys as well. But the line had to be drawn somewhere. It was drawn at the Kelveys. Many of the children, including the Burnells, were not allowed even to speak to them. They walked past the Kelveys with their heads in the air, and as they set the fashion in all matters of behaviour, the Kelveys were shunned by everybody. Even the teacher had a special voice for them, and a special smile for the other children when Lil Kelvey came up to her desk with a bunch of dreadfully common-looking flowers.

They were the daughters of a spry, hardworking little washerwoman, who went about from house to house by the day. This was awful enough. But where was Mr. Kelvey? Nobody knew for certain. But everybody said he was in prison. So they were the daughters of a washerwoman and a gaolbird. Very nice company for other people's children! And they looked it. Why Mrs. Kelvey made them so conspicuous was hard to understand. The truth was they were dressed in "bits" given to her by the people for whom she worked. Lil, for instance, who was a stout, plain child, with big freckles, came to school in a dress made from a green art-serge tablecloth of the Burnells', with red plush sleeves from the Logans' curtains. Her hat, perched on top of her high forehead, was a grown-up woman's hat, once the property of Miss Lecky, the postmistress. It was turned up at the back and trimmed with a large scarlet quill. What a little guy she looked! It was impossible not to laugh. And her little sister, our Else, wore a long white dress, rather like a nightgown, and a pair of little boy's boots. But whatever our Else wore she would have looked strange. She was a tiny wishbone of a child, with cropped hair and enormous solemn eyes—a little white owl. Nobody had ever seen her smile; she scarcely ever spoke. She went through life holding on to Lil, with a piece of Lil's skirt screwed up in her hand. Where Lil went our Else followed. In the playground, on the road going to and from school, there was Lil marching in front and our Else holding on behind. Only when she wanted anything, or when she was out of breath, our Else gave Lil a tug, a twitch, and Lil stopped and turned round. The Kelveys never failed to understand each other.

Now they hovered at the edge; you couldn't stop them listening. When the little girls turned round and sneered, Lil, as usual, gave her silly, shamefaced smile, but our Else only looked.

And Isabel's voice, so very proud, went on telling. The carpet made a great sensation, but so did the beds with real bedclothes, and the stove with an oven door.

When she finished Kezia broke in. "You've forgotten the lamp, Isabel."

"Oh, yes," said Isabel, "and there's a teeny little lamp, all made of yellow glass, with a white globe that stands on the dining-room table. You couldn't tell it from a real one."

"The lamp's best of all," cried Kezia. She thought Isabel wasn't making half enough of the little lamp. But nobody paid any attention. Isabel was choosing the two who were to come back with them that afternoon and see it. She chose Emmie Cole and Lena Logan. But when the others knew they were all to have a chance, they couldn't be nice enough to Isabel. One by one they put their arms round Isabel's waist and walked her off. They had something to whisper to her, a secret. "Isabel's my friend."

Only the little Kelveys moved away forgotten; there was nothing more for them to hear.

Days passed, and as more children saw the doll's house, the fame of it spread. It became the one subject, the rage. The one question was, "Have you seen Burnells' doll's house?" "Oh, ain't it lovely!" "Haven't you seen it? Oh, I say!"

Even the dinner hour was given up to talking about it. The little girls sat under the pines eating their thick mutton sandwiches and big slabs of johnny cake spread with butter. While always, as near as they could get, sat the Kelveys, our Else holding on to Lil, listening too, while they chewed their jam sandwiches out of a newspaper soaked with large red blobs.

"Mother," said Kezia, "can't I ask the Kelveys just once?"

"Certainly not, Kezia."

"But why not?"

"Run away, Kezia; you know quite well why not."

At last everybody had seen it except them. On that day the subject rather flagged. It was the dinner hour. The children stood together under the pine trees, and suddenly, as they looked at the Kelveys eating out of their paper, always by themselves, always listening, they wanted to be horrid to them. Emmie Cole started the whisper.

"Lil Kelvey's going to be a servant when she grows up."

"O-oh, how awful!" said Isabel Burnell, and she made eyes at Emmie.

Emmie swallowed in a very meaning way and nodded to Isabel as she'd seen her mother do on those occasions.

"It's true—it's true—it's true," she said.

Then Lena Logan's little eyes snapped. "Shall I ask her?" she whispered.

"Bet you don't," said Jessie May.

"Pooh, I'm not frightened," said Lena. Suddenly she gave a little squeal and danced in front of the other girls. "Watch! Watch me! Watch me now!" said Lena. And sliding, gliding, dragging one foot, giggling behind her hand, Lena went over to the Kelveys.

Lil looked up from her dinner. She wrapped the rest quickly away. Our Else stopped chewing. What was coming now?

"Is it true you're going to be a servant when you grow up, Lil Kelvey?" shrilled Lena.

Dead silence. But instead of answering, Lil only gave her silly, shame-faced smile. She didn't seem to mind the question at all. What a sell for Lena! The girls began to titter.

Lena couldn't stand that. She put her hands on her hips; she shot forward. "Yah, yer father's in prison!" she hissed, spitefully.

This was such a marvellous thing to have said that the little girls rushed away in a body, deeply, deeply excited, wild with joy. Someone found a long rope, and they began skipping. And never did they skip so high, run in and out so fast, or do such daring things as on that morning.

In the afternoon Pat called for the Burnell children with the buggy and they drove home. There were visitors. Isabel and Lottie, who liked visitors, went upstairs to change their pinafores. But Kezia thieved out at the back. Nobody was about; she began to swing on the big white gates of the courtyard. Presently, looking along the road, she saw two little dots. They grew bigger, they were coming towards her. Now she could see that one was in front and one close behind. Now she could see that they were the Kelveys. Kezia stopped swinging. She slipped off the gate as if she was going to run away. Then she hesitated. The Kelveys came nearer, and beside them walked their shadows, very long, stretching right across the road with their heads in the buttercups. Kezia clambered back on the gate; she had made up her mind; she swung out.

"Hullo," she said to the passing Kelveys.

They were so astounded that they stopped. Lil gave her silly smile. Our Else stared.

"You can come and see our doll's house if you want to," said Kezia, and she dragged one toe on the ground. But at that Lil turned red and shook her head quickly.

"Why not?" asked Kezia.

Lil gasped, then she said, "Your ma told our ma you wasn't to speak to us."

"Oh, well," said Kezia. She didn't know what to reply. "It doesn't matter. You can come and see our doll's house all the same. Come on. Nobody's looking."

But Lil shook her head still harder.

"Don't you want to?" asked Kezia.

Suddenly there was a twitch, a tug at Lil's skirt. She turned round. Our Else was looking at her with big, imploring eyes; she was frowning; she wanted to go. For a moment Lil looked at our Else very doubtfully. But then our Else twitched her skirt again. She started forward. Kezia led the way. Like two little stray cats they followed across the courtyard to where the doll's house stood.

"There it is," said Kezia.

There was a pause. Lil breathed loudly, almost snorted; our Else was still as a stone.

"I'll open it for you," said Kezia kindly. She undid the hook and they looked inside.

"There's the drawing-room and the dining-room, and that's the—"

"Kezia!"

Oh, what a start they gave!

"Kezia!"

It was Aunt Beryl's voice. They turned round. At the back door stood Aunt Beryl, staring as if she couldn't believe what she saw.

"How dare you ask the little Kelveys into the courtyard?" said her cold, furious voice. "You know as well as I do, you're not allowed to talk to them. Run away, children, run away at once. And don't come back again," said Aunt Beryl. And she stepped into the yard and shooed them out as if they were chickens.

"Off you go immediately!" she called, cold and proud.

They did not need telling twice. Burning with shame, shrinking together, Lil huddling along like her mother, our Else dazed, somehow they crossed the big courtyard and squeezed through the white gate.

"Wicked, disobedient little girl!" said Aunt Beryl bitterly to Kezia, and she slammed the doll's house to.

The afternoon had been awful. A letter had come from Willie Brent, a terrifying, threatening letter, saying if she did not meet him that evening in Pulman's Bush, he'd come to the front door and ask the reason why! But now that she had frightened those little rats of Kelveys and given Kezia a good scolding, her heart felt lighter. That ghastly pressure was gone. She went back to the house humming.

When the Kelveys were well out of sight of Burnells', they sat down to rest on a big red drain-pipe by the side of the road. Lil's cheeks were still burning; she took off the hat with the quill and held it on her knee. Dreamily they looked over the hay paddocks, past the creek, to the group of wattles where Logan's cows stood waiting to be milked. What were their thoughts?

Presently our Else nudged up close to her sister. But now she had forgotten the cross lady. She put out a finger and stroked her sister's quill; she smiled her rare smile.

"I seen the little lamp," she said, softly.

Then both were silent once more.

AT THE BAY

I

Very early morning. The sun was not yet risen, and the whole of Crescent Bay was hidden under a white sea-mist. The big bush-covered hills at the back were smothered. You could not see where they ended and the paddocks and bungalows began. The sandy road was gone and the paddocks and bungalows the other side of it; there were no white dunes covered with reddish grass beyond them; there was nothing to mark which was beach and where was the sea. A heavy dew had fallen. The grass was blue. Big drops hung on the bushes and just did not fall; the silvery, fluffy toi-toi was limp on its long stalks, and all the marigolds and the pinks in the bungalow gardens were bowed to the earth with wetness. Drenched were the cold fuchsias, round pearls of dew lay on the flat nasturtium leaves. It looked as though the sea had beaten up softly in the darkness, as though one immense wave had come rippling, rippling—how far? Perhaps if you had waked up in the middle of the night you might have seen a big fish flicking in at the window and gone again....

Ah-Aah! sounded the sleepy sea. And from the bush there came the sound of little streams flowing, quickly, lightly, slipping between the smooth stones, gushing into ferny basins and out again; and there was the splashing of big drops on large leaves, and something else—what was it?—a faint stirring and shaking, the snapping of a twig and then such silence that it seemed some one was listening.

Round the corner of Crescent Bay, between the piled-up masses of broken rock, a flock of sheep came pattering. They were huddled together, a small, tossing, woolly mass, and their thin, stick-like legs trotted along quickly as if the cold and the quiet had frightened them. Behind them an old sheep-dog, his soaking paws covered with sand, ran along with his nose to the ground, but carelessly, as if thinking of something else. And then in the rocky gateway the shepherd himself appeared. He was a lean, upright old man, in a frieze coat that was covered with a web of tiny drops, velvet trousers tied under the knee, and a wide-awake with a folded blue handkerchief round the brim. One hand was crammed into his belt, the other grasped a beautifully smooth yellow stick. And as he walked, taking his time, he kept up a very soft light whistling, an airy, far-away fluting that sounded mournful and tender. The old dog cut an ancient caper or two and then drew up sharp, ashamed of his levity, and walked a few dignified paces by his master's side. The sheep ran forward in little pattering rushes; they began to bleat, and ghostly flocks and herds answered them from under the sea. "Baa! Baaa!" For a time they seemed to be always on the same piece of ground. There ahead was stretched the sandy road with shallow puddles; the same soaking bushes showed on either side and the same shadowy palings. Then something immense came into view; an enormous shock-haired giant with his arms stretched out. It was the big gum-tree outside Mrs. Stubbs' shop, and as they passed by there was a strong whiff of eucalyptus. And now big spots of light gleamed in the mist. The shepherd stopped whistling; he rubbed his red nose and wet beard on his wet sleeve and, screwing up his eyes, glanced in the direction of the sea. The sun was rising. It was marvellous how quickly the mist thinned, sped away, dissolved from the shallow plain, rolled up from the bush and was gone as if in a hurry to escape; big twists and curls jostled and shouldered each other as the silvery beams broadened. The far-away sky—a bright, pure blue-was reflected in the puddles, and the drops, swimming along the telegraph poles, flashed into points of light. Now the leaping, glittering sea was so bright it made one's eyes ache to look at it. The shepherd drew a pipe, the bowl as small as an acorn, out of his breast pocket, fumbled for a chunk of speckled tobacco, pared off a few shavings and stuffed the bowl. He was a grave, fine-looking old man. As he lit up and the blue smoke wreathed his head, the dog, watching, looked proud of him.

"Baa! Baaa!" The sheep spread out into a fan. They were just clear of the summer colony before the first sleeper turned over and lifted a drowsy head; their cry sounded in the dreams of little children...who lifted their arms to drag down, to cuddle the darling little woolly lambs of sleep. Then the first inhabitant appeared; it was the Burnells' cat Florrie, sitting on the gatepost, far too early as usual, looking for their milk-girl. When she saw the old sheep-dog she sprang up quickly, arched her back, drew in her tabby head, and seemed to give a little fastidious shiver. "Ugh! What a coarse, revolting creature!" said Florrie. But the old sheep-dog, not looking up, waggled past, flinging out his legs from side to side. Only one of his ears twitched to prove that he saw, and thought her a silly young female.

The breeze of morning lifted in the bush and the smell of leaves and wet black earth mingled with the sharp smell of the sea. Myriads of birds were singing. A goldfinch flew over the shepherd's head and, perching on the tiptop of a spray, it turned to the sun, ruffling its small breast feathers. And now they had passed the fisherman's hut, passed the charred-looking little *whare* where Leila the milk-girl lived with her old Gran. The sheep strayed over a yellow swamp and Wag, the sheep-dog, padded after, rounded them up and headed them for the steeper, narrower rocky pass that led out of Crescent Bay and towards Daylight Cove. "Baa! Baaa!" Faint the cry came as they rocked along the fast-drying road. The shepherd put away his pipe, dropping it into his breast-pocket so that the little bowl hung over. And straightway the soft airy whistling began again. Wag ran out along a ledge of rock after something that smelled, and ran back again disgusted. Then pushing, nudging, hurrying, the sheep rounded the bend and the shepherd followed after out of sight.

II

A few moments later the back door of one of the bungalows opened, and a figure in a broad-striped bathing suit flung down the paddock, cleared the stile, rushed through the tussock grass into the hollow, staggered up the sandy hillock, and raced for dear life over the big porous stones, over the cold, wet pebbles, on to the hard sand that gleamed like oil. Splish-Splosh! Splish-Splosh! The water bubbled round his legs as Stanley Burnell waded out exulting. First man in as usual! He'd beaten them all again. And he swooped down to souse his head and neck.

"Hail, brother! All hail, Thou Mighty One!" A velvety bass voice came booming over the water.

Great Scott! Damnation take it! Stanley lifted up to see a dark head bobbing far out and an arm lifted. It was Jonathan Trout—there before him! "Glorious morning!" sang the voice.

"Yes, very fine!" said Stanley briefly. Why the dickens didn't the fellow stick to his part of the sea? Why should he come barging over to this exact spot? Stanley gave a kick, a lunge and struck out, swimming overarm. But Jonathan was a match for him. Up he came, his black hair sleek on his forehead, his short beard sleek.

"I had an extraordinary dream last night!" he shouted.

What was the matter with the man? This mania for conversation irritated Stanley beyond words. And it was always the same—always some piffle about a dream he'd had, or some cranky idea he'd got hold of, or some rot he'd been reading. Stanley turned over on his back and kicked with his legs till he was a living waterspout. But even then... "I dreamed I was hanging over a terrifically high cliff, shouting to someone below." You would be! thought Stanley. He could stick no more of it. He stopped splashing. "Look here, Trout," he said, "I'm in rather a hurry this morning."

"You're *what*?" Jonathan was so surprised—or pretended to be—that he sank under the water, then reappeared again blowing.

"All I mean is," said Stanley, "I've no time to—to—to fool about. I want to get this over. I'm in a hurry. I've work to do this morning—see?"

Jonathan was gone before Stanley had finished. "Pass, friend!" said the bass voice gently, and he slid away through the water with scarcely a ripple... But curse the fellow! He'd ruined Stanley's bathe. What an unpractical idiot the man was! Stanley struck out to sea again, and then as quickly swam in again, and away he rushed up the beach. He felt cheated.

Jonathan stayed a little longer in the water. He floated, gently moving his hands like fins, and letting the sea rock his long, skinny body. It was curious, but in spite of everything he was fond of Stanley Burnell. True, he had a fiendish desire to tease him sometimes, to poke fun at him, but at bottom he was sorry for the fellow. There was something pathetic in his determination to make a job of everything. You couldn't help feeling he'd be caught out one day, and then what an almighty cropper he'd come! At that moment an immense wave lifted Jonathan, rode past him, and broke along the beach with a joyful sound. What a beauty! And now there came another. That was the way to live—carelessly, recklessly, spending oneself. He got on to his feet and began to wade towards the shore, pressing his toes into the firm, wrinkled sand. To take things easy, not to fight against the ebb and flow of life, but to give way to it—that was what was needed. It was this tension that was all wrong. To live—to live! And the perfect morning, so fresh and fair, basking in the light, as though laughing at its own beauty, seemed to whisper, "Why not?"

But now he was out of the water Jonathan turned blue with cold. He ached all over; it was as though someone was wringing the blood out of him. And stalking up the beach, shivering, all his muscles tight, he too felt his bathe was spoilt. He'd stayed in too long.

III

Beryl was alone in the living-room when Stanley appeared, wearing a blue serge suit, a stiff collar and a spotted tie. He looked almost uncannily clean and brushed; he was going to town for the day. Dropping into his chair, he pulled out his watch and put it beside his plate.

"I've just got twenty-five minutes," he said. "You might go and see if the porridge is ready, Beryl?"

"Mother's just gone for it," said Beryl. She sat down at the table and poured out his tea.

"Thanks!" Stanley took a sip. "Hallo!" he said in an astonished voice, "you've forgotten the sugar."

"Oh, sorry!" But even then Beryl didn't help him; she pushed the basin across. What did this mean? As Stanley helped himself his blue eyes widened; they seemed to quiver. He shot a quick glance at his sister-in-law and leaned back.

"Nothing wrong, is there?" he asked carelessly, fingering his collar.

Beryl's head was bent; she turned her plate in her fingers.

"Nothing," said her light voice. Then she too looked up, and smiled at Stanley. "Why should there be?"

"O-oh! No reason at all as far as I know. I thought you seemed rather—"

At that moment the door opened and the three little girls appeared, each carrying a porridge plate. They were dressed alike in blue jerseys and knickers; their brown legs were bare, and each had her hair plaited and pinned up in what was called a horse's tail. Behind them came Mrs. Fairfield with the tray.

"Carefully, children," she warned. But they were taking the very greatest care. They loved being allowed to carry things. "Have you said good morning to your father?"

"Yes, grandma." They settled themselves on the bench opposite Stanley and Beryl.

"Good morning, Stanley!" Old Mrs. Fairfield gave him his plate.

"Morning, mother! How's the boy?"

"Splendid! He only woke up once last night. What a perfect morning!" The old woman paused, her hand on the loaf of bread, to gaze out of the open door into the garden. The sea sounded. Through the wide-open window streamed the sun on to the yellow varnished walls and bare floor. Everything on the table flashed and glittered. In the middle there was an old salad bowl filled with yellow and red nasturtiums. She smiled, and a look of deep content shone in her eyes.

"You might *cut* me a slice of that bread, mother," said Stanley. "I've only twelve and a half minutes before the coach passes. Has anyone given my shoes to the servant girl?"

"Yes, they're ready for you." Mrs. Fairfield was quite unruffled.

"Oh, Kezia! Why are you such a messy child!" cried Beryl despairingly.

"Me, Aunt Beryl?" Kezia stared at her. What had she done now? She had only dug a river down the middle of her porridge, filled it, and was eating the banks away. But she did that every single morning, and no one had said a word up till now.

"Why can't you eat your food properly like Isabel and Lottie?" How unfair grown-ups are!

"But Lottie always makes a floating island, don't you, Lottie?"

"I don't," said Isabel smartly. "I just sprinkle mine with sugar and put on the milk and finish it. Only babies play with their food."

Stanley pushed back his chair and got up.

"Would you get me those shoes, mother? And, Beryl, if you've finished, I wish you'd cut down to the gate and stop the coach. Run in to your mother, Isabel, and ask her where my bowler hat's been put. Wait a minute—have you children been playing with my stick?"

"No, father!"

"But I put it here," Stanley began to bluster. "I remember distinctly putting it in this corner. Now, who's had it? There's no time to lose. Look sharp! The stick's got to be found."

Even Alice, the servant-girl, was drawn into the chase. "You haven't been using it to poke the kitchen fire with by any chance?"

Stanley dashed into the bedroom where Linda was lying. "Most extraordinary thing. I can't keep a single possession to myself. They've made away with my stick, now!"

"Stick, dear? What stick?" Linda's vagueness on these occasions could not be real, Stanley decided. Would nobody sympathize with him?

"Coach! Coach, Stanley!" Beryl's voice cried from the gate.

Stanley waved his arm to Linda. "No time to say good-bye!" he cried. And he meant that as a punishment to her.

He snatched his bowler hat, dashed out of the house, and swung down the garden path. Yes, the coach was there waiting, and Beryl, leaning over the open gate, was laughing up at somebody or other just as if nothing had happened. The heartlessness of women! The way they took it for granted it was your job to slave away for them while they didn't even take the trouble to see that your walking-stick wasn't lost. Kelly trailed his whip across the horses.

"Good-bye, Stanley," called Beryl, sweetly and gaily. It was easy enough to say good-bye! And there she stood, idle, shading her eyes with her hand. The worst of it was Stanley had to shout good-bye too, for the sake of appearances. Then he saw her turn, give a little skip and run back to the house. She was glad to be rid of him!

Yes, she was thankful. Into the living-room she ran and called "He's gone!" Linda cried from her room: "Beryl! Has Stanley gone?" Old Mrs. Fairfield appeared, carrying the boy in his little flannel coatee.

"Gone?"

"Gone!"

Oh, the relief, the difference it made to have the man out of the house. Their very voices were changed as they called to one another; they sounded warm and loving and as if they shared a secret. Beryl went over to the table. "Have another cup of tea, mother. It's still hot." She wanted, somehow, to celebrate the fact that they could do what they liked now. There was no man to disturb them; the whole perfect day was theirs.

"No, thank you, child," said old Mrs. Fairfield, but the way at that moment she tossed the boy up and said "a-goos-a-goos-a-ga!" to him meant that she felt the same. The little girls ran into the paddock like chickens let out of a coop.

Even Alice, the servant-girl, washing up the dishes in the kitchen, caught the infection and used the precious tank water in a perfectly reckless fashion.

"Oh, these men!" said she, and she plunged the teapot into the bowl and held it under the water even after it had stopped bubbling, as if it too was a man and drowning was too good for them.

IV

"Wait for me, Isa-bel! Kezia, wait for me!"

There was poor little Lottie, left behind again, because she found it so fearfully hard to get over the stile by herself. When she stood on the first step her knees began to wobble; she grasped the post. Then you had to put one leg over. But which leg? She never could decide. And when she did finally put one leg over with a sort of stamp of despair—then the feeling was awful. She was half in the paddock still and half in the tussock grass. She clutched the post desperately and lifted up her voice. "Wait for me!"

"No, don't you wait for her, Kezia!" said Isabel. "She's such a little silly. She's always making a fuss. Come on!" And she tugged Kezia's jersey. "You can use my bucket if you come with me," she said kindly. "It's bigger than yours." But Kezia couldn't leave Lottie all by herself. She ran back to her. By this time Lottie was very red in the face and breathing heavily.

"Here, put your other foot over," said Kezia.

"Where?"

Lottie looked down at Kezia as if from a mountain height.

"Here where my hand is." Kezia patted the place.

"Oh, *there* do you mean!" Lottie gave a deep sigh and put the second foot over.

"Now—sort of turn round and sit down and slide," said Kezia.

"But there's nothing to sit down *on*, Kezia," said Lottie.

She managed it at last, and once it was over she shook herself and began to beam.

"I'm getting better at climbing over stiles, aren't I, Kezia?"

Lottie's was a very hopeful nature.

The pink and the blue sunbonnet followed Isabel's bright red sunbonnet up that sliding, slipping hill. At the top they paused to decide where to go and to have a good stare at who was there already. Seen from behind, standing against the skyline, gesticulating largely with their spades, they looked like minute puzzled explorers.

The whole family of Samuel Josephs was there already with their lady-help, who sat on a camp-stool and kept order with a whistle that she wore tied round her neck, and a small cane with which she directed operations. The Samuel Josephs never played by themselves or managed their own game. If they did, it ended in the boys pouring water down the girls' necks or the girls trying to put little black crabs into the boys' pockets. So Mrs. S. J. and the poor lady-help drew up what she called a "brogramme" every morning to keep them "abused and out of bischief." It was all competitions or races or round games. Everything began with a piercing blast of the lady-help's whistle and ended with another. There were even prizes—large, rather dirty paper parcels which the lady-help with a sour little smile drew out of a bulging string kit. The Samuel Josephs fought fearfully for the prizes and cheated and pinched one another's arms—they were all expert pinchers. The only time the Burnell children ever played with them Kezia had got a prize, and when she undid three bits of paper she found a very small rusty button-hook. She couldn't understand why they made such a fuss....

But they never played with the Samuel Josephs now or even went to their parties. The Samuel Josephs were always giving children's parties at the Bay and there was always the same food. A big washhand basin of very brown fruit-salad, buns cut into four and a washhand jug full of something the lady-help called "Limonadear." And you went away in the evening with half the frill torn off your frock or something spilled all down the front of your open-work pinafore, leaving the Samuel Josephs leaping like savages on their lawn. No! They were too awful.

On the other side of the beach, close down to the water, two little boys, their knickers rolled up, twinkled like spiders. One was digging, the other pattered in and out of the water, filling a small bucket. They were the Trout boys, Pip and Rags. But Pip was so busy digging and Rags was so busy helping that they didn't see their little cousins until they were quite close.

"Look!" said Pip. "Look what I've discovered." And he showed them an old wet, squashed-looking boot. The three little girls stared.

"Whatever are you going to do with it?" asked Kezia.

"Keep it, of course!" Pip was very scornful. "It's a find—see?"

Yes, Kezia saw that. All the same...

"There's lots of things buried in the sand," explained Pip. "They get chucked up from wrecks. Treasure. Why—you might find—"

"But why does Rags have to keep on pouring water in?" asked Lottie.

"Oh, that's to moisten it," said Pip, "to make the work a bit easier. Keep it up, Rags."

And good little Rags ran up and down, pouring in the water that turned brown like cocoa.

"Here, shall I show you what I found yesterday?" said Pip mysteriously, and he stuck his spade into the sand. "Promise not to tell."

They promised.

"Say, cross my heart straight dinkum."

The little girls said it.

Pip took something out of his pocket, rubbed it a long time on the front of his jersey, then breathed on it and rubbed it again.

"Now turn round!" he ordered.

They turned round.

"All look the same way! Keep still! Now!"

And his hand opened; he held up to the light something that flashed, that winked, that was a most lovely green.

"It's a nemeral," said Pip solemnly.

"Is it really, Pip?" Even Isabel was impressed.

The lovely green thing seemed to dance in Pip's fingers. Aunt Beryl had a nemeral in a ring, but it was a very small one. This one was as big as a star and far more beautiful.

V

As the morning lengthened whole parties appeared over the sand-hills and came down on the beach to bathe. It was understood that at eleven o'clock the women and children of the summer colony had the sea to themselves. First the women undressed, pulled on their bathing dresses and covered their heads in hideous caps like sponge bags; then the children were unbuttoned. The beach was strewn with little heaps of clothes and shoes; the big summer hats, with stones on them to keep them from blowing away, looked like immense shells. It was strange that even the sea seemed to sound differently when all those leaping, laughing figures ran into the waves. Old Mrs. Fairfield, in a lilac cotton dress and a black hat tied under the chin, gathered her little brood and got them ready. The little Trout boys whipped their shirts over their heads, and away the five sped, while their grandma sat with one hand in her knitting-bag ready to draw out the ball of wool when she was satisfied they were safely in.

The firm compact little girls were not half so brave as the tender, delicate-looking boys. Pip and Rags, shivering, crouching down, slapping the water, never hesitated. But Isabel, who could swim twelve strokes, and Kezia, who could nearly swim eight, only followed on the strict understanding they were not to be splashed. As for Lottie, she didn't follow at all. She liked to be left to go in her own way, please. And that way was to sit down at the edge of the water, her legs straight, her knees pressed together, and to make vague motions with her arms as if she expected to be wafted out to sea. But when a bigger wave than usual, an old whiskery one, came lolloping along in her direction, she scrambled to her feet with a face of horror and flew up the beach again.

"Here, mother, keep those for me, will you?"

Two rings and a thin gold chain were dropped into Mrs Fairfield's lap.

"Yes, dear. But aren't you going to bathe here?"

"No-o," Beryl drawled. She sounded vague. "I'm undressing farther along. I'm going to bathe with Mrs. Harry Kember."

"Very well." But Mrs. Fairfield's lips set. She disapproved of Mrs Harry Kember. Beryl knew it.

Poor old mother, she smiled, as she skimmed over the stones. Poor old mother! Old! Oh, what joy, what bliss it was to be young....

"You look very pleased," said Mrs. Harry Kember. She sat hunched up on the stones, her arms round her knees, smoking.

"It's such a lovely day," said Beryl, smiling down at her.

"Oh my *dear!*" Mrs. Harry Kember's voice sounded as though she knew better than that. But then her voice always sounded as though she knew something more about you than you did yourself. She was a long, strange-looking woman with narrow hands and feet. Her face, too, was long and narrow and exhausted-looking; even her fair curled fringe looked burnt out and withered. She was the only woman at the Bay who smoked, and she smoked incessantly, keeping the cigarette between her lips while she talked, and only taking it out when the ash was so long you could not understand why it did not fall. When she was not playing bridge—she played bridge every day of her life—she spent her time lying in the full glare of the sun. She could stand any amount of it; she never had enough. All the same, it did not seem to warm her. Parched, withered, cold, she stretched on the stones like a piece of tossed-up driftwood. The women at the Bay thought she was very, very fast. Her lack of vanity, her slang, the way she treated men as though she was one of them, and the fact that she didn't care twopence about her house and called the servant Gladys "Glad-eyes," was disgraceful. Standing on the veranda steps Mrs. Kember would call in her indifferent, tired voice, "I say, Glad-eyes, you might heave me a handkerchief if I've got one, will you?" And Glad-eyes, a red bow in her hair instead of a cap, and white shoes, came running with an impudent smile. It was an absolute scandal! True, she had no children, and her husband.... Here the voices were always raised; they became fervent. How can he have married her? How can he, how can he? It must have been money, of course, but even then!

Mrs. Kember's husband was at least ten years younger than she was, and so incredibly handsome that he looked like a mask or a most perfect illustration in an American novel rather than a man. Black hair, dark blue eyes, red lips, a slow sleepy smile, a fine tennis player, a perfect dancer, and with it all a mystery. Harry Kember was like a man walking in his sleep. Men couldn't stand him, they couldn't get a word out of the chap; he ignored his wife just as she ignored him. How did he live? Of course there were stories, but such stories! They simply couldn't be told. The women he's been seen with, the places he'd been seen in...but nothing was ever certain, nothing definite. Some of the women at the Bay privately thought he'd commit a murder one day. Yes, even while they talked to

Mrs. Kember and took in the awful concoction she was wearing, they saw her, stretched as she lay on the beach; but cold, bloody, and still with a cigarette stuck in the corner of her mouth.

Mrs. Kember rose, yawned, unsnapped her belt buckle, and tugged at the tape of her blouse. And Beryl stepped out of her skirt and shed her jersey, and stood up in her short white petticoat, and her camisole with ribbon bows on the shoulders.

"Mercy on us," said Mrs. Harry Kember, "what a little beauty you are!"

"Don't!" said Beryl softly; but, drawing off one stocking and then the other, she felt a little beauty.

"My dear—why not?" said Mrs. Harry Kember, stamping on her own petticoat. Really—her underclothes! A pair of blue cotton knickers and a linen bodice that reminded one somehow of a pillow-case.... "And you don't wear stays, do you?" She touched Beryl's waist, and Beryl sprang away with a small affected cry. Then "Never!" she said firmly.

"Lucky little creature," sighed Mrs. Kember, unfastening her own.

Beryl turned her back and began the complicated movements of someone who is trying to take off her clothes and to pull on her bathing-dress all at one and the same time.

"Oh, my dear—don't mind me," said Mrs. Harry Kember. "Why be shy? I shan't eat you. I shan't be shocked like those other ninnies." And she gave her strange neighing laugh and grimaced at the other women.

But Beryl was shy. She never undressed in front of anybody. Was that silly? Mrs. Harry Kember made her feel it was silly, even something to be ashamed of. Why be shy indeed! She glanced quickly at her friend standing so boldly in her torn chemise and lighting a fresh cigarette; and a quick, bold, evil feeling started up in her breast. Laughing recklessly, she drew on the limp, sandy-feeling bathing-dress that was not quite dry and fastened the twisted buttons.

"That's better," said Mrs. Harry Kember. They began to go down the beach together. "Really, it's a sin for you to wear clothes, my dear. Somebody's got to tell you some day."

The water was quite warm. It was that marvellous transparent blue, flecked with silver, but the sand at the bottom looked gold; when you kicked with your toes there rose a little puff of gold-dust. Now the waves just reached her breast. Beryl stood, her arms outstretched, gazing out, and as each wave came she gave the slightest little jump, so that it seemed it was the wave which lifted her so gently.

"I believe in pretty girls having a good time," said Mrs. Harry Kember. "Why not? Don't you make a mistake, my dear. Enjoy yourself." And suddenly she turned turtle, disappeared, and swam away quickly, quickly, like a rat. Then she flicked round and began swimming back. She was going to say something else. Beryl felt that she was being poisoned by this cold woman, but she longed to hear. But oh, how strange, how horrible! As Mrs. Harry Kember came up close she looked, in her black waterproof bathing-cap, with her sleepy face lifted above the water, just her chin touching, like a horrible caricature of her husband.

VI

In a steamer chair, under a manuka tree that grew in the middle of the front grass patch, Linda Burnell dreamed the morning away. She did nothing. She looked up at the dark, close, dry leaves of the manuka, at the chinks of blue between, and now and again a tiny yellowish flower dropped on her. Pretty—yes, if you held one of those flowers on the palm of your hand and looked at it closely, it was an exquisite small thing. Each pale yellow petal shone as if each was the careful work of a loving hand. The tiny tongue in the centre gave it the shape of a bell. And when you turned it over the outside was a deep bronze colour. But as soon as they flowered, they fell and were scattered. You brushed them off your frock as you talked; the horrid little things got caught in one's hair. Why, then, flower at all? Who takes the trouble—or the joy—to make all these things that are wasted, wasted…. It was uncanny.

On the grass beside her, lying between two pillows, was the boy. Sound asleep he lay, his head turned away from his mother. His fine dark hair looked more like a shadow than like real hair, but his ear was a bright, deep coral. Linda clasped her hands above her head and crossed her feet. It was very pleasant to know that all these bungalows were empty, that everybody was down on the beach, out of sight, out of hearing. She had the garden to herself; she was alone.

Dazzling white the picotees shone; the golden-eyed marigold glittered; the nasturtiums wreathed the veranda poles in green and gold flame. If only one had time to look at these flowers long enough, time to get over the sense of novelty and strangeness, time to know them! But as soon as one paused to part the petals, to discover the under-side of the leaf, along came Life and one was swept away. And, lying in her cane chair, Linda felt so light; she felt like a leaf. Along came Life like a wind and she was seized and shaken; she had to go. Oh dear, would it always be so? Was there no escape?

…Now she sat on the veranda of their Tasmanian home, leaning against her father's knee. And he promised, "As soon as you and I are old enough, Linny, we'll cut off somewhere, we'll escape. Two boys together. I have a fancy I'd like to sail up a river in China." Linda saw that river, very wide, covered with little rafts and boats. She saw the yellow hats of the boatmen and she heard their high, thin voices as they called…

"Yes, papa."

But just then a very broad young man with bright ginger hair walked slowly past their house, and slowly, solemnly even, uncovered. Linda's father pulled her ear teasingly, in the way he had.

"Linny's beau," he whispered.

"Oh, papa, fancy being married to Stanley Burnell!"

Well, she was married to him. And what was more she loved him. Not the Stanley whom everyone saw, not the everyday one; but a timid, sensitive, innocent Stanley who knelt down every night to say his prayers, and who longed to be good. Stanley was simple. If he believed in people—as he believed in her, for instance—it was with his whole heart. He could not be disloyal; he could not tell a lie. And how terribly he suffered if he thought anyone—she—was not being dead straight, dead sincere with him! "This is too subtle for me!" He flung out the words, but his open quivering, distraught look was like the look of a trapped beast.

But the trouble was—here Linda felt almost inclined to laugh, though Heaven knows it was no laughing matter—she saw *her* Stanley so seldom. There were glimpses, moments, breathing spaces of calm, but all the rest of the time it was like living in a house that couldn't be cured of the habit of catching on fire, on a ship that got wrecked every day. And it was always Stanley who was in the thick of the danger. Her whole time was spent in rescuing him, and restoring him, and calming him down, and listening to his story. And what was left of her time was spent in the dread of having children.

Linda frowned; she sat up quickly in her steamer chair and clasped her ankles. Yes, that was her real grudge against life; that was what she could not understand. That was the question she asked and asked, and listened in vain for the answer. It was all very well to say it was the common lot of women to bear children. It wasn't true. She, for one, could prove that wrong. She was broken, made weak, her courage was gone, through child-bearing. And what made it doubly hard to bear was, she did not love her children. It was useless pretending. Even if she had had the strength she never would have nursed and played with the little girls. No, it was as though a cold breath had chilled her through and through on each of those awful journeys; she had no warmth left to give them. As to the boy—well, thank Heaven, mother had taken him; he was mother's, or Beryl's, or anybody's who wanted him. She had hardly held him in her arms. She was so indifferent about him that as he lay there... Linda glanced down.

The boy had turned over. He lay facing her, and he was no longer asleep. His dark-blue, baby eyes were open; he looked as though he was peeping at his mother. And suddenly his face dimpled; it broke into a wide, toothless smile, a perfect beam, no less.

"I'm here!" that happy smile seemed to say. "Why don't you like me?"

There was something so quaint, so unexpected about that smile that Linda smiled herself. But she checked herself and said to the boy coldly, "I don't like babies."

"Don't like babies?" The boy couldn't believe her. "Don't like *me?*" He waved his arms foolishly at his mother.

Linda dropped off her chair on to the grass.

"Why do you keep on smiling?" she said severely. "If you knew what I was thinking about, you wouldn't."

But he only squeezed up his eyes, slyly, and rolled his head on the pillow. He didn't believe a word she said.

"We know all about that!" smiled the boy.

Linda was so astonished at the confidence of this little creature.... Ah no, be sincere. That was not what she felt; it was something far different, it was something so new, so... The tears danced in her eyes; she breathed in a small whisper to the boy, "Hallo, my funny!"

But by now the boy had forgotten his mother. He was serious again. Something pink, something soft waved in front of him. He made a grab at it and it immediately disappeared. But when he lay back, another, like the first, appeared. This time he determined to catch it. He made a tremendous effort and rolled right over.

The tide was out; the beach was deserted; lazily flopped the warm sea. The sun beat down, beat down hot and fiery on the fine sand, baking the grey and blue and black and white-veined pebbles. It sucked up the little drop of water that lay in the hollow of the curved shells; it bleached the pink convolvulus that threaded through and through the sand-hills. Nothing seemed to move but the small sand-hoppers. Pit-pit-pit! They were never still.

Over there on the weed-hung rocks that looked at low tide like shaggy beasts come down to the water to drink, the sunlight seemed to spin like a silver coin dropped into each of the small rock pools. They danced, they quivered, and minute ripples laved the porous shores. Looking down, bending over, each pool was like a lake with pink and blue houses clustered on the shores; and oh! the vast mountainous country behind those houses—the ravines, the passes, the dangerous creeks and fearful tracks that led to the water's edge. Underneath waved the sea-forest—pink thread-like trees, velvet anemones, and orange berry-spotted weeds. Now a stone on the bottom moved, rocked, and there was a glimpse of a black feeler; now a thread-like creature wavered by and was lost. Something was happening to the pink, waving trees; they were changing to a cold moonlight blue. And now there sounded the faintest "plop." Who made that sound? What was going on down there? And how strong, how damp the seaweed smelt in the hot sun....

The green blinds were drawn in the bungalows of the summer colony. Over the verandas, prone on the paddock, flung over the fences, there were exhausted-looking bathing-dresses and rough striped towels. Each back window seemed to have a pair of sand-shoes on the sill and some lumps of rock or a bucket or a collection of pawa shells. The bush quivered in a haze of heat; the sandy road was empty except for the Trouts' dog Snooker, who lay stretched in the very middle of it. His blue eye was turned up, his legs stuck out stiffly, and he gave an occasional desperate-sounding puff, as much as to say he had decided to make an end of it and was only waiting for some kind cart to come along.

"What are you looking at, my grandma? Why do you keep stopping and sort of staring at the wall?"

Kezia and her grandmother were taking their siesta together. The little girl, wearing only her short drawers and her under-bodice, her arms and legs bare, lay on one of the puffed-up pillows of her grandma's bed, and the old woman, in a white ruffled dressing-gown sat in a rocker at the window, with a long piece of pink knitting in her lap. This room that they shared, like the other rooms of her bungalow, was of light varnished wood and the floor was bare. The furniture was of the shabbiest, the simplest. The dressing-table, for instance, was a packing-case in a sprigged muslin petticoat, and the mirror above was very strange; it was as though a little piece of forked lightning was imprisoned in it. On the table there stood a jar of sea-pinks, pressed so tightly together they looked more like a velvet pincushion, and a special shell which Kezia had given her grandma for a pin-tray, and another even more special which she had thought would make a very nice place for a watch to curl up in.

"Tell me, grandma," said Kezia.

The old woman sighed, whipped the wool twice round her thumb, and drew the bone needle through. She was casting on.

"I was thinking of your Uncle William, darling," she said quietly.

"My Australian Uncle William?" said Kezia. She had another.

"Yes, of course."

"The one I never saw?"

"That was the one."

"Well, what happened to him?" Kezia knew perfectly well, but she wanted to be told again.

"He went to the mines, and he got a sunstroke there and died," said old Mrs. Fairfield.

Kezia blinked and considered the picture again...a little man fallen over like a tin soldier by the side of the big black hole.

"Does it make you sad to think about him, grandma?" She hated her grandma to be sad.

It was the old woman's turn to consider. Did it make her sad? To look back, back. To stare down the years, as Kezia had seen her doing. To look after *them* as a woman does, long after *they* were out of sight. Did it make her sad? No, life was like that.

"No, Kezia."

"But why?" asked Kezia. She lifted one bare arm and began to draw things in the air. "Why did Uncle William have to die? He wasn't old."

Mrs. Fairfield began counting the stitches in threes. "It just happened," she said in an absorbed voice.

"Does everybody have to die?" asked Kezia.

"Everybody!"

"*Me?*" Kezia sounded fearfully incredulous.

"Some day, my darling."

"But, grandma." Kezia waved her left leg and waggled the toes. They felt sandy. "What if I just won't?"

The old woman sighed again and drew a long thread from the ball.

"We're not asked, Kezia," she said sadly. "It happens to all of us sooner or later."

Kezia lay still thinking this over. She didn't want to die. It meant she would have to leave here, leave everywhere, for ever, leave—leave her grandma. She rolled over quickly.

"Grandma," she said in a startled voice.

"What, my pet!"

"*You're* not to die." Kezia was very decided.

"Ah, Kezia"—her grandma looked up and smiled and shook her head—"don't let's talk about it."

"But you're not to. You couldn't leave me. You couldn't not be there." This was awful. "Promise me you won't ever do it, grandma," pleaded Kezia.

The old woman went on knitting.

"Promise me! Say never!"

But still her grandma was silent.

Kezia rolled off her bed; she couldn't bear it any longer, and lightly she leapt on to her grandma's knees, clasped her hand round the old woman's throat and began kissing her, under the chin, behind the ear, and blowing down her neck.

"Say never…say never…say never—" She gasped between the kisses. And then she began, very softly and lightly, to tickle her grandma.

"Kezia!" The old woman dropped her knitting. She swung back in the rocker. She began to tickle Kezia. "Say never, say never, say never," gurgled Kezia, while they lay there laughing in each other's arms. "Come, that's enough, my squirrel! That's enough, my wild pony!" said old Mrs. Fairfield, setting her cap straight. "Pick up my knitting."

Both of them had forgotten what the "never" was about.

VIII

The sun was still full on the garden when the back door of the Burnells' shut with a bang, and a very gay figure walked down the path to the gate. It was Alice, the servant-girl, dressed for her afternoon out. She wore a white cotton dress with such large red spots on it and so many that they made you shudder, white shoes and a leghorn turned up under the brim with poppies. Of course she wore gloves, white ones, stained at the fastenings with iron-mould, and in one hand she carried a very dashed-looking sunshade which she referred to as her *perishall*.

Beryl, sitting in the window, fanning her freshly-washed hair, thought she had never seen such a guy. If Alice had only blacked her face with a piece of cork before she started out, the picture would have been complete. And where did a girl like that go to in a place like this? The heart-shaped Fijian fan beat scornfully at that lovely bright mane. She supposed Alice had picked up some horrible common larrikin and they'd go off into the bush together. Pity to have made herself so conspicuous; they'd have hard work to hide with Alice in that rig-out.

But no, Beryl was unfair. Alice was going to tea with Mrs Stubbs, who'd sent her an "invite" by the little boy who called for orders. She had taken ever such a liking to Mrs. Stubbs ever since the first time she went to the shop to get something for her mosquitoes.

"Dear heart!" Mrs. Stubbs had clapped her hand to her side. "I never seen anyone so eaten. You might have been attacked by canningbals."

Alice did wish there'd been a bit of life on the road though. Made her feel so queer, having nobody behind her. Made her feel all weak in the spine. She couldn't believe that someone wasn't watching her. And yet it was silly to turn round; it gave you away. She pulled up her gloves, hummed to herself and said to the distant gum-tree, "Shan't be long now." But that was hardly company.

Mrs. Stubbs's shop was perched on a little hillock just off the road. It had two big windows for eyes, a broad veranda for a hat, and the sign on the roof, scrawled MRS. STUBBS'S, was like a little card stuck rakishly in the hat crown.

On the veranda there hung a long string of bathing-dresses, clinging together as though they'd just been rescued from the sea rather than waiting to go in, and beside them there hung a cluster of sand-shoes so extraordinarily mixed that to get at one pair you had to tear apart and forcibly separate at least fifty. Even then it was the rarest thing to find the left that belonged to the right. So many people had lost patience and gone off with one shoe that fitted and one that was a little too big.... Mrs. Stubbs prided herself on keeping something of everything. The two windows, arranged in the form of precarious pyramids, were crammed so tight, piled so high, that it seemed only a conjurer could prevent them from toppling over. In the left-hand corner of one window, glued to the pane by four gelatine lozenges, there was—and there had been from time immemorial—a notice.

LOST! HANSOME GOLD BROOCH
SOLID GOLD
ON OR NEAR BEACH
REWARD OFFERED

Alice pressed open the door. The bell jangled, the red serge curtains parted, and Mrs. Stubbs appeared. With her broad smile and the long bacon knife in her hand, she looked like a friendly brigand. Alice was welcomed so warmly that she found it quite difficult to keep up her "manners." They consisted of persistent little coughs and hems, pulls at her gloves, tweaks at her skirt, and a curious difficulty in seeing what was set before her or understanding what was said.

Tea was laid on the parlour table—ham, sardines, a whole pound of butter, and such a large johnny cake that it looked like an advertisement for somebody's baking-powder. But the Primus stove roared so loudly that it was useless to try to talk above it. Alice sat down on the edge of a basket-chair while Mrs. Stubbs pumped the stove still higher. Suddenly Mrs. Stubbs whipped the cushion off a chair and disclosed a large brown-paper parcel.

"I've just had some new photers taken, my dear," she shouted cheerfully to Alice. "Tell me what you think of them."

In a very dainty, refined way Alice wet her finger and put the tissue back from the first one. Life! How many there were! There were three dozzing at least. And she held it up to the light.

Mrs. Stubbs sat in an arm-chair, leaning very much to one side. There was a look of mild astonishment on her large face, and well there might be. For though the arm-chair stood on a carpet, to the left of it, miraculously skirting the carpet-border, there was a dashing water-fall. On her right stood a Grecian pillar with a giant fern-tree on either side of it, and in the background towered a gaunt mountain, pale with snow.

"It is a nice style, isn't it?" shouted Mrs. Stubbs; and Alice had just screamed "Sweetly" when the roaring of the Primus stove died down, fizzled out, ceased, and she said "Pretty" in a silence that was frightening.

"Draw up your chair, my dear," said Mrs. Stubbs, beginning to pour out. "Yes," she said thoughtfully, as she handed the tea, "but I don't care about the size. I'm having an enlargemint. All very well for Christmas cards, but I never was the one for small photers myself. You get no comfort out of them. To say the truth, I find them dis'eartening."

Alice quite saw what she meant.

"Size," said Mrs. Stubbs. "Give me size. That was what my poor dear husband was always saying. He couldn't stand anything small. Gave him the creeps. And, strange as it may seem my dear"—here Mrs. Stubbs creaked and seemed to expand herself at the memory—"it was dropsy that carried him off at the larst. Many's the time they drawn one and a half pints from 'im at the 'ospital... It seemed like a judgemint."

Alice burned to know exactly what it was that was drawn from him. She ventured, "I suppose it was water."

But Mrs. Stubbs fixed Alice with her eyes and replied meaningly, "It was *liquid*, my dear."

Liquid! Alice jumped away from the word like a cat and came back to it, nosing and wary.

"That's 'im!" said Mrs. Stubbs, and she pointed dramatically to the life-size head and shoulders of a burly man with a dead white rose in the button-hole of his coat that made you think of a curl of cold mutting fat. Just below, in silver letters on a red cardboard ground, were the words, "Be not afraid, it is I."

"It's ever such a fine face," said Alice faintly.

The pale-blue bow on the top of Mrs. Stubbs's fair frizzy hair quivered. She arched her plump neck. What a neck she had! It was bright pink where it began and then it changed to warm apricot, and that faded to the colour of a brown egg and then to a deep creamy.

"All the same, my dear," she said surprisingly, "freedom's best!" Her soft, fat chuckle sounded like a purr. "Freedom's best," said Mrs. Stubbs again.

Freedom! Alice gave a loud, silly little titter. She felt awkward. Her mind flew back to her own kitching. Ever so queer! She wanted to be back in it again.

IX

A strange company assembled in the Burnells' washhouse after tea. Round the table there sat a bull, a rooster, a donkey that kept forgetting it was a donkey, a sheep and a bee. The washhouse was the perfect place for such a meeting because they could make as much noise as they liked, and nobody ever interrupted. It was a small tin shed standing apart from the bungalow. Against the wall there was a deep trough and in the corner a copper with a basket of clothes-pegs on top of it. The little window, spun over with cobwebs, had a piece of candle and a mouse-trap on the dusty sill. There were clothes-lines criss-crossed overhead and, hanging from a peg on the wall, a very big, a huge, rusty horseshoe. The table was in the middle with a form at either side.

"You can't be a bee, Kezia. A bee's not an animal. It's a ninseck."

"Oh, but I do want to be a bee frightfully," wailed Kezia.... A tiny bee, all yellow-furry, with striped legs. She drew her legs up under her and leaned over the table. She felt she was a bee.

"A ninseck must be an animal," she said stoutly. "It makes a noise. It's not like a fish."

"I'm a bull, I'm a bull!" cried Pip. And he gave such a tremendous bellow—how did he make that noise?—that Lottie looked quite alarmed.

"I'll be a sheep," said little Rags. "A whole lot of sheep went past this morning."

"How do you know?"

"Dad heard them. Baa!" He sounded like the little lamb that trots behind and seems to wait to be carried.

"Cock-a-doodle-do!" shrilled Isabel. With her red cheeks and bright eyes she looked like a rooster.

"What'll I be?" Lottie asked everybody, and she sat there smiling, waiting for them to decide for her. It had to be an easy one.

"Be a donkey, Lottie." It was Kezia's suggestion. "Hee-haw! You can't forget that."

"Hee-haw!" said Lottie solemnly. "When do I have to say it?"

"I'll explain, I'll explain," said the bull. It was he who had the cards. He waved them round his head. "All be quiet! All listen!" And he waited for them. "Look here, Lottie." He turned up a card. "It's got two spots on it—see? Now, if you put that card in the middle and somebody else has one with two spots as well, you say 'Hee-haw,' and the card's yours."

"Mine?" Lottie was round-eyed. "To keep?"

"No, silly. Just for the game, see? Just while we're playing." The bull was very cross with her.

"Oh, Lottie, you *are* a little silly," said the proud rooster.

Lottie looked at both of them. Then she hung her head; her lip quivered. "I don't want to play," she whispered. The others glanced at one another like conspirators. All of them knew what that meant. She would go away and be discovered somewhere standing with her pinny thrown over her head, in a corner, or against a wall, or even behind a chair.

"Yes, you *do*, Lottie. It's quite easy," said Kezia.

And Isabel, repentant, said exactly like a grown-up, "Watch *me*, Lottie, and you'll soon learn."

"Cheer up, Lot," said Pip. "There, I know what I'll do. I'll give you the first one. It's mine, really, but I'll give it to you. Here you are." And he slammed the card down in front of Lottie.

Lottie revived at that. But now she was in another difficulty. "I haven't got a hanky," she said; "I want one badly, too."

"Here, Lottie, you can use mine." Rags dipped into his sailor blouse and brought up a very wet-looking one, knotted together. "Be very careful," he warned her. "Only use that corner. Don't undo it. I've got a little starfish inside I'm going to try and tame."

"Oh, come on, you girls," said the bull. "And mind—you're not to look at your cards. You've got to keep your hands under the table till I say 'Go.'"

Smack went the cards round the table. They tried with all their might to see, but Pip was too quick for them. It was very exciting, sitting there in the washhouse; it was all they could do not to burst into a little chorus of animals before Pip had finished dealing.

"Now, Lottie, you begin."

Timidly Lottie stretched out a hand, took the top card off her pack, had a good look at it—it was plain she was counting the spots—and put it down.

"No, Lottie, you can't do that. You mustn't look first. You must turn it the other way over."

"But then everybody will see it the same time as me," said Lottie. The game proceeded. Mooe-ooo-er! The bull was terrible. He charged over the table and seemed to eat the cards up.

Bss-ss! said the bee.

Cock-a-doodle-do! Isabel stood up in her excitement and moved her elbows like wings.

Baa! Little Rags put down the King of Diamonds and Lottie put down the one they called the King of Spain. She had hardly any cards left.

"Why don't you call out, Lottie?"

"I've forgotten what I am," said the donkey woefully.

"Well, change! Be a dog instead! Bow-wow!"

"Oh yes. That's *much* easier." Lottie smiled again. But when she and Kezia both had a one Kezia waited on purpose. The others made signs to Lottie and pointed. Lottie turned very red; she looked bewildered, and at last she said, "Hee-haw! Ke-zia."

"Ss! Wait a minute!" They were in the very thick of it when the bull stopped them, holding up his hand. "What's that? What's that noise?"

"What noise? What do you mean?" asked the rooster.

"Ss! Shut up! Listen!" They were mouse-still. "I thought I heard a—a sort of knocking," said the bull.

"What was it like?" asked the sheep faintly.

No answer.

The bee gave a shudder. "Whatever did we shut the door for?" she said softly. Oh, why, why had they shut the door?

While they were playing, the day had faded; the gorgeous sunset had blazed and died. And now the quick dark came racing over the sea, over the sand-hills, up the paddock. You were frightened to look in the corners of the washhouse, and yet you had to look with all your might. And somewhere, far away, grandma was lighting a lamp. The blinds were being pulled down; the kitchen fire leapt in the tins on the mantelpiece.

"It would be awful now," said the bull, "if a spider was to fall from the ceiling on to the table, wouldn't it?"

"Spiders don't fall from ceilings."

"Yes, they do. Our Min told us she'd seen a spider as big as a saucer, with long hairs on it like a gooseberry."

Quickly all the little heads were jerked up; all the little bodies drew together, pressed together.

"Why doesn't somebody come and call us?" cried the rooster.

Oh, those grown-ups, laughing and snug, sitting in the lamp-light, drinking out of cups! They'd forgotten about them. No, not really forgotten. That was what their smile meant. They had decided to leave them there all by themselves.

Suddenly Lottie gave such a piercing scream that all of them jumped off the forms, all of them screamed too. "A face—a face looking!" shrieked Lottie.

It was true, it was real. Pressed against the window was a pale face, black eyes, a black beard.

"Grandma! Mother! Somebody!"

But they had not got to the door, tumbling over one another, before it opened for Uncle Jonathan. He had come to take the little boys home.

X

He had meant to be there before, but in the front garden he had come upon Linda walking up and down the grass, stopping to pick off a dead pink or give a top-heavy carnation something to lean against, or to take a deep breath of something, and then walking on again, with her little air of remoteness. Over her white frock she wore a yellow, pink-fringed shawl from the Chinaman's shop.

"Hallo, Jonathan!" called Linda. And Jonathan whipped off his shabby panama, pressed it against his breast, dropped on one knee, and kissed Linda's hand.

"Greeting, my Fair One! Greeting, my Celestial Peach Blossom!" boomed the bass voice gently. "Where are the other noble dames?"

"Beryl's out playing bridge and mother's giving the boy his bath.... Have you come to borrow something?"

The Trouts were for ever running out of things and sending across to the Burnells' at the last moment.

But Jonathan only answered, "A little love, a little kindness;" and he walked by his sister-in-law's side.

Linda dropped into Beryl's hammock under the manuka tree, and Jonathan stretched himself on the grass beside her, pulled a long stalk and began chewing it. They knew each other well. The voices of children cried from the other gardens. A fisherman's light cart shook along the sandy road, and from far away they heard a dog barking; it was muffled as though the dog had its head in a sack. If you listened you could just hear the soft swish of the sea at full tide sweeping the pebbles. The sun was sinking.

"And so you go back to the office on Monday, do you, Jonathan?" asked Linda.

"On Monday the cage door opens and clangs to upon the victim for another eleven months and a week," answered Jonathan.

Linda swung a little. "It must be awful," she said slowly.

"Would ye have me laugh, my fair sister? Would ye have me weep?"

Linda was so accustomed to Jonathan's way of talking that she paid no attention to it.

"I suppose," she said vaguely, "one gets used to it. One gets used to anything."

"Does one? Hum!" the "Hum" was so deep it seemed to boom from underneath the ground. "I wonder how it's done," brooded Jonathan; "I've never managed it."

Looking at him as he lay there, Linda thought again how attractive he was. It was strange to think that he was only an ordinary clerk, that Stanley earned twice as much money as he. What was the matter with Jonathan? He had no ambition; she supposed that was it. And yet one felt he was gifted, exceptional. He was passionately fond of music; every spare penny he had went on books. He was always full of new ideas, schemes, plans. But nothing came of it all. The new fire blazed in Jonathan; you almost heard it roaring softly as he explained, described and dilated on the new thing; but a moment later it had fallen in and there was nothing but ashes, and Jonathan went about with a look like hunger in his black eyes. At these times he exaggerated his absurd manner of speaking, and he sang in church—he was the leader of the choir—with such fearful dramatic intensity that the meanest hymn put on an unholy splendour.

"It seems to me just as imbecile, just as infernal, to have to go to the office on Monday," said Jonathan, "as it always has done and always will do. To spend all the best years of one's life sitting on a stool from nine to five, scratching in somebody's ledger! It's a queer use to make of one's...one and only life, isn't it? Or do I fondly dream?" He rolled over on the grass and looked up at Linda. "Tell me, what is the difference between my life and that of an ordinary prisoner? The only difference I can see is that I put myself in jail and nobody's ever going to let me out. That's a more intolerable situation than the other. For if I'd been—pushed in, against my will—kicking, even—once the door was locked, or at any rate in five years or so, I might have accepted the fact and begun to take an interest in the flight of flies or counting the warder's steps along the passage with particular attention to variations of tread and so on. But as it is, I'm like an insect that's flown into a room of its own accord. I dash against the walls, dash against the windows, flop against the ceiling, do everything on God's earth, in fact, except fly out again. And all the while I'm thinking, like that moth, or that butterfly, or whatever it is, 'The shortness of life! The shortness of life!' I've only one night or one day, and there's this vast dangerous garden, waiting out there, undiscovered, unexplored."

"But, if you feel like that, why—" began Linda quickly.

"*Ah!*" cried Jonathan. And that "ah!" was somehow almost exultant. "There you have me. Why? Why indeed? There's the maddening, mysterious question. Why don't I fly out again? There's the window or the door or whatever it was I came in by. It's not hopelessly shut—is it? Why don't I find it and be off? Answer me that, little sister." But he gave her no time to answer.

"I'm exactly like that insect again. For some reason"Jonathan paused between the words"it's not allowed, it's forbidden, it's against the insect law, to stop banging and flopping and crawling up the pane even for an instant. Why don't I leave the office? Why don't I seriously consider, this moment, for instance, what it is that prevents me leaving? It's not as though I'm tremendously tied. I've two boys to provide for, but, after all, they're boys. I could cut off to sea, or get a job up-country, or" Suddenly he smiled at Linda and said in a changed voice, as if he were confiding a secret, "Weak...weak. No stamina. No anchor. No guiding principle, let us call it." But then the dark velvety voice rolled out:"

Would ye hear the story
How it unfolds itself...

and they were silent.

The sun had set. In the western sky there were great masses of crushed-up rose-coloured clouds. Broad beams of light shone through the clouds and beyond them as if they would cover the whole sky. Overhead the blue faded; it turned a pale gold, and the bush outlined against it gleamed dark and brilliant like metal. Sometimes when those beams of light show in the sky they are very awful. They remind you that up there sits Jehovah, the jealous God, the Almighty, Whose eye is upon you, ever watchful, never weary. You remember that at His coming the whole earth will shake into one ruined graveyard; the cold, bright angels will drive you this way and that, and there will be no time to explain what could be explained so simply.... But tonight it seemed to Linda there was something infinitely joyful and loving in those silver beams. And now no sound came from the sea. It breathed softly as if it would draw that tender, joyful beauty into its own bosom.

"It's all wrong, it's all wrong," came the shadowy voice of Jonathan. "It's not the scene, it's not the setting for...three stools, three desks, three ink pots and a wire blind."

Linda knew that he would never change, but she said, "Is it too late, even now?"

"I'm old—I'm old," intoned Jonathan. He bent towards her, he passed his hand over his head. "Look!" His black hair was speckled all over with silver, like the breast plumage of a black fowl.

Linda was surprised. She had no idea that he was grey. And yet, as he stood up beside her and sighed and stretched, she saw him, for the first time, not resolute, not gallant, not careless, but touched already with age. He looked very tall on the darkening grass, and the thought crossed her mind, "He is like a weed."

Jonathan stooped again and kissed her fingers.

"Heaven reward thy sweet patience, lady mine," he murmured. "I must go seek those heirs to my fame and fortune...." He was gone.

XI

Light shone in the windows of the bungalow. Two square patches of gold fell upon the pinks and the peaked marigolds. Florrie, the cat, came out on to the veranda, and sat on the top step, her white paws close together, her tail curled round. She looked content, as though she had been waiting for this moment all day.

"Thank goodness, it's getting late," said Florrie. "Thank goodness, the long day is over." Her greengage eyes opened.

Presently there sounded the rumble of the coach, the crack of Kelly's whip. It came near enough for one to hear the voices of the men from town, talking loudly together. It stopped at the Burnells' gate.

Stanley was half-way up the path before he saw Linda. "Is that you, darling?"

"Yes, Stanley."

He leapt across the flower-bed and seized her in his arms. She was enfolded in that familiar, eager, strong embrace.

"Forgive me, darling, forgive me," stammered Stanley, and he put his hand under her chin and lifted her face to him.

"Forgive you?" smiled Linda. "But whatever for?"

"Good God! You can't have forgotten," cried Stanley Burnell. "I've thought of nothing else all day. I've had the hell of a day. I made up my mind to dash out and telegraph, and then I thought the wire mightn't reach you before I did. I've been in tortures, Linda."

"But, Stanley," said Linda, "what must I forgive you for?"

"Linda!"—Stanley was very hurt—"didn't you realize—you must have realized—I went away without saying good-bye to you this morning? I can't imagine how I can have done such a thing. My confounded temper, of course. But—well"—and he sighed and took her in his arms again—"I've suffered for it enough today."

"What's that you've got in your hand?" asked Linda. "New gloves? Let me see."

"Oh, just a cheap pair of wash-leather ones," said Stanley humbly. "I noticed Bell was wearing some in the coach this morning, so, as I was passing the shop, I dashed in and got myself a pair. What are you smiling at? You don't think it was wrong of me, do you?"

"On the *contrary*, darling," said Linda, "I think it was most sensible."

She pulled one of the large, pale gloves on her own fingers and looked at her hand, turning it this way and that. She was still smiling.

Stanley wanted to say, "I was thinking of you the whole time I bought them." It was true, but for some reason he couldn't say it. "Let's go in," said he.

XII

Why does one feel so different at night? Why is it so exciting to be awake when everybody else is asleep? Late—it is very late! And yet every moment you feel more and more wakeful, as though you were slowly, almost with every breath, waking up into a new, wonderful, far more thrilling and exciting world than the daylight one. And what is this queer sensation that you're a conspirator? Lightly, stealthily you move about your room. You take something off the dressing-table and put it down again without a sound. And everything, even the bed-post, knows you, responds, shares your secret....

You're not very fond of your room by day. You never think about it. You're in and out, the door opens and slams, the cupboard creaks. You sit down on the side of your bed, change your shoes and dash out again. A dive down to the glass, two pins in your hair, powder your nose and off again. But now—it's suddenly dear to you. It's a darling little funny room. It's yours. Oh, what a joy it is to own things! Mine—my own!

"My very own for ever?"

"Yes." Their lips met.

No, of course, that had nothing to do with it. That was all nonsense and rubbish. But, in spite of herself, Beryl saw so plainly two people standing in the middle of her room. Her arms were round his neck; he held her. And now he whispered, "My beauty, my little beauty!" She jumped off her bed, ran over to the window and kneeled on the window-seat, with her elbows on the sill. But the beautiful night, the garden, every bush, every leaf, even the white palings, even the stars, were conspirators too. So bright was the moon that the flowers were bright as by day; the shadow of the nasturtiums, exquisite lily-like leaves and wide-open flowers, lay across the silvery veranda. The manuka-tree, bent by the southerly winds, was like a bird on one leg stretching out a wing.

But when Beryl looked at the bush, it seemed to her the bush was sad.

"We are dumb trees, reaching up in the night, imploring we know not what," said the sorrowful bush.

It is true when you are by yourself and you think about life, it is always sad. All that excitement and so on has a way of suddenly leaving you, and it's as though, in the silence, somebody called your name, and you heard your name for the first time. "Beryl!"

"Yes, I'm here. I'm Beryl. Who wants me?"

"Beryl!"

"Let me come."

It is lonely living by oneself. Of course, there are relations, friends, heaps of them; but that's not what she means. She wants someone who will find the Beryl they none of them know, who will expect her to be that Beryl always. She wants a lover.

"Take me away from all these other people, my love. Let us go far away. Let us live our life, all new, all ours, from the very beginning. Let us make our fire. Let us sit down to eat together. Let us have long talks at night."

And the thought was almost, "Save me, my love. Save me!"

…"Oh, go on! Don't be a prude, my dear. You enjoy yourself while you're young. That's my advice." And a high rush of silly laughter joined Mrs. Harry Kember's loud, indifferent neigh.

You see, it's so frightfully difficult when you've nobody. You're so at the mercy of things. You can't just be rude. And you've always this horror of seeming inexperienced and stuffy like the other ninnies at the Bay. And—and it's fascinating to know you've power over people. Yes, that is fascinating.…

Oh why, oh why doesn't "he" come soon?

If I go on living here, thought Beryl, anything may happen to me.

"But how do you know he is coming at all?" mocked a small voice within her.

But Beryl dismissed it. She couldn't be left. Other people, perhaps, but not she. It wasn't possible to think that Beryl Fairfield never married, that lovely fascinating girl.

"Do you remember Beryl Fairfield?"

"Remember her! As if I could forget her! It was one summer at the Bay that I saw her. She was standing on the beach in a blue"—no, pink—"muslin frock, holding on a big cream"—no, black—"straw hat. But it's years ago now."

"She's as lovely as ever, more so if anything."

Beryl smiled, bit her lip, and gazed over the garden. As she gazed, she saw somebody, a man, leave the road, step along the paddock beside their palings as if he was coming straight towards her. Her heart beat. Who was it? Who could it be? It couldn't be a burglar, certainly not a burglar, for he was smoking and he strolled lightly. Beryl's heart leapt; it seemed to turn right over, and then to stop. She recognized him.

"Good evening, Miss Beryl," said the voice softly.

"Good evening."

"Won't you come for a little walk?" it drawled.

Come for a walk—at that time of night! "I couldn't. Everybody's in bed. Everybody's asleep."

"Oh," said the voice lightly, and a whiff of sweet smoke reached her. "What does everybody matter? Do come! It's such a fine night. There's not a soul about."

Beryl shook her head. But already something stirred in her, something reared its head.

The voice said, "Frightened?" It mocked, "Poor little girl!"

"Not in the least," said she. As she spoke that weak thing within her seemed to uncoil, to grow suddenly tremendously strong; she longed to go!

And just as if this was quite understood by the other, the voice said, gently and softly, but finally, "Come along!"

Beryl stepped over her low window, crossed the veranda, ran down the grass to the gate. He was there before her.

"That's right," breathed the voice, and it teased, "You're not frightened, are you? You're not frightened?"

She was; now she was here she was terrified, and it seemed to her everything was different. The moonlight stared and glittered; the shadows were like bars of iron. Her hand was taken.

"Not in the least," she said lightly. "Why should I be?"

Her hand was pulled gently, tugged. She held back.

"No, I'm not coming any farther," said Beryl.

"Oh, rot!" Harry Kember didn't believe her. "Come along! We'll just go as far as that fuchsia bush. Come along!"

The fuchsia bush was tall. It fell over the fence in a shower. There was a little pit of darkness beneath.

"No, really, I don't want to," said Beryl.

For a moment Harry Kember didn't answer. Then he came close to her, turned to her, smiled and said quickly, "Don't be silly! Don't be silly!"

His smile was something she'd never seen before. Was he drunk? That bright, blind, terrifying smile froze her with horror. What was she doing? How had she got here? the stern garden asked her as the gate pushed open, and quick as a cat Harry Kember came through and snatched her to him.

"Cold little devil! Cold little devil!" said the hateful voice.

But Beryl was strong. She slipped, ducked, wrenched free.

"You are vile, vile," said she.

"Then why in God's name did you come?" stammered Harry Kember.

Nobody answered him.

A cloud, small, serene, floated across the moon. In that moment of darkness the sea sounded deep, troubled. Then the cloud sailed away, and the sound of the sea was a vague murmur, as though it waked out of a dark dream. All was still.

THE TIREDNESS OF ROSABEL

At the corner of Oxford Circus Rosabel bought a bunch of violets, and that was practically the reason why she had so little tea—for a scone and a boiled egg and a cup of cocoa at Lyons are not ample sufficiency after a hard day's work in a millinery establishment. As she swung on to the step of the Atlas bus, grabbed her skirt with one hand and clung to the railing with the other, Rosabel thought she would have sacrificed her soul for a good dinner—roast duck and green peas, chestnut stuffing, pudding with brandy sauce—something hot and strong and filling. She sat down next to a girl very much her own age who was reading Anna Lombard in a cheap, paper-covered edition, and the rain had tear-spattered the pages. Rosabel looked out of the windows; the street was blurred and misty, but light striking on the panes turned their dullness to opal and silver, and the jewellers' shops seen through this, were fairy palaces. Her feet were horribly wet, and she knew the bottom of her skirt and petticoat would be coated with black, greasy mud. There was a sickening smell of warm humanity—it seemed to be oozing out of everybody in the bus—and everybody had the same expression, sitting so still, staring in front of them. How many times had she read these advertisements—"Sapolio Saves Time, Saves Labour"—"Heinz's Tomato Sauce"—and the inane, annoying dialogue between doctor and judge concerning the superlative merits of "Lamplough's Pyretic Saline." She glanced at the book which the girl read so earnestly, mouthing the words in a way that Rosabel detested, licking her first finger and thumb each time that she turned the page. She could not see very clearly; it was something about a hot, voluptuous night, a band playing, and a girl with lovely, white shoulders. Oh, Heavens! Rosabel stirred suddenly and unfastened the two top buttons of her coat...she felt almost stifled. Through her half-closed eyes the whole row of people on the opposite seat seemed to resolve into one fatuous, staring face...

And this was her corner. She stumbled a little on her way out and lurched against the girl next her. "I beg your pardon," said Rosabel, but the girl did not even look up. Rosabel saw that she was smiling as she read.

Westbourne Grove looked as she had always imagined Venice to look at night, mysterious, dark, even the hansoms were like gondolas dodging up and down, and the lights trailing luridly—tongues of flame licking the wet street—magic fish swimming in the Grand Canal. She was more than glad to reach Richmond Road, but from the corner of the street until she came to No. 26 she thought of those four flights of stairs. Oh, why four flights! It was really criminal to expect people to live so high up. Every house ought to have a lift, something simple and inexpensive, or else an electric staircase like the one at Earl's Court—but four flights! When she stood in the hall and saw the first flight ahead of her and the stuffed albatross head on the landing, glimmering ghost-like in the light of the little gas jet, she almost cried. Well, they had to be faced; it was very like bicycling up a steep hill, but there was not the satisfaction of flying down the other side...

Her own room at last! She closed the door, lit the gas, took off her hat and coat, skirt, blouse, unhooked her old flannel dressing-gown from behind the door, pulled it on, then unlaced her boots—on consideration her stockings were not wet enough to change. She went over to the wash-stand. The jug had not been filled again today. There was just enough water to soak the sponge, and the enamel was coming off the basin—that was the second time she had scratched her chin.

It was just seven o'clock. If she pulled the blind up and put out the gas it was much more restful— Rosabel did not want to read. So she knelt down on the floor, pillowing her arms on the window-sill...just one little sheet of glass between her and the great wet world outside!

She began to think of all that had happened during the day. Would she ever forget that awful woman in the grey mackintosh who had wanted a trimmed motor-cap—"something purple with something rosy each side"—or the girl who had tried on every hat in the shop and then said she would "call in tomorrow and decide definitely." Rosabel could not help smiling; the excuse was worn so thin...

But there had been one other—a girl with beautiful red hair and a white skin and eyes the colour of that green ribbon shot with gold they had got from Paris last week. Rosabel had seen her electric brougham at the door; a man had come in with her, quite a young man, and so well dressed.

"What is it exactly that I want, Harry?" she had said, as Rosabel took the pins out of her hat, untied her veil, and gave her a hand-mirror.

"You must have a black hat," he had answered, "a black hat with a feather that goes right round it and then round your neck and ties in a bow under your chin, and the ends tuck into your belt—a decent-sized feather."

The girl glanced at Rosabel laughingly. "Have you any hats like that?"

They had been very hard to please; Harry would demand the impossible, and Rosabel was almost in despair. Then she remembered the big, untouched box upstairs.

"Oh, one moment, Madam," she had said. "I think perhaps I can show you something that will please you better." She had run up, breathlessly, cut the cords, scattered the tissue paper, and yes, there was the very hat—rather large, soft, with a great, curled feather, and a black velvet rose, nothing else. They had been charmed. The girl had put it on and then handed it to Rosabel.

"Let me see how it looks on you," she said, frowning a little, very serious indeed.

Rosabel turned to the mirror and placed it on her brown hair, then faced them.

"Oh, Harry, isn't it adorable," the girl cried, "I must have that!" She smiled again at Rosabel. "It suits you, beautifully."

A sudden, ridiculous feeling of anger had seized Rosabel. She longed to throw the lovely, perishable thing in the girl's face, and bent over the hat, flushing.

"It's exquisitely finished off inside, Madam," she said. The girl swept out to her brougham, and left Harry to pay and bring the box with him.

"I shall go straight home and put it on before I come out to lunch with you," Rosabel heard her say.

The man leant over her as she made out the bill, then, as he counted the money into her hand— "Ever been painted?" he said.

"No," said Rosabel, shortly, realising the swift change in his voice, the slight tinge of insolence, of familiarity.

"Oh, well you ought to be," said Harry. "You've got such a damned pretty little figure."

Rosabel did not pay the slightest attention. How handsome he had been! She had thought of no one else all day; his face fascinated her; she could see clearly his fine, straight eyebrows, and his hair grew back from his forehead with just the slightest suspicion of crisp curl, his laughing, disdainful mouth. She saw again his slim hands counting the money into hers... Rosabel suddenly pushed the hair back from her face, her forehead was hot...if those slim hands could rest one moment...the luck of that girl!

Suppose they changed places. Rosabel would drive home with him, of course they were in love with each other, but not engaged, very nearly, and she would say—"I won't be one moment." He would wait in the brougham while her maid took the hat-box up the stairs, following Rosabel. Then the great, white and pink bedroom with roses everywhere in dull silver vases. She would sit down before the mirror and the little French maid would fasten her hat and find her a thin, fine veil and another pair of white suède gloves—a button had come off the gloves she had worn that morning. She had scented her furs and gloves and handkerchief, taken a big muff and run down stairs. The butler opened the door, Harry was waiting, they drove away together... That was life, thought Rosabel! On the way to the Carlton they stopped at Gerard's, Harry bought her great sprays of Parma violets, filled her hands with them.

"Oh, they are sweet!" she said, holding them against her face.

"It is as you always should be," said Harry, "with your hands full of violets."

(Rosabel realised that her knees were getting stiff; she sat down on the floor and leant her head against the wall.) Oh, that lunch! The table covered with flowers, a band hidden behind a grove of palms playing music that fired her blood like wine—the soup, and oysters, and pigeons, and creamed potatoes, and champagne, of course, and afterwards coffee and cigarettes. She would lean over the table fingering her glass with one hand, talking with that charming gaiety which Harry so appreciated. Afterwards a matinee, something that gripped them both, and then tea at the "Cottage."

"Sugar? Milk? Cream?" The little homely questions seemed to suggest a joyous intimacy. And then home again in the dusk, and the scent of the Parma violets seemed to drench the air with their sweetness.

"I'll call for you at nine," he said as he left her.

The fire had been lighted in her boudoir, the curtains drawn, there were a great pile of letters waiting her—invitations for the Opera, dinners, balls, a week-end on the river, a motor tour—she glanced through them listlessly as she went upstairs to dress. A fire in her bedroom, too, and her beautiful, shining dress spread on the bed—white tulle over silver, silver shoes, silver scarf, a little silver fan. Rosabel knew that she was the most famous woman at the ball that night; men paid her homage, a foreign Prince desired to be presented to this English wonder. Yes, it was a voluptuous night, a band playing, and her lovely white shoulders...

But she became very tired. Harry took her home, and came in with her for just one moment. The fire was out in the drawingroom, but the sleepy maid waited for her in her boudoir. She took off her cloak, dismissed the servant, and went over to the fireplace, and stood peeling off her gloves; the firelight shone on her hair, Harry came across the room and caught her in his arms—"Rosabel, Rosabel, Rosabel"... Oh, the haven of those arms, and she was very tired.

(The real Rosabel, the girl crouched on the floor in the dark, laughed aloud, and put her hand up to her hot mouth.)

Of course they rode in the park next morning, the engagement had been announced in the Court Circular, all the world knew, all the world was shaking hands with her...

They were married shortly afterwards at St. George's, Hanover Square, and motored down to Harry's old ancestral home for the honeymoon; the peasants in the village curtseyed to them as they passed; under the folds of the rug he pressed her hands convulsively. And that night she wore again her white and silver frock. She was tired after the journey and went upstairs to bed...quite early...

The real Rosabel got up from the floor and undressed slowly, folding her clothes over the back of a chair. She slipped over her head her coarse, calico nightdress, and took the pins out of her hair—the soft, brown flood of it fell round her, warmly. Then she blew out the candle and groped her way into bed, pulling the blankets and grimy "honeycomb" quilt closely round her neck, cuddling down in the darkness...

So she slept and dreamed, and smiled in her sleep, and once threw out her arm to feel for something which was not there, dreaming still.

And the night passed. Presently the cold fingers of dawn closed over her uncovered hand; grey light flooded the dull room. Rosabel shivered, drew a little gasping breath, sat up. And because her heritage was that tragic optimism, which is all too often the only inheritance of youth, still half asleep, she smiled, with a little nervous tremor round her mouth.

HOW PEARL BUTTON WAS KIDNAPPED

Pearl Button swung on the little gate in front of the House of Boxes. It was the early afternoon of a sunshiny day with little winds playing hide-and-seek in it. They blew Pearl Button's pinafore frill into her mouth, and they blew the street dust all over the House of Boxes. Pearl watched it—like a cloud—like when mother peppered her fish and the top of the pepper-pot came off. She swung on the little gate, all alone, and she sang a small song. Two big women came walking down the street. One was dressed in red and the other was dressed in yellow and green. They had pink handkerchiefs over their heads, and both of them carried a big flax basket of ferns. They had no shoes and stockings on, and they came walking along, slowly, because they were so fat, and talking to each other and always smiling. Pearl stopped swinging, and when they saw her they stopped walking. They looked and looked at her and then they talked to each other, waving their arms and clapping their hands together. Pearl began to laugh.

The two women came up to her, keeping close to the hedge and looking in a frightened way towards the House of Boxes.

"Hallo, little girl!" said one.

Pearl said, "Hallo!"

"You all alone by yourself?"

Pearl nodded.

"Where's your mother?"

"In the kitching, ironing-because-its-Tues-day."

The women smiled at her and Pearl smiled back. "Oh," she said, "haven't you got very white teeth indeed! Do it again."

The dark women laughed, and again they talked to each other with funny words and wavings of the hands. "What's your name?" they asked her.

"Pearl Button."

"You coming with us, Pearl Button? We got beautiful things to show you," whispered one of the women. So Pearl got down from the gate and she slipped out into the road. And she walked between the two dark women down the windy road, taking little running steps to keep up, and wondering what they had in their House of Boxes.

They walked a long way. "You tired?" asked one of the women, bending down to Pearl. Pearl shook her head. They walked much further. "You not tired?" asked the other woman. And Pearl shook her head again, but tears shook from her eyes at the same time and her lips trembled. One of the women gave over her flax basket of ferns and caught Pearl Button up in her arms, and walked with Pearl Button's head against her shoulder and her dusty little legs dangling. She was softer than a bed and she had a nice smell—a smell that made you bury your head and breathe and breathe it...

They set Pearl Button down in a log room full of other people the same colour as they were—and all these people came close to her and looked at her, nodding and laughing and throwing up their eyes. The woman who had carried Pearl took off her hair ribbon and shook her curls loose. There was a cry from the other women, and they crowded close and some of them ran a finger through Pearl's yellow curls, very gently, and one of them, a young one, lifted all Pearl's hair and kissed the back of her little white neck. Pearl felt shy but happy at the same time. There were some men on the floor, smoking, with rugs and feather mats round their shoulders. One of them made a funny face at her and he pulled a great big peach out of his pocket and set it on the floor, and flicked it with his finger as though it were a marble. It rolled right over to her. Pearl picked it up. "Please can I eat it?" she asked. At that they all laughed and clapped their hands, and the man with the funny face made another at her and pulled a pear out of his pocket and sent it bobbling over the floor. Pearl laughed. The women sat on the floor and Pearl sat down too. The floor was very dusty. She carefully pulled up her pinafore and dress and sat on her petticoat as she had been taught to sit in dusty places, and she ate the fruit, the juice running all down her front.

"Oh!" she said in a very frightened voice to one of the women, "I've spilt all the juice!

"That doesn't matter at all," said the woman, patting her cheek. A man came into the room with a long whip in his hand. He shouted something. They all got up, shouting, laughing, wrapping themselves up in rugs and blankets and feather mats. Pearl was carried again, this time into a great cart, and she sat on the lap of one of her women with the driver beside her. It was a green cart with a red pony and a black pony. It went very fast out of the town. The driver stood up and waved the whip round his head. Pearl peered over the shoulder of her woman. Other carts were behind like a procession. She waved at them. Then the country came. First fields of short grass with sheep on them and little bushes of white flowers and pink briar rose baskets—then big trees on both sides of the road—and nothing to be seen except big trees. Pearl tried to look through them but it was quite dark. Birds were singing. She nestled closer in the big lap. The woman was warm as a cat, and she moved up and down when she breathed, just like purring. Pearl played with a green ornament round her neck, and the woman took the little hand and kissed each of her fingers and then turned it over and kissed the dimples. Pearl had never been happy like this before. On the top of a big hill they stopped. The driving man turned to Pearl and said, "Look, look!" and pointed with his whip.

And down at the bottom of the hill was something perfectly different—a great big piece of blue water was creeping over the land. She screamed and clutched at the big woman, "What is it, what is it?"

"Why," said the woman, "it's the sea."

"Will it hurt us—is it coming?"

"Ai-e, no, it doesn't come to us. It's very beautiful. You look again."

Pearl looked. "You're sure it can't come," she said.

"Ai-e, no. It stays in its place," said the big woman. Waves with white tops came leaping over the blue. Pearl watched them break on a long piece of land covered with gardenpath shells. They drove round a corner.

There were some little houses down close to the sea, with wood fences round them and gardens inside. They comforted her. Pink and red and blue washing hung over the fences, and as they came near more people came out, and five yellow dogs with long thin tails. All the people were fat and laughing, with little naked babies holding on to them or rolling about in the gardens like puppies. Pearl was lifted down and taken into a tiny house with only one room and a verandah. There was a girl there with two pieces of black hair down to her feet. She was setting the dinner on the floor. "It is a funny place," said Pearl, watching the pretty girl while the woman unbuttoned her little drawers for her. She was very hungry. She ate meat and vegetables and fruit and the woman gave her milk out of a green cup. And it was quite silent except for the sea outside and the laughs of the two women watching her.

"Haven't you got any Houses of Boxes?" she said. "Don't you all live in a row? Don't the men go to offices? Aren't there any nasty things?"

They took off her shoes and stockings, her pinafore and dress. She walked about in her petticoat and then she walked outside with the grass pushing between her toes. The two women came out with different sorts of baskets. They took her hands. Over a little paddock, through a fence, and then on warm sand with brown grass in it they went down to the sea. Pearl held back when the sand grew wet, but the women coaxed, "Nothing to hurt, very beautiful. You come." They dug in the sand and found some shells which they threw into the baskets. The sand was wet as mud pies. Pearl forgot her fright and began digging too. She got hot and wet, and suddenly over her feet broke a little line of foam. "Oo, oo!" she shrieked, dabbling with her feet, "Lovely, lovely!" She paddled in the shallow water. It was warm. She made a cup of her hands and caught some of it. But it stopped being blue in her hands. She was so excited that she rushed over to her woman and flung her little thin arms round the woman's neck, hugging her, kissing...

Suddenly the girl gave a frightful scream. The woman raised herself and Pearl slipped down on the sand and looked towards the land. Little men in blue coats—little blue men came running, running towards her with shouts and whistlings—a crowd of little blue men to carry her back to the House of Boxes.

THE JOURNEY TO BRUGES

"You got three-quarters of an hour," said the porter. "You got an hour mostly. Put it in the cloak-room, lady."

A German family, their luggage neatly buttoned into what appeared to be odd canvas trouser legs, filled the entire space before the counter, and a homoeopathic young clergyman, his black dicky flapping over his shirt, stood at my elbow. We waited and waited, for the cloak-room porter could not get rid of the German family, who appeared by their enthusiasm and gestures to be explaining to him the virtue of so many buttons. At last the wife of the party seized her particular packet and started to undo it. Shrugging his shoulders, the porter turned to me. "Where for?" he asked.

"Ostend."

"Wot are you putting it in here for?" I said, "Because I've a long time to wait."

He shouted, "Train's in 2.20. No good bringing it here. Hi, you there, lump it off!"

My porter lumped it. The young clergyman, who had listened and remarked, smiled at me radiantly. "The train is in," he said, "really in. You've only a few moments, you know." My sensitiveness glimpsed a symbol in his eye. I ran to the book-stall. When I returned I had lost my porter. In the teasing heat I ran up and down the platform. The whole travelling world seemed to possess a porter and glory in him except me. Savage and wretched I saw them watch me with that delighted relish of the hot in the very much hotter. "One could have a fit running in weather like this," said a stout lady, eating a farewell present of grapes. Then I was informed that the train was not yet in. I had been running up and down the Folkstone express. On a higher platform I found my porter sitting on the suit case.

"I knew you'd be doin' that," he said, airily.

"I nearly come and stop you. I seen you from' ere."

I dropped into a smoking compartment with four young men, two of whom were saying good-bye to a pale youth with a cane. "Well, good-bye, old chap. It's frightfully good of you to have come down. I knew you. I knew the same old slouch. Now, look here, when we come back we'll have a night of it. What? Ripping of you to have come, old man." This from an enthusiast, who lit a cigar as the train swung out, turned to his companion and said, "Frightfully nice chap, but—lord—what a bore!" His companion, who was dressed entirely in mole, even unto his socks and hair, smiled gently. I think his brain must have been the same colour: he proved so gentle and sympathetic a listener. In the opposite corner to me sat a beautiful young Frenchman with curly hair and a watch-chain from which dangled a silver fish, a ring, a silver shoe, and a medal. He stared out of the window the whole time, faintly twitching his nose. Of the remaining member there was nothing to be seen from behind his luggage but a pair of tan shoes and a copy of The Snark's Summer Annual.

"Look here, old man," said the Enthusiast, "I want to change all our places. You know those arrangements you've made—I want to cut them out altogether. Do you mind?"

"No," said the Mole, faintly. "But why?"

"Well, I was thinking it over in bed last night, and I'm hanged if I can see the good of us paying fifteen bob if we don't want to. You see what I mean?" The Mole took off his pince-nez and breathed on them. "Now I don't want to unsettle you," went on the Enthusiast, "because, after all, it's your party—you asked me. I wouldn't upset it for anything, but—there you are—you see—what?"

Suggested the Mole: "I'm afraid people will be down on me for taking you abroad."

Straightway the other told him how sought after he had been. From far and near, people who were full up for the entire month of August had written and begged for him. He wrung the Mole's heart by enumerating those longing homes and vacant chairs dotted all over England, until the Mole deliberated between crying and going to sleep. He chose the latter.

They all went to sleep except the young Frenchman, who took a little pocket edition out of his coat and nursed it on his knee while he gazed at the warm, dusty country. At Shorncliffe the train stopped. Dead silence. There was nothing to be seen but a large white cemetery. Fantastic it looked in the late afternoon sun, its full-length marble angels appearing to preside over a cheerless picnic of the Shorncliffe departed on the brown field. One white butterfly flew over the railway lines. As we crept out of the station I saw a poster advertising the Athenaeum. The Enthusiast grunted and yawned, shook himself into existence by rattling the money in his trouser pockets. He jabbed the Mole in the ribs. "I say, we're nearly there! Can you get down those beastly golf-clubs of mine from the rack?" My heart yearned over the Mole's immediate future, but he was cheerful and offered to find me a porter at Dover, and strapped my parasol in with my rugs. We saw the sea. "It's going to be beastly rough," said the Enthusiast, "Gives you a head, doesn't it? Look here, I know a tip for sea-sickness, and it's this: You lie on your back—flat—you know, cover your face, and eat nothing but biscuits."

"Dover!" shouted a guard.

In the act of crossing the gangway we renounced England. The most blatant British female produced her mite of French: we "S'il vous plaît'd" one another on the deck, "Merci'd" one another on the stairs, and "Pardon'd" to our heart's content in the saloon. The stewardess stood at the foot of the stairs, a stout, forbidding female, pockmarked, her hands hidden under a businesslike-looking apron. She replied to our salutations with studied indifference, mentally ticking off her prey. I descended to the cabin to remove my hat. One old lady was already established there.

She lay on a rose and white couch, a black shawl tucked round her, fanning herself with a black feather fan. Her grey hair was half covered with a lace cap and her face gleamed from the black drapings and rose pillows with charming old-world dignity. There was about her a faint rustling and the scents of camphor and lavender. As I watched her, thinking of Rembrandt and, for some reason, Anatole France, the stewardess bustled up, placed a canvas stool at her elbow, spread a newspaper upon it, and banged down a receptacle rather like a baking tin. I went up on deck. The sea was bright green, with rolling waves. All the beauty and artificial flower of France had removed their hats and bound their heads in veils. A number of young German men, displaying their national bulk in light-coloured suits cut in the pattern of pyjamas, promenaded. French family parties—the female element in chairs, the male in graceful attitudes against the ship's side—talked already with that brilliance which denotes friction! I found a chair in a corner against a white partition, but unfortunately this partition had a window set in it for the purpose of providing endless amusement for the curious, who peered through it, watching those bold and brave spirits who walked "for'ard" and were drenched and beaten by the waves. In the first half-hour the excitement of getting wet and being pleaded with, and rushing into dangerous places to return and be rubbed down, was all-absorbing. Then it palled—the parties drifted into silence. You would catch them staring intently at the ocean—and yawning. They grew cold and snappy. Suddenly a young lady in a white woollen hood with cherry bows got up from her chair and swayed over to the railings. We watched her, vaguely sympathetic. The young man with whom she had been sitting called to her.

"Are you better?" Negative expressed.

He sat up in his chair. "Would you like me to hold your head?"

"No," said her shoulders

"Would you care for a coat round you?... Is it over?... Are you going to remain there?"... He looked at her with infinite tenderness. I decided never again to call men unsympathetic, and to believe in the all conquering power of love until I died—but never put it to the test. I went down to sleep.

I lay down opposite the old lady, and watched the shadows spinning over the ceilings and the wave-drops shining on the portholes.

In the shortest sea voyage there is no sense of time. You have been down in the cabin for hours or days or years. Nobody knows or cares. You know all the people to the point of indifference. You do not believe in dry land any more—you are caught in the pendulum itself, and left there, idly swinging. The light faded.

I fell asleep, to wake to find the stewardess shaking me. "We are there in two minutes," said she. Forlorn ladies, freed from the embrace of Neptune, knelt upon the floor and searched for their shoes and hairpins—only the old and dignified one lay passive, fanning herself. She looked at me and smiled.

"Grâce de Dieu, c'est fini," she quavered in a voice so fine it seemed to quaver on a thread of lace.

I lifted up my eyes. "*Oui, c'est fini!*"

"*Vous allez à Strasbourg, Madame?*"

"No," I said. "Bruges."

"That is a great pity," said she, closing her fan and the conversation. I could not think why, but I had visions of myself perhaps travelling in the same railway carriage with her, wrapping her in the black shawl, of her falling in love with me and leaving me unlimited quantities of money and old lace... These sleepy thoughts pursued me until I arrived on deck.

The sky was indigo blue, and a great many stars were shining: our little ship stood black and sharp in the clear air. "Have you the tickets?... Yes, they want the tickets... Produce your tickets!"... We were squeezed over the gangway, shepherded into the custom house, where porters heaved our luggage on to long wooden slabs, and an old man wearing horn spectacles checked it without a word.

"Follow me!" shouted the villainous-looking creature whom I had endowed with my worldly goods. He leapt on to a railway line, and I leapt after him. He raced along a platform, dodging the passengers and fruit wagons, with the security of a cinematograph figure. I reserved a seat and went to buy fruit at a little stall displaying grapes and greengages. The old lady was there, leaning on the arm of a large blond man, in white, with a flowing tie. We nodded.

"Buy me," she said in her delicate voice, "three ham sandwiches, mon cher!"

"And some cakes," said he.

"Yes, and perhaps a bottle of lemonade."

"Romance is an imp!" thought I, climbing up into the carriage. The train swung out of the station; the air, blowing through the open windows, smelled of fresh leaves. There were sudden pools of light in the darkness; when I arrived at Bruges the bells were ringing, and white and mysterious shone the moon over the Grand' Place.

A TRUTHFUL ADVENTURE

"The little town lies spread before the gaze of the eager traveller like a faded tapestry threaded with the silver of its canals, made musical by the great chiming belfry. Life is long since asleep in Bruges; fantastic dreams alone breathe over tower and mediaeval house front, enchanting the eye, inspiring the soul and filling the mind with the great beauty of contemplation."

I read this sentence from a guide-book while waiting for Madame in the hotel sitting-room. It sounded extremely comforting, and my tired heart, tucked away under a thousand and one grey city wrappings, woke and exulted within me... I wondered if I had enough clothes with me to last for at least a month. "I shall dream away whole days," I thought, "take a boat and float up and down the canals, or tether it to a green bush tangling the water side, and absorb mediaeval house fronts. At evensong I shall lie in the long grass of the Béguinage meadow and look up at the elm trees—their leaves touched with gold light and quivering in the blue air—listening the while to the voices of nuns at prayer in the little chapel, and growing full enough of grace to last me the whole winter."

While I soared magnificently upon these very new feathers Madame came in and told me that there was no room at all for me in the hotel—not a bed, not a corner. She was extremely friendly and seemed to find a fund of secret amusement in the fact; she looked at me as though expecting me to break into delighted laughter. "Tomorrow," she said, "there may be. I am expecting a young gentleman who is suddenly taken ill to move from number eleven. He is at present at the chemist's—perhaps you would care to see the room?"

"Not at all," said I. "Neither shall I wish tomorrow to sleep in the bedroom of an indisposed young gentleman."

"But he will be gone," cried Madame, opening her blue eyes wide and laughing with that French cordiality so enchanting to English hearing. I was too tired and hungry to feel either appreciative or argumentative. "Perhaps you can recommend me another hotel?"

"Impossible!" She shook her head and turned up her eyes, mentally counting over the blue bows painted on the ceiling. "You see, it is the season in Bruges, and people do not care to let their rooms for a very short time"—not a glance at my little suit case lying between us, but I looked at it gloomily, and it seemed to dwindle before my desperate gaze—become small enough to hold nothing but a collapsible folding tooth-brush.

"My large box is at the station," I said coldly, buttoning my gloves.

Madame started. "You have more luggage… Then you intend to make a long stay in Bruges, perhaps?"

"At least a fortnight—perhaps a month." I shrugged my shoulders.

"One moment," said Madame. "I shall see what I can do." She disappeared, I am sure not further than the other side of the door, for she reappeared immediately and told me I might have a room at her private house—"ust round the corner and kept by an old servant who, although she has a wall eye, has been in our family for fifteen years. The porter will take you there, and you can have supper before you go."

I was the only guest in the dining-room. A tired waiter provided me with an omelette and a pot of coffee, then leaned against a sideboard and watched me while I ate, the limp table napkin over his arm seeming to symbolise the very man. The room was hung with mirrors reflecting unlimited empty tables and watchful waiters and solitary ladies finding sad comfort in omelettes, and sipping coffee to the rhythm of Mendelssohn's Spring Song played over three times by the great chiming belfry.

"Are you ready, Madame?" asked the waiter. "It is I who carry your luggage."

"Quite ready."

He heaved the suit case on to his shoulder and strode before me—past the little pavement cafés where men and women, scenting our approach, laid down their beer and their post-cards to stare after us, down a narrow street of shuttered houses, through the Place van Eyck, to a red-brick house. The door was opened by the wall-eyed family treasure, who held a candle like a miniature frying-pan in her hand. She refused to admit us until we had both told the whole story.

"C'est ça, c'est ça," said she. "Jean, number five!"

She shuffled up the stairs, unlocked a door and lit another miniature frying-pan upon the bed-table. The room was papered in pink, having a pink bed, a pink door and a pink chair. On pink mats on the mantelpiece obese young cherubs burst out of pink eggshells with trumpets in their mouths. I was brought a can of hot water; I shut and locked the door. "Bruges at last," I thought as I climbed into a bed so slippery with fine linen that one felt like a fish endeavouring to swim over an ice pond, and this quiet house with the old "typical" servant,—the Place van Eyck, with the white statue surrounded by those dark and heavy trees,—there was almost a touch of Verlaine in that…

Bang! went a door. I started up in terror and felt for the frying-pan, but it was the room next to mine suddenly invaded. "Ah! home at last," cried a female voice. "Mon Dieu, my feet! Would you go down to Marie, mon cher, and ask her for the tin bath and some hot water?"

"No, that is too much," boomed the answer. "You have washed them three times today already."

"But you do not know the pain I suffer; they are quite inflamed. Look only!"

"I have looked three times already; I am tired. I beg of you come to bed."

"It would be useless; I could not sleep. Mon Dieu, mon Dieu, how a woman suffers!" A masculine snort accompanied by the sounds of undressing.

"Then, if I wait until the morning will you promise not to drag me to a picture gallery?"

"Yes, yes, I promise."

"But truly?"

"I have said so."

"Now can I believe you?"

A long groan.

"It is absurd to make that noise, for you know yourself the same thing happened last evening and this morning."

...There was only one thing to be done. I coughed and cleared my throat in that unpleasant and obtrusive way of strange people in next door bedrooms. It acted like a charm, their conversation sifted into a whisper for female voice only! I fell asleep.

"Barquettes for hire. Visit the Venice of the North by boat. Explore the little known and fascinating by-ways." With the memory of the guide book clinging about me I went into the shop and demanded a boat. "Have you a small canoe?"

"No, Mademoiselle, but a little boat—very suitable."

"I wish to go alone and return when I like."

"Then you have been here before?"

"No."

The boatman looked puzzled. "It is not safe for Mademoiselle to go without a guide for the first time."

"Then I will take one on the condition that he is silent and points out no beauties to me."

"But the names of the bridges?" cried the boatman—"the famous house fronts?"

I ran down to the landing stage. "Pierre, Pierre!" called the waterman. A burly young Belgian, his arms full of carpet strips and red velvet pillows, appeared and tossed his spoil into an immense craft. On the bridge above the landing stage a crowd collected, watching the proceedings, and just as I took my seat a fat couple who had been hanging over the parapet rushed down the steps and declared they must come too. "Certainly, certainly," said Pierre, handing in the lady with charming grace. "Mademoiselle will not mind at all." They sat in the stern, the gentleman held the lady's hand, and we twisted among these "silver ribbons" while Pierre threw out his chest and chanted the beauties of Bruges with the exultant abandon of a Latin lover. "Turn your head this way—to the left—to the right—now, wait one moment—look up at the bridge—observe this house front. Mademoiselle do you wish to see the Lac d'Amour?"

I looked vague; the fat couple answered for me.

"Then we shall disembark."

We rowed close into a little parapet. We caught hold of a bush and I jumped out. "Now, Monsieur," who successfully followed, and, kneeling on the bank, gave Madame the crook of his walking-stick for support. She stood up, smiling and vigorous, clutched the walking-stick, strained against the boat side, and the next moment had fallen flat into the water. "Ah! what has happened—what has happened!" screamed Monsieur, clutching her arm, for the water was not deep, reaching only to her waist mark. Somehow or other we fished her up on to the bank where she sat and gasped, wringing her black alpaca skirt.

"It is all over—a little accident!" said she, amazingly cheerful.

But Pierre was furious. "It is the fault of Mademoiselle for wishing to see the Lac d'Amour," said he. "Madame had better walk through the meadow and drink something hot at the little café opposite."

"No, no," said she, but Monsieur seconded Pierre.

"You will await our return," said Pierre, loathing me. I nodded and turned my back, for the sight of Madame flopping about on the meadow grass like a large, ungainly duck, was too much. One cannot expect to travel in upholstered boats with people who are enlightened enough to understand laughter that has its wellspring in sympathy. When they were out of sight I ran as fast as I could over the meadow, crawled through a fence, and never went near the Lac d'Amour again. "They may think me as drowned as they please," thought I, "I have had quite enough of canals to last me a lifetime."

In the Béguinage meadow at evensong little groups of painters are dotted about in the grass with spindle-legged easels which seem to possess a separate individuality, and stand rudely defying their efforts and returning their long, long gaze with an unfinished stare. English girls wearing flower-wreathed hats and the promise of young American manhood, give expression to their souls with a gaiety and "camaraderie," a sort of "the world is our shining playground" spirit—theoretically delightful. They call to one another, and throw cigarettes and fruit and chocolates with youthful naïveté, while parties of tourists who have escaped the clutches of an old woman lying in wait for them in the shadow of the chapel door, pause thoughtfully in front of the easels to "see and remark, and say whose?"

I was lying under a tree with the guilty consciousness of no sketch book—watching the swifts wheel and dip in the bright air, and wondering if all the brown dogs resting in the grass belonged to the young painters, when two people passed me, a man and a girl, their heads bent over a book. There was something vaguely familiar in their walk. Suddenly they looked down at me—we stared—opened our mouths. She swooped down upon me, and he took off his immaculate straw hat and placed it under his left arm.

"Katherine! How extraordinary! How incredible after all these years!" cried she. Turning to the man: "Guy, can you believe it?—It's Katherine, in Bruges of all places in the world!"

"Why not?" said I, looking very bright and trying to remember her name.

"But, my dear, the last time we met was in New Zealand—only think of the miles!"

Of course, she was Betty Sinclair; I'd been to school with her.

"Where are you staying; have you been here long? Oh, you haven't changed a day—not a day. I'd have known you anywhere."

She beckoned to the young man, and said, blushing as though she were ashamed of the fact, but it had to be faced, "This is my husband." We shook hands. He sat down and chewed a grass twig. Silence fell while Betty recovered breath and squeezed my hand.

"I didn't know you were married," I said stupidly.

"Oh, my dear—got a baby!" said Betty. "We live in England now. We're frightfully keen on the Suffrage, you know."

Guy removed the straw. "Are you with us?" he asked, intensely.

I shook my head. He put the straw back again and narrowed his eyes.

"Then here's the opportunity," said Betty. "My dear, how long are you going to stay? We must go about together and have long talks. Guy and I aren't a honeymoon couple, you know. We love to have other people with us sometimes."

The belfry clashed into See the Conquering Hero Comes!

"Unfortunately I have to go home quite soon. I've had an urgent letter."

"How disappointing! You know Bruges is simply packed with treasures and churches and pictures. There's an out-door concert tonight in the Grand' Place, and a competition of bell ringers tomorrow to go on for a whole week."

"Go I must," I said so firmly that my soul felt imperative marching orders, stimulated by the belfry.

"But the quaint streets and the Continental smells, and the lace makers—if we could just wander about—we three—and absorb it all." I sighed and bit my underlip.

"What's your objection to the vote?" asked Guy, watching the nuns wending their way in sweet procession among the trees.

"I always had the idea you were so frightfully keen on the future of women," said Betty. "Come to dinner with us tonight. Let's thrash the whole subject out. You know, after the strenuous life in London, one does seem to see things in such a different light in this old world city."

"Oh, a very different light indeed," I answered, shaking my head at the familiar guide book emerging from Guy's pocket.

Mrs. Carsfield and her mother sat at the dining-room table putting the finishing touches to some green cashmere dresses. They were to be worn by the two Misses Carsfield at church on the following day, with apple-green sashes, and straw hats with ribbon tails. Mrs. Carsfield had set her heart on it, and this being a late night for Henry, who was attending a meeting of the Political League, she and the old mother had the dining-room to themselves, and could make "a peaceful litter" as she expressed it. The red cloth was taken off the table—where stood the wedding-present sewing machine, a brown work-basket, the "material," and some torn fashion journals. Mrs. Carsfield worked the machine, slowly, for she feared the green thread would give out, and had a sort of tired hope that it might last longer if she was careful to use a little at a time; the old woman sat in a rocking chair, her skirt turned back, and her felt-slippered feet on a hassock, tying the machine threads and stitching some narrow lace on the necks and cuffs. The gas jet flickered. Now and again the old woman glanced up at the jet and said, "There's water in the pipe, Anne, that's what's the matter," then was silent, to say again a moment later, "There must be water in that pipe, Anne," and again, with quite a burst of energy, "Now there is—I'm certain of it."

Anne frowned at the sewing machine. "The way mother harps on things—it gets frightfully on my nerves," she thought. "And always when there's no earthly opportunity to better a thing...I suppose it's old age—but most aggravating." Aloud she said: "Mother, I'm having a really substantial hem in this dress of Rose's—the child has got so leggy, lately. And don't put any lace on Helen's cuffs; it will make a distinction, and besides she's so careless about rubbing her hands on anything grubby."

"Oh there's plenty," said the old woman. "I'll put it a little higher up." And she wondered why Anne had such a down on Helen—Henry was just the same. They seemed to want to hurt Helen's feelings—the distinction was merely an excuse.

"Well," said Mrs. Carsfield, "you didn't see Helen's clothes when I took them off tonight, Black from head to foot after a week. And when I compared them before her eyes with Rose's she merely shrugged, you know that habit she's got, and began stuttering. I really shall have to see Dr. Malcolm about her stuttering, if only to give her a good fright. I believe it's merely an affectation she's picked up at school—that she can help it."

"Anne, you know she's always stuttered. You did just the same when you were her age, she's highly strung." The old woman took off her spectacles, breathed on them, and rubbed them with a corner of her sewing apron.

"Well, the last thing in the world to do her any good is to let her imagine that" answered Anne, shaking out one of the green frocks, and pricking at the pleats with her needle. "She is treated exactly like Rose, and the Boy hasn't a nerve. Did you see him when I put him on the rocking-horse today, for the first time? He simply gurgled with joy. He's more the image of his father every day."

"Yes, he certainly is a thorough Carsfield," assented the old woman, nodding her head.

"Now that's another thing about Helen," said Anne. "The peculiar way she treats Boy, staring at him and frightening him as she does. You remember when he was a baby how she used to take away his bottle to see what he would do? Rose is perfect with the child—but Helen..."

The old woman put down her work on the table. A little silence fell, and through the silence the loud ticking of the dining-room clock. She wanted to speak her mind to Anne once and for all about the way she and Henry were treating Helen, ruining the child, but the ticking noise distracted her. She could not think of the words and sat there stupidly, her brain going tick, tick, to the dining-room clock.

"How loudly that clock ticks," was all she said.

"Oh there's mother—off the subject again—giving me no help or encouragement," thought Anne. She glanced at the clock.

"Mother, if you've finished that frock, would you go into the kitchen and heat up some coffee, and perhaps cut a plate of ham. Henry will be in directly. I'm practically through with this second frock by myself." She held it up for inspection. "Aren't they charming? They ought to last the children a good two years, and then I expect they'll do for school—lengthened, and perhaps dyed."

"I'm glad we decided on the more expensive material," said the old woman.

Left alone in the dining-room Anne's frown deepened, and her mouth drooped—a sharp line showed from nose to chin. She breathed deeply, and pushed back her hair. There seemed to be no air in the room, she felt stuffed up, and it seemed so useless to be tiring herself out with fine sewing for Helen. One never got through with children, and never had any gratitude from them—except Rose—who was exceptional. Another sign of old age in mother was her absurd point of view about Helen, and her "touchiness" on the subject. There was one thing, Mrs. Carsfield said to herself. She was determined to keep Helen apart from Boy. He had all his father's sensitiveness to unsympathetic influences. A blessing that the girls were at school all day!

At last the dresses were finished and folded over the back of the chair. She carried the sewing machine over to the book-shelves, spread the table-cloth, and went over to the window. The blind was up, she could see the garden quite plainly: there must be a moon about. And then she caught sight of something shining on the garden seat. A book, yes, it must be a book, left there to get soaked through by the dew. She went out into the hall, put on her goloshes, gathered up her skirt, and ran into the garden. Yes, it was a book. She picked it up carefully. Damp already—and the cover bulging. She shrugged her shoulders in the way that her little daughter had caught from her. In the shadowy garden that smelled of grass and rose leaves, Anne's heart hardened. Then the gate clicked and she saw Henry striding up the front path.

"Henry!" she called.

"Hullo," he cried, "what on earth are you doing down there... Moon-gazing, Anne?" She ran forward and kissed him.

"Oh, look at this book," she said. "Helen's been leaving it about, again. My dear, how you smell of cigars!"

Said Henry: "You've got to smoke a decent cigar when you're with, these other chaps. Looks so bad if you don't. But come inside, Anne; you haven't got anything on. Let the book go hang! You're cold, my dear, you're shivering." He put his arm round her shoulder. "See the moon over there, by the chimney? Fine night. By jove! I had the fellows roaring tonight—I made a colossal joke. One of them said: 'Life is a game of cards,' and I, without thinking, just straight out..." Henry paused by the door and held up a finger. "I said...well I've forgotten the exact words, but they shouted, my dear, simply shouted. No, I'll remember what I said in bed tonight; you know I always do."

"I'll take this book into the kitchen to dry on the stove-rack," said Anne, and she thought, as she banged the pages, "Henry has been drinking beer again, that means indigestion tomorrow. No use mentioning Helen tonight."

When Henry had finished the supper, he lay back in the chair, picking his teeth, and patted his knee for Anne to come and sit there.

"Hullo," he said, jumping her up and down, "what's the green fandangles on the chair back? What have you and mother been up to, eh?"

Said Anne, airily, casting a most careless glance at the green dresses, "Only some frocks for the children. Remnants for Sunday."

The old woman put the plate and cup and saucer together, then lighted a candle.

"I think I'll go to bed," she said, cheerfully.

"Oh, dear me, how unwise of Mother," thought Anne. "She makes Henry suspect by going away like that, as she always does if there's any unpleasantness brewing."

"No, don't go to bed yet, mother," cried Henry, jovially. "Let's have a look at the things." She passed him over the dresses, faintly smiling. Henry rubbed them through his fingers.

"So these are the remnants, are they, Anne? Don't feel much like the Sunday trousers my mother used to make me out of an ironing blanket. How much did you pay for this a yard, Anne?"

Anne took the dresses from him, and played with a button of his waistcoat.

"Forget the exact price, darling. Mother and I rather skimped them, even though they were so cheap. What can great big men bother about clothes…? Was Lumley there, tonigh?"

"Yes, he says their kid was a bit bandylegged at just the same age as Boy. He told me of a new kind of chair for children that the draper has just got in—makes them sit with their legs straight. By the way, have you got this month's draper's bill?"

She had been waiting for that—had known it was coming. She slipped off his knee and yawned.

"Oh, dear me," she said, "I think I'll follow mother. Bed's the place for me." She stared at Henry, vacantly. "Bill—bill did you say, dear? Oh, I'll look it out in the morning."

"No, Anne, hold on." Henry got up and went over to the cupboard where the bill file was kept. "Tomorrow's no good—because it's Sunday. I want to get that account off my chest before I turn in. Sit down there—in the rocking-chair—you needn't stand!"

She dropped into the chair, and began humming, all the while her thoughts coldly busy, and her eyes fixed on her husband's broad back as he bent over the cupboard door. He dawdled over finding the file.

"He's keeping me in suspense on purpose," she thought. "We can afford it—otherwise why should I do it? I know our income and our expenditure. I'm not a fool. They're a hell upon earth every month, these bills." And she thought of her bed upstairs, yearned for it, imagining she had never felt so tired in her life.

"Here we are!" said Henry. He slammed the file on to the table.

"Draw up your chair..."

"Clayton: Seven yards green cashmere at five shillings a yard—thirty-five shillings." He read the item twice—then folded the sheet over, and bent towards Anne. He was flushed and his breath smelt of beer. She knew exactly how he took things in that mood, and she raised her eyebrows and nodded.

"Do you mean to tell me," stormed Henry, "that lot over there cost thirty-five shillings—that stuff you've been mucking up for the children. Good God! Anybody would think you'd married a millionaire. You could buy your mother a trousseau with that money. You're making yourself a laughing-stock for the whole town. How do you think I can buy Boy a chair or anything else—if you chuck away my earnings like that? Time and again you impress upon me the impossibility of keeping Helen decent; and then you go decking her out the next moment in thirty-five shillings worth of green cashmere..."

On and on stormed the voice.

"He'll have calmed down in the morning, when the beer's worked off," thought Anne, and later, as she toiled up to bed, "When he sees how they'll last, he'll understand..."

A brilliant Sunday morning. Henry and Anne quite reconciled, sitting in the dining-room waiting for church time to the tune of Carsfield junior, who steadily thumped the shelf of his high-chair with a gravy spoon given him from the breakfast table by his father.

"That beggar's got muscle," said Henry, proudly. "I've timed him by my watch. He's kept that up for five minutes without stopping."

"Extraordinary," said Anne, buttoning her gloves. "I think he's had that spoon almost long enough now, dear, don't you? I'm so afraid of him putting it into his mouth."

"Oh, I've got an eye on him." Henry stood over his small son. "Go it, old man. Tell Mother boys like to kick up a row."

Anne kept silence. At any rate it would keep his eye off the children when they came down in those cashmeres. She was still wondering if she had drummed into their minds often enough the supreme importance of being careful and of taking them off immediately after church before dinner, and why Helen was fidgety when she was pulled about at all, when the door opened and the old woman ushered them in, complete to the straw hats with ribbon tails.

She could not help thrilling, they looked so very superior—Rose carrying her prayer-book in a white case embroidered with a pink woollen cross. But she feigned indifference immediately, and the lateness of the hour. Not a word more on the subject from Henry, even with the thirty-five shillings worth walking hand in hand before him all the way to church. Anne decided that was really generous and noble of him. She looked up at him, walking with the shoulders thrown back. How fine he looked in that long black coat, with the white silk tie just showing! And the children looked worthy of him. She squeezed his hand in church, conveying by that silent pressure, "It was for your sake I made the dresses; of course you can't understand that, but really, Henry." And she fully believed it.

On their way home the Carsfield family met Doctor Malcolm, out walking with a black dog carrying his stick in its mouth. Doctor Malcolm stopped and asked after Boy so intelligently that Henry invited him to dinner.

"Come and pick a bone with us and see Boy for yourself," he said. And Doctor Malcolm accepted. He walked beside Henry and shouted over his shoulder, "Helen, keep an eye on my boy baby, will you, and see he doesn't swallow that walking-stick. Because if he does, a tree will grow right out of his mouth or it will go to his tail and make it so stiff that a wag will knock you into kingdom come!"

"Oh, Doctor Malcolm!" laughed Helen, stooping over the dog, "Come along, doggie, give it up, there's a good boy!"

"Helen, your dress!" warned Anne.

"Yes, indeed," said Doctor Malcolm. "They are looking top-notchers today—the two young ladies."

"Well, it really is Rose's colour," said Anne.

"Her complexion is so much more vivid than Helen's."

Rose blushed. Doctor Malcolm's eyes twinkled, and he kept a tight rein on himself from saying she looked like a tomato in a lettuce salad.

"That child wants taking down a peg," he decided. "Give me Helen every time. She'll come to her own yet, and lead them just the dance they need."

Boy was having his mid-day sleep when they arrived home, and Doctor Malcolm begged that Helen might show him round the garden. Henry, repenting already of his generosity, gladly assented, and Anne went into the kitchen to interview the servant girl.

"Mumma, let me come too and taste the gravy," begged Rose.

"Huh!" muttered Doctor Malcolm. "Good riddance."

He established himself on the garden bench—put up his feet and took off his hat, to give the sun "a chance of growing a second crop," he told Helen.

She asked, soberly: "Doctor Malcolm, do you really like my dress."

"Of course I do, my lady. Don't you?"

"Oh yes, I'd like to be born and die in it. But it was such a fuss—tryings on, you know, and pullings, and 'don'ts.' I believe mother would kill me if it got hurt. I even knelt on my petticoat all through church because of dust on the hassock."

"Bad as that!" asked Doctor Malcolm, rolling his eyes at Helen.

"Oh, far worse," said the child, then burst into laughter and shouted, "Hellish!" dancing over the lawn.

"Take care, they'll hear you, Helen."

"Oh, booh! It's just dirty old cashmere—serve them right. They can't see me if they're not here to see and so it doesn't matter. It's only with them I feel funny."

"Haven't you got to remove your finery before dinner."

"No, because you're here."

"O my prophetic soul!" groaned Doctor Malcolm.

Coffee was served in the garden. The servant girl brought out some cane chairs and a rug for Boy. The children were told to go away and play.

"Leave off worrying Doctor Malcolm, Helen," said Henry. "You mustn't be a plague to people who are not members of your own family." Helen pouted, and dragged over to the swing for comfort. She swung high, and thought Doctor Malcolm was a most beautiful man—and wondered if his dog had finished the plate of bones in the back yard. Decided to go and see. Slower she swung, then took a flying leap; her tight skirt caught on a nail—there was a sharp, tearing sound—quickly she glanced at the others—they had not noticed—and then at the frock—at a hole big enough to stick her hand through. She felt neither frightened nor sorry. "I'll go and change it," she thought.

"Helen, where are you going to?" called Anne.

"Into the house for a book."

The old woman noticed that the child held her skirt in a peculiar way. Her petticoat string must have come untied. But she made no remark. Once in the bedroom Helen unbuttoned the frock, slipped out of it, and wondered what to do next. Hide it somewhere—she glanced all round the room— there was nowhere safe from them. Except the top of the cupboard—but even standing on a chair she could not throw so high—it fell back on top of her every time—the horrid, hateful thing. Then her eyes lighted on her school satchel hanging on the end of the bed post. Wrap it in her school pinafore—put it in the bottom of the bag with the pencil case on top. They'd never look there. She returned to the garden in the every-day dress—but forgot about the book.

"A-ah," said Anne, smilingironically. "What a new leaf for Doctor Malcolm's benefit! Look, Mother, Helen has changed without being told to."

"Come here, dear, and be done up properly."

She whispered to Helen: "Where did you leave your dress?"

"Left it on the side of the bed. Where I took it off," sang Helen.

Doctor Malcolm was talking to Henry of the advantages derived from public school education for the sons of commercial men, but he had his eye on the scene, and watching Helen, he smelt a rat—smelt a Hamelin tribe of them.

Confusion and consternation reigned. One of the green cashmeres had disappeared—spirited off the face of the earth—during the time that Helen took it off and the children's tea.

"Show me the exact spot," scolded Mrs. Carsfield for the twentieth time. "Helen, tell the truth."

"Mumma, I swear I left it on the floor."

"Well, it's no good swearing if it's not there. It can't have been stolen!"

"I did see a very funny-looking man in a white cap walking up and down the road and staring in the windows as I came up to change." Sharply Anne eyed her daughter.

"Now," she said. "I know you are telling lies."

She turned to the old woman, in her voice something of pride and joyous satisfaction.

"You hear, Mother—this cock-and-bull story?"

When they were near the end of the bed Helen blushed and turned away from them. And now and again she wanted to shout "I tore it, I tore it," and she fancied she had said it and seen their faces, just as sometimes in bed she dreamed she had got up and dressed. But as the evening wore on she grew quite careless—glad only of one thing—people had to go to sleep at night. Viciously she stared at the sun shining through the window space and making a pattern of the curtain on the bare nursery floor. And then she looked at Rose, painting a text at the nursery table with a whole egg cup full of water to herself…

Henry visited their bedroom the last thing. She heard him come creaking into their room and hid under the bedclothes. But Rose betrayed her.

"Helen's not asleep," piped Rose.

Henry sat by the bedside pulling his moustache.

"If it were not Sunday, Helen, I would whip you. As it is, and I must be at the office early tomorrow, I shall give you a sound smacking after tea in the evening… Do you hear me?"

She grunted.

"You love your father and mother, don't you?"

No answer.

Rose gave Helen a dig with her foot.

"Well," said Henry, sighing deeply, "I suppose you love Jesus?"

"Rose has scratched my leg with her toe nail," answered Helen.

Henry strode out of the room and flung himself on to his own bed, with his outdoor boots on the starched bolster, Anne noticed, but he was too overcome for her to venture a protest. The old woman was in the bedroom too, idly combing the hairs from Anne's brush. Henry told them the story, and was gratified to observe Anne's tears.

"It is Rose's turn for her toe-nails after the bath next Saturday," commented the old woman.

In the middle of the night Henry dug his elbow into Mrs. Carsfield.

"I've got an idea," he said. "Malcolm's at the bottom of this."

"No...how...why...where...bottom of what?"

"Those damned green dresses."

"Wouldn't be surprised," she managed to articulate, thinking, "imagine his rage if I woke him up to tell him an idiotic thing like that!"

"Is Mrs. Carsfield at home," asked Doctor Malcolm.

"No, sir, she's out visiting," answered the servant girl.

"Is Mr. Carsfield anywhere about?"

"Oh, no, sir, he's never home midday."

"Show me into the drawing-room."

The servant girl opened the drawing-room door, cocked her eye at the doctor's bag. She wished he would leave it in the hall—even if she could only feel the outside without opening it... But the doctor kept it in his hand.

The old woman sat in the drawing-room, a roll of knitting on her lap. Her head had fallen back—her mouth was open—she was asleep and quietly snoring. She started up at the sound of the doctor's footsteps and straightened her cap.

"Oh, Doctor—you did, take me by surprise. I was dreaming that Henry had bought Anne five little canaries. Please sit down!"

"No, thanks. I just popped in on the chance of catching you alone... You see this bag?"

The old woman nodded.

"Now, are you any good at opening bags?"

"Well, my husband was a great traveller and once I spent a whole night in a railway train."

"Well, have a go at opening this one."

The old woman knelt on the floor—her fingers trembled.

"There's nothing startling inside?" she asked.

"Well, it won't bite exactly," said Doctor Malcolm.

The catch sprang open—the bag yawned like a toothless mouth, and she saw, folded in its depths—green cashmere—with narrow lace on the neck and sleeves.

"Fancy that!" said the old woman mildly.

"May I take it out, Doctor?" She professed neither astonishment nor pleasure—and Malcolm felt disappointed.

"Helen's dress," he said, and bending towards her, raised his voice. "That young spark's Sunday rig-out."

"I'm not deaf, Doctor," answered the old woman. "Yes, I thought it looked like it. I told Anne only this morning it was bound to turn up somewhere." She shook the crumpled frock, and looked it over. "Things always do if you give them time; I've noticed that so often—it's such a blessing."

"You know Lindsay—the postman? Gastric ulcers—called there this morning... Saw this brought in by Lena, who'd got it from Helen on her way to school. Said the kid fished it out of her satchel rolled in a pinafore, and said her mother had told her to give it away because it did not fit her. When I saw the tear I understood yesterday's 'new leaf,' as Mrs. Carsfield put it. Was up to the dodge in a jiffy. Got the dress—bought some stuff at Clayton's and made my sister Bertha sew it while I had dinner. I knew what would be happening this end of the line—and I knew you'd see Helen through for the sake of getting one in at Henry."

"How thoughtful of you, Doctor!" said the old woman. "I'll tell Anne I found it under my dolman."

"Yes, that's your ticket," said Doctor Malcolm.

"But of course Helen would have forgotten the whipping by tomorrow morning, and I'd promised her a new doll..." The old woman spoke regretfully.

Doctor Malcolm snapped his bag together.

"It's no good talking to the old bird," he thought, "she doesn't take in half I say. Don't seem to have got any forrader than doing Helen out of a doll."

THE WOMAN AT THE STORE

All that day the heat was terrible. The wind blew close to the ground; it rooted among the tussock grass, slithered along the road, so that the white pumice dust swirled in our faces, settled and sifted over us and was like a dry-skin itching for growth on our bodies. The horses stumbled along, coughing and chuffing. The pack horse was sick—with a big, open sore rubbed under the belly. Now and again she stopped short, threw back her head, looked at us as though she were going to cry, and whinnied. Hundreds of larks shrilled; the sky was slate colour, and the sound of the larks reminded me of slate pencils scraping over its surface. There was nothing to be seen but wave after wave of tussock grass, patched with purple orchids and manuka bushes covered with thick spider webs.

Jo rode ahead. He wore a blue galatea shirt, corduroy trousers and riding boots. A white handkerchief, spotted with red—it looked as though his nose had been bleeding on it—was knotted round his throat. Wisps of white hair straggled from under his wideawake—his moustache and eyebrows were called white—he slouched in the saddle, grunting. Not once that day had he sung

"I don't care, for don't you see,   My wife's mother was in front of me!"

It was the first day we had been without it for a month, and now there seemed something uncanny in his silence. Jim rode beside me, white as a clown; his black eyes glittered, and he kept shooting out his tongue and moistening his lips. He was dressed in a Jaeger vest, and a pair of blue duck trousers, fastened round the waist with a plaited leather belt. We had hardly spoken since dawn. At noon we had lunched off fly biscuits and apricots by the side of a swampy creek.

"My stomach feels like the crop of a hen," said Jo. "Now then, Jim, you're the bright boy of the party—where's this 'ere store you kep' on talking about. 'Oh, yes,' you says, 'I know a fine store, with a paddock for the horses and a creek runnin' through, owned by a friend of mine who'll give yer a bottle of whisky before 'e shakes hands with yer.' I'd like ter see that place—merely as a matter of curiosity—not that I'd ever doubt yer word—as yer know very well—but..."

Jim laughed. "Don't forget there's a woman too, Jo, with blue eyes and yellow hair, who'll promise you something else before she shakes hands with you. Put that in your pipe and smoke it."

"The heat's making you balmy," said Jo. But he dug his knees into the horse. We shambled on. I half fell asleep, and had a sort of uneasy dream that the horses were not moving forward at all—then that I was on a rocking-horse, and my old mother was scolding me for raising such a fearful dust from the drawing-room carpet. "You've entirely worn off the pattern of the carpet," I heard her saying, and she gave the reins a tug. I snivelled and woke to find Jim leaning over me, maliciously smiling.

"That was a case of all but," said he. "I just caught you. What'sup? Been bye-bye?"

"No!" I raised my head. "Thank the Lord we're arriving somewhere."

We were on the brow of the hill, and below us there was a whare roofed with corrugated iron. It stood in a garden, rather far back from the road—a big paddock opposite, and a creek and a clump of young willow trees. A thin line of blue smoke stood up straight from the chimney of the whare; and as I looked a woman came out, followed by a child and a sheep dog—the woman carrying what appeared to me a black stick. She made gestures at us.

The horses put on a final spurt, Jo took off his wideawake, shouted, threw out his chest, and began singing, "I don't care, for don't you see..." The sun pushed through the pale clouds and shed a vivid light over the scene. It gleamed on the woman's yellow hair, over her flapping pinafore and the rifle she was carrying. The child hid behind her, and the yellow dog, a mangy beast, scuttled back into the whare, his tail between his legs. We drew rein and dismounted.

"Hallo," screamed the woman. "I thought you was three' awks. My kid comes runnin' in ter me. 'Mumma,' says she, 'there's three brown things comin' over the 'ill,' says she. An' I comes out smart, I can tell yer. 'They'll be' awks,' I says to her. Oh, the' awks about 'ere, yer wouldn't believe."

The "kid" gave us the benefit of one eye from behind the woman's pinafore—then retired again.

"Where's your old man?" asked Jim.

The woman blinked rapidly, screwing up her face.

"Away shearin'. Bin away a month. I suppose yer not goin' to stop, are yer? There's a storm comin' up."

"You bet we are," said Jo. "So you're on your lonely, missus?"

She stood, pleating the frills of her pinafore, and glancing from one to the other of us, like a hungry bird. I smiled at the thought of how Jim had pulled Jo's leg about her. Certainly her eyes were blue, and what hair she had was yellow, but ugly. She was a figure of fun. Looking at her, you felt there was nothing but sticks and wires under that pinafore—her front teeth were knocked out, she had red pulpy hands, and she wore on her feet a pair of dirty Bluchers.

"I'll go and turn out the horses," said Jim.

"Got any embrocation? Poi's rubbed herself to hell!"

"Arf a mo!" The woman stood silent a moment, her nostrils expanding as she breathed. Then she shouted violently. "I'd rather you didn't stop... You can't, and there's the end of it. I don't let out that paddock any more. You'll have to go on; I ain't got nothing!"

"Well, I'm blest!" said Jo, heavily. He pulled me aside. "Gone a bit off'er dot," he whispered. "Too much alone, you know" very significantly. "Turn the sympathetic tap on' er, she'll come round all right."

But there was no need—she had come round by herself.

"Stop if yer like!" she muttered, shrugging her shoulders. To me—"I'll give yer the embrocation if yer come along."

"Right-o, I'll take it down to them." We walked together up the garden path. It was planted on both sides with cabbages. They smelled like stale dish-water. Of flowers there were double poppies and sweet-williams. One little patch was divided off by pawa shells—presumably it belonged to the child—for she ran from her mother and began to grub in it with a broken clothes-peg. The yellow dog lay across the doorstep, biting fleas; the woman kicked him away.

"Gar-r, get away, you beast the place ain't tidy. I 'aven't 'ad time ter fix things today—been ironing. Come right in."

It was a large room, the walls plastered with old pages of English periodicals. Queen Victoria's Jubilee appeared to be the most recent number. A table with an ironing board and wash tub on it, some wooden forms, a black horsehair sofa, and some broken cane chairs pushed against the walls. The mantelpiece above the stove was draped in pink paper, further ornamented with dried grasses and ferns and a coloured print of Richard Seddon. There were four doors—one, judging from the smell, let into the "Store," one on to the "backyard," through a third I saw the bedroom. Flies buzzed in circles round the ceiling, and treacle papers and bundles of dried clover were pinned to the window curtains.

I was alone in the room; she had gone into the store for the embrocation. I heard her stamping about and muttering to herself: "I got some, now where did I put that bottle? It's behind the pickles no, it ain't." I cleared a place on the table and sat there, swinging my legs. Down in the paddock I could hear Jo singing and the sound of hammer strokes as Jim drove in the tent pegs. It was sunset. There is no twilight in our New Zealand days, but a curious half-hour when everything appears grotesque—it frightens—as though the savage spirit of the country walked abroad and sneered at what it saw. Sitting alone in the hideous room I grew afraid. The woman next door was a long time finding that stuff. What was she doing in there? Once I thought I heard her bang her hands down on the counter, and once she half moaned, turning it into a cough and clearing her throat. I wanted to shout "Buck up!" but I kept silent.

"Good Lord, what a life!" I thought. "Imagine being here day in, day out, with that rat of a child and a mangy dog. Imagine bothering about ironing. Mad, of course she's mad! Wonder how long she's been here—wonder if I could get her to talk."

At that moment she poked her head round the door.

"Wot was it yer wanted?" she asked.

"Embrocation."

"Oh, I forgot. I got it, it was in front of the pickle jars."

She handed me the bottle.

"My, you do look tired, you do! Shall I knock yer up a few scones for supper! There's some tongue in the store, too, and I'll cook yer a cabbage if you fancy it."

"Right-o." I smiled at her. "Come down to the paddock and bring the kid for tea."

She shook her head, pursing up her mouth.

"Oh no. I don't fancy it. I'll send the kid down with the things and a billy of milk. Shall I knock up a few extry scones to take with yer ter-morrow?"

"Thanks."

She came and stood by the door.

"How old is the kid?"

"Six—come next Christmas. I 'ad a bit of trouble with 'er one way an' another. I 'adn't any milk till a month after she was born and she sickened like a cow."

"She's not like you—takes after her father?"

Just as the woman had shouted her refusal at us before, she shouted at me then.

"No, she don't! She's the dead spit of me. Any fool could see that. Come on in now, Else, you stop messing in the dirt."

I met Jo climbing over the paddock fence.

"What's the old bitch got in the store?" he asked.

"Don't know—didn't look."

"Well, of all the fools. Jim's slanging you. What have you been doing all the time?"

"She couldn't find this stuff. Oh, my shakes, you are smart!"

Jo had washed, combed his wet hair in a line across his forehead, and buttoned a coat over his shirt. He grinned.

Jim snatched the embrocation from me. I went to the end of the paddock where the willows grew and bathed in the creek. The water was clear and soft as oil. Along the edges held by the grass and rushes, white foam tumbled and bubbled. I lay in the water and looked up at the trees that were still a moment, then quivered lightly, and again were still. The air smelt of rain. I forgot about the woman and the kid until I came back to the tent. Jim lay by the fire, watching the billy boil.

I asked where Jo was, and if the kid had brought our supper.

"Pooh," said Jim, rolling over and looking up at the sky. "Didn't you see how Jo had been titivating? He said to me before he went up to the whare, 'Dang it! she'll look better by night light—at any rate, my buck, she's female flesh!'"

"You had Jo about her looks—you had me, too."

"No—look here. I can't make it out. It's four years since I came past this way, and I stopped here two days. The husband was a pal of mine once, down the West Coast—a fine, big chap, with a voice on him like a trombone. She'd been barmaid down the Coast—as pretty as a wax doll. The coach used to come this way then once a fortnight, that was before they opened the railway up Napier way, and she had no end of a time! Told me once in a confidential moment that she knew one hundred and twenty-five different ways of kissing!"

"Oh, go on, Jim! She isn't the same woman!"

"Course she is I can't make it out. What I think is the old man's cleared out and left her: that's all my eye about shearing. Sweet life! The only people who come through now are Maoris and sundowners!"

Through the dark we saw the gleam of the kid's pinafore. She trailed over to us with a basket in her hand, the milk billy in the other. I unpacked the basket, the child standing by.

"Come over here," said Jim, snapping his fingers at her.

She went, the lamp from the inside of the tent cast a bright light over her. A mean, undersized brat, with whitish hair, and weak eyes. She stood, legs wide apart and her stomach protruding.

"What do you do all day?" asked Jim.

She scraped out one tear with her little finger, looked at the result and said, "Draw."

"Huh! What do you draw? Leave your ears alone!"

"Pictures."

"What on?"

"Bits of butter paper an' a pencil of my Mumma's."

"Boh! What a lot of words at one time!" Jim rolled his eyes at her. "Baa-lambs and moo-cows?"

"No, everything. I'll draw all of you when you're gone, and your horses and the tent, and that one"— she pointed to me—"with no clothes on in the creek. I looked at her where she couldn't see me from."

"Thanks very much. How ripping of you," said Jim. "Where's Dad?"

The kid pouted. "I won't tell you because I don't like yer face!" She started operations on the other ear.

"Here," I said. "Take the basket, get along home and tell the other man supper's ready."

"I don't want to."

"I'll give you a box on the ear if you don't," said Jim, savagely.

"Hie! I'll tell Mumma. I'll tell Mumma." The kid fled.

We ate until we were full, and had arrived at the smoke stage before Jo came back, very flushed and jaunty, a whisky bottle in his hand.

"'Ave a drink—you two!" he shouted, carrying off matters with a high hand. "'Ere, shove along the cups."

"One hundred and twenty-five different ways," I murmured to Jim.

"What's that? Oh! stow it!" said Jo.

"Why 'ave you always got your knife into me. You gas like a kid at a Sunday School beano. She wants us to go up there tonight, and have a comfortable chat. "I"—he waved his hand airily—"I got 'er round."

"Trust you for that," laughed Jim. "But did she tell you where the old man's got to?"

Jo looked up. "Shearing! You 'eard 'er, you fool!"

The woman had fixed up the room, even to a light bouquet of sweet-williams on the table. She and I sat one side of the table, Jo and Jim the other. An oil lamp was set between us, the whisky bottle and glasses, and a jug of water. The kid knelt against one of the forms, drawing on butter paper; I wondered, grimly, if she was attempting the creek episode. But Jo had been right about night time. The woman's hair was tumbled—two red spots burned in her cheeks—her eyes shone—and we knew that they were kissing feet under the table. She had changed the blue pinafore for a white calico dressing jacket and a black skirt—the kid was decorated to the extent of a blue sateen hair ribbon. In the stifling room, with the flies buzzing against the ceiling and dropping on to the table, we got slowly drunk.

"Now listen to me," shouted the woman, banging her fist on the table. "It's six years since I was married, and four miscarriages. I says to 'im, I says, what do you think I'm doin' up 'ere? If you was back at the coast, I'd 'ave you lynched for child murder. Over and over I tells 'im—you've broken my spirit and spoiled my looks, and wot for—that's wot I'm driving at." She clutched her head with her hands and stared round at us. Speaking rapidly, "Oh, some days—an' months of them—I 'ear them two words knockin' inside me all the time—'Wot for!' but sometimes I'll be cooking the spuds an' I lifts the lid off to give 'em a prong and I 'ears, quite suddin again, 'Wot for!' Oh! I don't mean only the spuds and the kid—I mean—I mean," she hiccoughed—"you know what I mean, Mr. Jo."

"I know," said Jo, scratching his head.

"Trouble with me is," she leaned across the table, "he left me too much alone. When the coach stopped coming, sometimes he'd go away days, sometimes he'd go away weeks, and leave me ter look after the store. Back 'e'd come—pleased as Punch. 'Oh, 'allo, 'e'd say. ''Ow are you gettin' on. Come and give us a kiss.' Sometimes I'd turn a bit nasty, and then 'e'd go off again, and if I took it all right, 'e'd wait till 'e could twist me round 'is finger, then 'e'd say, 'Well, so long, I'm off,' and do you think I could keep 'im?—not me!"

"Mumma," bleated the kid, "I made a picture of them on the 'ill, an' you an' me, an' the dog down below."

"Shut your mouth!" said the woman.

A vivid flash of lightning played over the room—we heard the mutter of thunder.

"Good thing that's broke loose," said Jo. "I've 'ad it in me 'ead for three days."

"Where's your old man now?" asked Jim, slowly.

The woman blubbered and dropped her head on to the table. "Jim, 'e's gone shearin' and left me alone again," she wailed.

"'Ere, look out for the glasses," said Jo. "Cheer-o, 'ave another drop. No good cryin' over spilt 'usbands! You Jim, you blasted cuckoo!"

"Mr. Jo," said the woman, drying her eyes on her jacket frill, "you're a gent, an' if I was a secret woman, I'd place any confidence in your 'ands. I don't mind if I do 'ave a glass on that."

Every moment the lightning grew more vivid and the thunder sounded nearer. Jim and I were silent—the kid never moved from her bench. She poked her tongue out and blew on her paper as she drew.

"It's the loneliness," said the woman, addressing Jo—he made sheep's eyes at her—"and bein' shut up 'ere like a broody 'en." He reached his hand across the table and held hers, and though the position looked most uncomfortable when they wanted to pass the water and whisky, their hands stuck together as though glued. I pushed back my chair and went over to the kid, who immediately sat flat down on her artistic achievements and made a face at me.

"You're not to look," said she.

"Oh, come on, don't be nasty!" Jim came over to us, and we were just drunk enough to wheedle the kid into showing us. And those drawings of hers were extraordinary and repulsively vulgar. The creations of a lunatic with a lunatic's cleverness. There was no doubt about it, the kid's mind was diseased. While she showed them to us, she worked herself up into a mad excitement, laughing and trembling, and shooting out her arms.

"Mumma," she yelled. "Now I'm going to draw them what you told me I never was to—now I am."

The woman rushed from the table and beat the child's head with the flat of her hand.

"I'll smack you with yer clothes turned up if yer dare say that again," she bawled.

Jo was too drunk to notice, but Jim caught her by the arm. The kid did not utter a cry. She drifted over to the window and began picking flies from the treacle paper.

We returned to the table—Jim and I sitting one side, the woman and Jo, touching shoulders, the other. We listened to the thunder, saying stupidly, "That was a near one," "There it goes again," and Jo, at a heavy hit, "Now we're off," "Steady on the brake," until rain began to fall, sharp as cannon shot on the iron roof.

"You'd better doss here for the night," said the woman.

"That's right," assented Jo, evidently in the know about this move.

"Bring up yer things from the tent. You two can doss in the store along with the kid—she's used to sleep in there and won't mind you."

"Oh Mumma, I never did," interrupted the kid.

"Shut yer lies! An' Mr. Jo can 'ave this room."

It sounded a ridiculous arrangement, but it was useless to attempt to cross them, they were too far gone. While the woman sketched the plan of action, Jo sat, abnormally solemn and red, his eyes bulging, and pulling at his moustache.

"Give us a lantern," said Jim, "I'll go down to the paddock." We two went together. Rain whipped in our faces, the land was light as though a bush fire was raging. We behaved like two children let loose in the thick of an adventure, laughed and shouted to each other, and came back to the whare to find the kid already bedded in the counter of the store.

The woman brought us a lamp. Jo took his bundle from Jim, the door was shut.

"Good-night all," shouted Jo.

Jim and I sat on two sacks of potatoes. For the life of us we could not stop laughing. Strings of onions and half-hams dangled from the ceiling—wherever we looked there were advertisements for "Camp Coffee" and tinned meats. We pointed at them, tried to read them aloud—overcome with laughter and hiccoughs. The kid in the counter stared at us. She threw off her blanket and scrambled to the floor, where she stood in her grey flannel night-gown, rubbing one leg against the other. We paid no attention to her.

"Wot are you laughing at?" she said, uneasily.

"You!" shouted Jim. "The red tribe of you, my child."

She flew into a rage and beat herself with her hands. "I won't be laughed at, you curs—you." He swooped down upon the child and swung her on to the counter.

"Go to sleep, Miss Smarty—or make a drawing—here's a pencil—you can use Mumma's account book."

Through the rain we heard Jo creak over the boarding of the next room—the sound of a door being opened—then shut to.

"It's the loneliness," whispered Jim.

"One hundred and twenty-five different ways—alas! my poor brother!"

The kid tore out a page and flung it at me.

"There you are," she said. "Now I done it ter spite Mumma for shutting me up 'ere with you two. I done the one she told me I never ought to. I done the one she told me she'd shoot me if I did. Don't care! Don't care!"

The kid had drawn the picture of the woman shooting at a man with a rook rifle and then digging a hole to bury him in.

She jumped off the counter and squirmed about on the floor biting her nails.

Jim and I sat till dawn with the drawing beside us. The rain ceased, the little kid fell asleep, breathing loudly. We got up, stole out of the whare, down into the paddock. White clouds floated over a pink sky—a chill wind blew; the air smelled of wet grass. Just as we swung into the saddle Jo came out of the whare—he motioned to us to ride on.

"I'll pick you up later," he shouted.

A bend in the road, and the whole place disappeared.

OLE UNDERWOOD

To Anne Estelle Rice

Down the windy hill stalked Ole Underwood. He carried a black umbrella in one hand, in the other a red and white spotted handkerchief knotted into a lump. He wore a black peaked cap like a pilot; gold rings gleamed in his ears and his little eyes snapped like two sparks. Like two sparks they glowed in the smoulder of his bearded face. On one side of the hill grew a forest of pines from the road right down to the sea. On the other side short tufted grass and little bushes of white manuka flower. The pine-trees roared like waves in their topmost branches, their stems creaked like the timber of ships; in the windy air flew the white manuka flower. "Ah-k!" shouted Ole Underwood, shaking his umbrella at the wind bearing down upon him, beating him, half strangling him with his black cape. "Ah-k!" shouted the wind a hundred times as loud, and filled his mouth and nostrils with dust. Something inside Ole Underwood's breast beat like a hammer. One, two—one, two—never stopping, never changing. He couldn't do anything. It wasn't loud. No, it didn't make a noise—only a thud. One, two—one, two—like some one beating on an iron in a prison, some one in a secret place—bang—bang—bang—trying to get free. Do what he would, fumble at his coat, throw his arms about, spit, swear, he couldn't stop the noise. Stop! Stop! Stop! Stop! Ole Underwood began to shuffle and run.

Away below, the sea heaving against the stone walls, and the little town just out of its reach close packed together, the better to face the grey water. And up on the other side of the hill the prison with high red walls. Over all bulged the grey sky with black web-like clouds streaming.

Ole Underwood slackened his pace as he neared the town, and when he came to the first house he flourished his umbrella like a herald's staff and threw out his chest, his head glancing quickly from right to left. They were ugly little houses leading into the town, built of wood—two windows and a door, a stumpy verandah and a green mat of grass before. Under one verandah yellow hens huddled out of the wind. "Shoo!" shouted Ole Underwood, and laughed to see them fly, and laughed again at the woman who came to the door and shook a red, soapy fist at him. A little girl stood in another yard untwisting some rags from a clothes-line. When she saw Ole Underwood she let the clothes-prop fall and rushed screaming to the door, beating it, screaming "Mumma—Mumma!" That started the hammer in Ole Underwood's heart. Mum-ma—Mum-ma! He saw an old face with a trembling chin and grey hair nodding out of the window as they dragged him past. Mumma—Mum-ma! He looked up at the big red prison perched on the hill and he pulled a face as if he wanted to cry.

At the corner in front of the pub some carts were pulled up, and some men sat in the porch of the pub drinking and talking. Ole Underwood wanted a drink. He slouched into the bar. It was half full of old and young men in big coats and top boots with stock whips in their hands. Behind the counter a big girl with red hair pulled the beer handles and cheeked the men. Ole Underwood sneaked to one side, like a cat. Nobody looked at him, only the men looked at each other, one or two of them nudged. The girl nodded and winked at the fellow she was serving. He took some money out of his knotted handkerchief and slipped it on to the counter. His hand shook. He didn't speak. The girl took no notice; she served everybody, went on with her talk, and then as if by accident shoved a mug towards him. A great big jar of red pinks stood on the bar counter. Ole Underwood stared at them as he drank and frowned at them. Red—red—red—red! beat the hammer. It was very warm in the bar and quiet as a pond, except for the talk and the girl. She kept on laughing. Ha! Ha! That was what the men liked to see, for she threw back her head and her great breasts lifted and shook to her laughter.

In one corner sat a stranger. He pointed at Ole Underwood. "Cracked!" said one of the men. "When he was a young fellow, thirty years ago, a man 'ere done in 'is woman, and 'e foun' out an' killed 'er. Got twenty years in quod up on the 'ill. Came out cracked."

"Oo done 'er in?" asked the man.

"Dunno. 'E dunno, nor nobody. 'E was a sailor till 'e marrid 'er. Cracked!" The man spat and smeared the spittle on the floor, shrugging his shoulders. "'E's 'armless enough."

Ole Underwood heard; he did not turn, but he shot out an old claw and crushed up the red pinks. "Uh-Uh! You ole beast! Uh! You ole swine!" screamed the girl, leaning across the counter and banging him with a tin jug. "Get art! Get art! Don' you never come 'ere no more!" Somebody kicked him: he scuttled like a rat.

He walked past the Chinamen's shops. The fruit and vegetables were all piled up against the windows. Bits of wooden cases, straw, and old newspapers were strewn over the pavement. A woman flounced out of a shop and slushed a pail of slops over his feet. He peered in at the windows, at the Chinamen sitting in little groups on old barrels playing cards. They made him smile. He looked and looked, pressing his face against the glass and sniggering. They sat still with their long pigtails bound round their heads and their faces yellow as lemons. Some of them had knives in their belts, and one old man sat by himself on the floor plaiting his long crooked toes together. The Chinamen didn't mind Ole Underwood. When they saw him they nodded. He went to the door of a shop and cautiously opened it. In rushed the wind with him, scattering the cards. "Ya-Ya! Ya-Ya!" screamed the Chinamen, and Ole Underwood rushed off, the hammer beating quick and hard. Ya-Ya! He turned a corner out of sight. He thought he heard one of the Chinks after him, and he slipped into a timber-yard. There he lay panting...

Close by him, under another stack there was a heap of yellow shavings. As he watched them they moved and a little grey cat unfolded herself and came out waving her tail. She trod delicately over to Ole Underwood and rubbed against his sleeve. The hammer in Ole Underwood's heart beat madly. It pounded up into his throat, and then it seemed to half stop and beat very, very faintly. "Kit! Kit! Kit!" That was what she used to call the little cat he brought her off the ship—"Kit! Kit! Kit!"—and stoop down with the saucer in her hands. "Ah! my God! my Lord!" Ole Underwood sat up and took the kitten in his arms and rocked to and fro, crushing it against his face. It was warm and soft, and it mewed faintly. He buried his eyes in its fur. My God! My Lord! He tucked the little cat in his coat and stole out of the woodyard, and slouched down towards the wharves. As he came near the sea, Ole Underwood's nostrils expanded. The mad wind smelled of tar and ropes and slime and salt. He crossed the railway line, he crept behind the wharf-sheds and along a little cinder path that threaded through a patch of rank fennel to some stone drain pipes carrying the sewage into the sea. And he stared up at the wharves and at the ships with flags flying, and suddenly the old, old lust swept over Ole Underwood. "I will! I will! I will!" he muttered.

He tore the little cat out of his coat and swung it by its tail and flung it out to the sewer opening. The hammer beat loud and strong. He tossed his head, he was young again. He walked on to the wharves, past the wool-bales, past the loungers and the loafers to the extreme end of the wharves. The sea sucked against the wharf-poles as though it drank something from the land. One ship was loading wool. He heard a crane rattle and the shriek of a whistle. So he came to the little ship lying by herself with a bit of a plank for a gangway, and no sign of anybody—anybody at all. Ole Underwood looked once back at the town, at the prison perched like a red bird, at the black webby clouds trailing. Then he went up the gangway and on to the slippery deck. He grinned, and rolled in his walk, carrying high in his hand the red and white handkerchief. His ship! Mine! Mine! Mine! beat the hammer. There was a door latched open on the lee-side, labelled "State-room." He peered in. A man lay sleeping on a bunk—his bunk—a great big man in a seaman's coat with a long fair beard and hair on the red pillow. And looking down upon him from the wall there shone her picture—his woman's picture—smiling and smiling at the big sleeping man.

THE LITTLE GIRL

To the little girl he was a figure to be feared and avoided. Every morning before going to business he came into the nursery and gave her a perfunctory kiss, to which she responded with "Good-bye, father." And oh, the glad sense of relief when she heard the noise of the buggy growing fainter and fainter down the long road!

In the evening, leaning over the banisters at his home-coming, she heard his loud voice in the hall. "Bring my tea into the smoking-room... Hasn't the paper come yet? Have they taken it into the kitchen again? Mother, go and see if my paper's out there—and bring me my slippers."

"Kezia," mother would call to her, "if you're a good girl you can come down and take off father's boots." Slowly the girl would slip down the stairs, holding tightly to the banisters with one hand— more slowly still, across the hall, and push open the smoking-room door.

By that time he had his spectacles on and looked at her over them in a way that was terrifying to the little girl.

"Well, Kezia, get a move on and pull off these boots and take them outside. Been a good girl today?"

"I d-d-don't know, father."

"You d-d-don't know? If you stutter like that mother will have to take you to the doctor."

She never stuttered with other people—had quite given it up—but only with father, because then she was trying so hard to say the words properly.

"What's the matter? What are you looking so wretched about? Mother, I wish you would teach this child not to appear on the brink of suicide... Here, Kezia, carry my teacup back to the table— carefully; your hands jog like an old lady's. And try to keep your handkerchief in your pocket, not up your sleeve."

"Y-y-yes, father."

On Sundays she sat in the same pew with him in church, listening while he sang in a loud, clear voice, watching while he made little notes during the sermon with the stump of a blue pencil on the back of an envelope—his eyes narrowed to a slit—one hand beating a silent tattoo on the pew ledge. He said his prayers so loudly she was certain God heard him above the clergyman.

He was so big—his hands and his neck, especially his mouth when he yawned. Thinking about him alone in the nursery was like thinking about a giant.

On Sunday afternoons grandmother sent her down to the drawing-room, dressed in her brown velvet, to have a "nice talk with father and mother." But the little girl always found mother reading The Sketch and father stretched out on the couch, his handkerchief on his face, his feet propped on one of the best sofa pillows, and so soundly sleeping that he snored.

She, perched on the piano-stool, gravely watched him until he woke and stretched, and asked the time—then looked at her.

"Don't stare so, Kezia. You look like a little brown owl."

One day, when she was kept indoors with a cold, the grandmother told her that father's birthday was next week, and suggested she should make him a pincushion for a present out of a beautiful piece of yellow silk.

Laboriously, with a double cotton, the little girl stitched three sides. But what to fill it with? That was the question. The grandmother was out in the garden, and she wandered into mother's bedroom to look for "scraps." On the bed table she discovered a great many sheets of fine paper, gathered them up, shredded them into tiny pieces, and stuffed her case, then sewed up the fourth side.

That night there was a hue and cry over the house. Father's great speech for the Port Authority had been lost. Rooms were ransacked—servants questioned. Finally mother came into the nursery.

"Kezia, I suppose you didn't see some papers on a table in our room?"

"Oh, yes," she said. "I tore them up for my s'prise."

"What!" screamed mother. "Come straight down to the dining-room this instant."

And she was dragged down to where father was pacing to and fro, hands behind his back.

"Well?" he said sharply.

Mother explained.

He stopped and stared in a stupefied manner at the child.

"Did you do that?"

"N-n-no," she whispered.

"Mother, go up to the nursery and fetch down the damned thing—see that the child's put to bed this instant."

Crying too much to explain, she lay in the shadowed room watching the evening light sift through the Venetian blinds and trace a sad little pattern on the floor.

Then father came into the room with a ruler in his hands.

"I am going to whip you for this," he said.

"Oh, no, no!" she screamed, cowering down under the bedclothes.

He pulled them aside.

"Sit up," he commanded, "and hold out your hands. You must be taught once and for all not to touch what does not belong to you."

"But it was for your b-b-birthday."

Down came the ruler on her little, pink palms.

Hours later, when the grandmother had wrapped her in a shawl and rocked her in the rocking-chair the child cuddled close to her soft body.

"What did Jesus make fathers for?" she sobbed.

"Here's a clean hanky, darling, with some of my lavender water on it. Go to sleep, pet; you'll forget all about it in the morning. I tried to explain to father, but he was too upset to listen tonight."

But the child never forgot. Next time she saw him she whipped both hands behind her back, and a red colour flew into her cheeks.

The Macdonalds lived in the next-door house. Five children there were. Looking through a hole in the vegetable garden fence the little girl saw them playing "tag" in the evening. The father with the baby Mac on his shoulders, two little girls hanging on to his coat tails, ran round and round the flower beds, shaking with laughter. Once she saw the boys turn the hose on him—turn the hose on him—and he made a great grab at them, tickling them until they got hiccoughs. Then it was she decided there were different sorts of fathers.

Suddenly, one day, mother became ill, and she and grandmother drove into town in a closed carriage.

The little girl was left alone in the house with Alice, the "general." That was all right in the daytime, but while Alice was putting her to bed she grew suddenly afraid.

"What'll I do if I have nightmare?" she asked. "I often have nightmare, and then grannie takes me into her bed—I can't stay in the dark—it all gets 'whispery.'… What'll I do if I do?"

"You just go to sleep, child," said Alice, pulling off her socks and whacking them against the bedrail, "and don't you holler out and wake your poor pa."

But the same old nightmare came—the butcher with a knife and a rope who grew nearer and nearer, smiling that dreadful smile, while she could not move, could only stand still, crying out, "Grandma, Grandma!" She woke shivering, to see father beside her bed, a candle in his hand.

"What's the matter?" he said.

"Oh, a butcher—a knife—I want grannie." He blew out the candle, bent down and caught up the child in his arms, carrying her along the passage to the big bedroom. A newspaper was on the bed— a half-smoked cigar balanced against his reading-lamp. He pitched the paper on the floor, threw the cigar into the fireplace, then carefully tucked up the child. He lay down beside her. Half asleep still, still with the butcher's smile all about her, it seemed, she crept close to him, snuggled her head under his arm, held tightly to his pyjama jacket.

Then the dark did not matter; she lay still. "Here, rub your feet against my legs and get them warm," said father.

Tired out, he slept before the little girl. A funny feeling came over her. Poor father! Not so big, after all—and with no one to look after him… He was harder than the grandmother, but it was a nice hardness… And every day he had to work and was too tired to be a Mr. Macdonald… She had torn up all his beautiful writing… She stirred suddenly, and sighed.

"What's the matter?" asked father. "Another dream?"

"Oh," said the little girl, "my head's on your heart; I can hear it going. What a big heart you've got, father dear."

MILLIE

Millie stood leaning against the verandah, until the men were out of sight. When they were far down the road Willie Cox turned round on his horse and waved. But she didn't wave back. She nodded her head a little and made a grimace. Not a bad young fellow, Willie Cox, but a bit too free and easy for her taste. Oh, my word! it was hot. Enough to fry your hair!

Millie put her handkerchief over her head and shaded her eyes with her hand. In the distance along the dusty road she could see the horses, like brown spots dancing up and down, and when she looked away from them and over the burnt paddocks she could see them still—just before her eyes, jumping like mosquitoes. It was half-past two in the afternoon. The sun hung in the faded blue sky like a burning mirror, and away beyond the paddocks the blue mountains quivered and leapt like sea.

Sid wouldn't be back until half-past ten. He had ridden over to the township with four of the boys to help hunt down the young fellow who'd murdered Mr. Williamson. Such a dreadful thing! And Mrs. Williamson left all alone with all those kids. Funny! she couldn't think of Mr. Williamson being dead! He was such a one for a joke. Always having a lark. Willie Cox said they found him in the barn, shot bang through the head, and the young English "johnny" who'd been on the station learning farming—disappeared. Funny! she couldn't think of anyone shooting Mr. Williamson, and him so popular and all. My word! when they caught that young man! Well, you couldn't be sorry for a young fellow like that. As Sid said, if he wasn't strung up where would they all be? A man like that doesn't stop at one go. There was blood all over the barn. And Willie Cox said he was that knocked out he picked a cigarette up out of the blood and smoked it. My word! he must have been half dotty.

Millie went back into the kitchen. She put some ashes on the stove and sprinkled them with water. Languidly, the sweat pouring down her face, and dropping off her nose and chin, she cleared away the dinner, and going into the bedroom, stared at herself in the fly-specked mirror, and wiped her face and neck with a towel. She didn't know what was the matter with herself that afternoon. She could have a good cry—just for nothing—and then change her blouse and have a good cup of tea. Yes, she felt like that!

She flopped down on the side of the bed and stared at the coloured print on the wall opposite, Garden Party at Windsor Castle. In the foreground emerald lawns planted with immense oak trees, and in their grateful shade, a muddle of ladies and gentlemen and parasols and little tables. The background was filled with the towers of Windsor Castle, flying three Union Jacks, and in the middle of the picture the old Queen, like a tea cosy with a head on top of it.

"I wonder if it really looked like that." Millie stared at the flowery ladies, who simpered back at her. "I wouldn't care for that sort of thing. Too much side. What with the Queen an' one thing an' another."

Over the packing-case dressing-table there was a large photograph of her and Sid, taken on their wedding day. Nice picture that—if you do like. She was sitting down in a basket chair, in her cream cashmere and satin ribbons, and Sid, standing with one hand on her shoulder, looking at her bouquet. And behind them there were some fern trees, and a waterfall, and Mount Cook in the distance, covered with snow. She had almost forgotten her wedding day; time did pass so, and if you hadn't any one to talk things over with, they soon dropped out of your mind. "I wunner why we never had no kids…" She shrugged her shoulders—gave it up. "Well, I've never missed them. I wouldn't be surprised if Sid had, though. He's softer than me."

And then she sat quiet, thinking of nothing at all, her red swollen hands rolled in her apron, her feet stuck out in front of her, her little head with the thick screw of dark hair drooped on her chest. Tick-tick went the kitchen clock, the ashes clinked in the grate, and the venetian blind knocked against the kitchen window. Quite suddenly Millie felt frightened. A queer trembling started inside her—in her stomach—and then spread all over to her knees and hands. "There's somebody about." She tiptoed to the door and peered into the kitchen. Nobody there; the verandah doors were closed, the blinds were down, and in the dusky light the white face of the clock shone, and the furniture seemed to bulge and breathe…and listen, too. The clock—the ashes—and the venetian—and then again—something else, like steps in the back yard. "Go an' see what it is, Millie Evans."

She darted to the back door, opened it, and at the same moment some one ducked behind the wood pile. "Who's that?" she cried, in a loud, bold voice. "Come out o' that! I seen yer. I know where y'are. I got my gun. Come out from behind of that wood stack!" She was not frightened any more. She was furiously angry. Her heart banged like a drum.

"I'll teach you to play tricks with a woman," she yelled, and she took a gun from the kitchen corner, and dashed down the verandah steps, across the glaring yard to the other side of the wood stack. A young man lay there, on his stomach, one arm across his face. "Get up! You're shamming!" Still holding the gun she kicked him in the shoulders. He gave no sign. "Oh, my God, I believe he's dead." She knelt down, seized hold of him, and turned him over on his back. He rolled like a sack. She crouched back on her haunches, staring; her lips and nostrils fluttered with horror.

He was not much more than a boy, with fair hair, and a growth of fair down on his lips and chin. His eyes were open, rolled up, showing the whites, and his face was patched with dust caked with sweat. He wore a cotton shirt and trousers, with sandshoes on his feet. One of the trousers was stuck to his leg with a patch of dark blood. "I can't," said Millie, and then, "You've got to." She bent over and felt his heart. "Wait a minute," she stammered, "wait a minute," and she ran into the house for brandy and a pail of water. "What are you going to do, Millie Evans? Oh, I don't know. I never seen anyone in a dead faint before." She knelt down, put her arm under the boy's head and poured some brandy between his lips. It spilled down both sides of his mouth. She dipped a corner of her apron in the water and wiped his face and his hair and his throat, with fingers that trembled. Under the dust and sweat his face gleamed, white as her apron, and thin, and puckered in little lines. A strange dreadful feeling gripped Millie Evans' bosom—some seed that had never flourished there, unfolded and struck deep roots and burst into painful leaf. "Are yer coming round? Feeling all right again?" The boy breathed sharply, half choked, his eyelids quivered, and he moved his head from side to side. "You're better," said Millie, smoothing his hair. "Feeling fine now again, ain't you?" The pain in her bosom half suffocated her. "It's no good you crying, Millie Evans. You got to keep your head." Quite suddenly he sat up and leaned against the wood pile, away from her, staring on the ground. "There now!" cried Millie Evans, in a strange, shaking voice.

The boy turned and looked at her, still not speaking, but his eyes were so full of pain and terror that she had to shut her teeth and clench her hands to stop from crying. After a long pause he said in the little voice of a child talking in his sleep, "I'm hungry."

His lips quivered. She scrambled to her feet and stood over him.

"You come right into the house and have a sit down meal," she said. "Can you walk?"

"Yes," he whispered, and swaying he followed her across the glaring yard to the verandah.

At the bottom step he paused, looking at her again. "I'm not coming in," he said. He sat on the verandah step in the little pool of shade that lay round the house. Millie watched him. "When did yer last 'ave anythink to eat?" He shook his head. She cut a chunk off the greasy corned beef and a round of bread plastered with butter; but when she brought it he was standing up, glancing round him, and paid no attention to the plate of food. "When are they coming back?" he stammered.

At that moment she knew. She stood, holding the plate, staring. He was Harrison. He was the English johnny who'd killed Mr. Williamson.

"I know who you are," she said, very slowly, "yer can't fox me. That's who you are. I must have been blind in me two eyes not to 'ave known from the first."

He made a movement with his hands as though that was all nothing. "When are they coming back?"

And she meant to say, "Any minute. They're on their way now." Instead she said to the dreadful, frightened face, "Not till 'arf past ten."

He sat down, leaning against one of the verandah poles. His face broke up into little quivers. He shut his eyes and tears streamed down his cheeks.

"Nothing but a kid. An' all them fellows after 'im. 'E don't stand any more of a chance than a kid would."

"Try a bit of beef," said Millie. "It's the food you want. Somethink to steady your stomach." She moved across the verandah and sat down beside him, the plate on her knees. "'Ere—try a bit." She broke the bread and butter into little pieces, and she thought, "They won't ketch him. Not if I can 'elp it. Men is all beasts. I don' care wot 'e's done, or wot 'e 'asn't done. See 'im through, Millie Evans. 'E's nothink but a sick kid."

Millie lay on her back, her eyes wide open, listening. Sid turned over, hunched the quilt round his shoulders, muttered "Good-night, ole girl." She heard Willie Cox and the other chap drop their clothes onto the kitchen floor, and then their voices, and Willie Cox saying, "Lie down, Gumboil. Lie down, yer little devil," to his dog. The house dropped quiet. She lay and listened. Little pulses tapped in her body, listening, too. It was hot. She was frightened to move because of Sid. "'E must get off. 'E must. I don' care anythink about justice an' all the rot they've bin spoutin' tonight," she thought, savagely. "'Ow are yer to know what anythink's like till yer do know. It's all rot." She strained to the silence. He ought to be moving... Before there was a sound from outside, Willie Cox's Gumboil got up and padded sharply across the kitchen floor and sniffed at the back door. Terror started up in Millie. "What's that dog doing? Uh! What a fool that young fellow is with a dog 'anging about. Why don't 'e lie down an'sleep." The dog stopped, but she knew it was listening.

Suddenly, with a sound that made her cry out in horror the dog started barking and rushing to and fro. "What's that? What's up?" Sid flung out of bed. "It ain't nothink. It's only Gumboil. Sid, Sid!" She clutched his arm, but he shook her off. "My Christ, there's somethink up. My God!" Sid flung into his trousers. Willie Cox opened the back door. Gumboil in a fury darted out into the yard, round the corner of the house. "Sid, there's some one in the paddock," roared the other chap. "What is it—what's that?" Sid dashed out on to the front verandah. "'Ere, Millie, take the lantin. Willie, some skunk's got 'old of one of the 'orses." The three men bolted out of the house, and at the same moment Millie saw Harrison dash across the paddock on Sid's horse and down the road. "Millie, bring that blasted lantin." She ran in her bare feet, her nightdress flicking her legs. They were after him in a flash. And at the sight of Harrison in the distance, and the three men hot after, a strange mad joy smothered everything else. She rushed into the road—she laughed and shrieked and danced in the dust, jigging the lantern. "A—ah! Arter 'im, Sid! A—a—a—h! Ketch him, Willie. Go it! Go it! A—ah, Sid! Shoot 'im down. Shoot 'im!"

PENSION SÉGUIN

The servant who opened the door was twin sister to that efficient and hideous creature bearing a soup tureen into the First French Picture. Her round red face shone like freshly washed china. She had a pair of immense bare arms to match, and a quantity of mottled hair arranged in a sort of bow. I stammered in a ridiculous, breathless fashion, as though a pack of Russian wolves were behind me, rather than five flights of beautifully polished French stairs.

"Have you a room?" The servant girl did not know. She would ask Madame. Madame was at dinner.

"Will you come in, please?"

Through the dark hall, guarded by a large black stove that had the appearance of a headless cat with one red all-seeing eye in the middle of its stomach, I followed her into the salon.

"Please to sit down," said the servant girl, closing the door behind her. I heard her list slippers shuffle along the corridor, the sound of another door opening—a little clamour—instantly suppressed. Silence followed.

The salon was long and narrow, with a yellow floor dotted with white mats. White muslin curtains hid the windows: the walls were white, decorated with pictures of pale ladies drifting down cypress avenues to forsaken temples, and moons rising over boundless oceans. You would have thought that all the long years of Madame's virginity had been devoted to the making of white mats—that her childish voice had lisped its numbers in crochet-work stitches. I did not dare to begin counting them. They rained upon me from every possible place, like impossible snowflakes. Even the piano stool was buttoned into one embroidered with P.F.

I had been looking for a resting place all the morning. At the start I flew up innumerable stairs as though they were major scales—the most cheerful things in the world—but after repeated failures the scales had resolved into the minor, and my heart, which was quite cast down by this time, leapt up again at these signs and tokens of virtue and sobriety. "A woman with such sober passions," thought I, "is bound to be quiet and clean, with few babies and a much absent husband. Mats are not the sort of things that lend themselves in their making to cheerful singing. Mats are essentially the fruits of pious solitude. I shall certainly take a room here." And I began to dream of unpacking my clothes in a little white room, and getting into a kimono and lying on a white bed, watching the curtains float out from the windows in the delicious autumn air that smelled of apples and honey...until the door opened and a tall thin woman in a lilac pinafore came in, smiling in a vague fashion.

"Madame Séguin?"

"Yes, Madame."

I repeated the familiar story. A quiet room, removed from any church bells, or crowing cocks, or little boys' schools, or railway stations.

"There are none of such things anywhere near here," said Madame, looking very surprised. "I have a very beautiful room to let, and quite unexpectedly. It has been occupied by a young gentleman from Buenos Ayres whose father died, unfortunately, and implored him to return home immediately. Quite natural, indeed."

"Oh, very!" said I, hoping that the Hamlet-like apparition was at rest again and would not invade my solitude to make certain of his son's obedience.

"If Madame will follow me."

Down a dark corridor, round a corner I felt my way. I wanted to ask Madame if this was where Buenos Ayres père appeared unto his son, but I did not dare to.

"Here—you see. Quite away from everything," said Madame.

I have always viewed with a proper amount of respect and abhorrence those penetrating spirits who are not susceptible to appearances. What is there to believe in except appearances? I have nearly always found that they are the only things worth enjoying at all, and if ever an innocent child lays its head upon my knee and begs for the truth of the matter, I shall tell it the story of my one and only nurse, who, knowing my horror of gooseberry jam, spread a coat of apricot over the top of the jam jar. As long as I believed it apricot I was happy, and learning wisdom, I contrived to eat the apricot and leave the gooseberry behind. "So, you see, my little innocent creature," I shall end, "the great thing to learn in this life is to be content with appearances, and shun the vulgarities of the grocer and philosopher."

Bright sunlight streamed through the windows of the delightful room. There was an alcove for the bed, a writing table was placed against the window, a couch against the wall. And outside the window I looked down upon an avenue of gold and red trees and up at a range of mountains white with fresh fallen snow.

"One hundred and eighty francs a month," murmured Madame, smiling at nothing, but seeming to imply by her manner, "Of course this has nothing to do with the matter." I said, "That is too much. I cannot afford more than one hundred and fifty francs."

"But," explained Madame, "the size! the alcove! And the extreme rarity of being overlooked by so many mountains."

"Yes," I said.

"And then the food. There are four meals a day, and breakfast in your room if you wish it."

"Yes," I said, more feebly.

"And my husband a Professor at the Conservatoire—that again is so rare."

Courage is like a disobedient dog, once it starts running away it flies all the faster for your attempts to recall it.

"One hundred and sixty," I said.

"If you agree to take it for two months I will accept," said Madame, very quickly. I agreed.

Marie helped to unstrap my boxes. She knelt on the floor, grinning and scratching her big red arms.

"Ah, how glad I am Madame has come," she said. "Now we shall have some life again. Monsieur Arthur, who lived in this room—he was a gay one. Singing all day and sometimes dancing. Many a time Mademoiselle Ambatielos would be playing and he'd dance for an hour without stopping."

"Who is Mademoiselle Ambatielos?" I asked.

"A young lady studying at the Conservatoire," said Marie, sniffing in a very friendly fashion. "But she gives lessons too. Ah, mon Dieu, sometimes when I am dusting in her room I think her fingers will drop off. She plays all day long. But I like that—that's life, noise is. That's what I say. You'll hear her soon. Up and down she goes!" said Marie, with extreme heartiness.

"But," I cried, loathing Marie, "how many other people are staying here?"

Marie shrugged. "Nobody to speak of. There's the Russian gentleman, a priest he is, and Madame's three children—and that's all. The children are lively enough," she said, filling the wash-stand pitcher, "but then there's the baby—the boy! Ah, you'll know about him, poor little one, soon enough!" She was so detestable I would not ask her anything further.

I waited until she was gone, and leaned against the window sill, watching the sun deepen in the trees until they seemed full and trembling with gold, and wondering what was the matter with the mysterious baby.

All through the afternoon Mademoiselle Ambatielos and the piano warred with the Appassionata Sonata. They shattered it to bits and re-made it to their heart's desire—they unpicked it—and tried it in various styles. They added a little touch—caught up something. Finally they decided that the only thing of importance was the loud pedal. The mysterious baby, hidden behind Heaven knows how many doors, cried with such curious persistence that I had to strain my ears, wondering if it was a baby or an engine or a far-off whistle. At dusk Marie, accompanied by the two little girls, brought me a lamp. My appearance disturbed these charming children to such an extent that they rushed up and down the corridor in a frenzied state for half-an-hour afterwards, bumping themselves against the walls, and shrieking with derisive laughter.

At eight the gong sounded for supper. I was hungry. The corridor was filled with the warm, strong smell of cooked meat. "Well," I thought, "at any rate, judging by the smell, the food must be good." And feeling very frightened I entered the dining-room.

Two rows of faces turned to watch me. M. Séguin introduced me, rapped on the table with the soup spoon, and the two little girls, impudent and scornful, cried: "Bon soir, Madame," while the baby, half washed away by his afternoon's performance, emptied his cup of milk over his head while Madame Séguin showed me my seat. In the confusion caused by this last episode, and by his being carried away by Marie, screaming and spitting with rage, I sat down next to the Russian priest and opposite Mademoiselle Ambatielos. M. Séguin took a loaf of bread from a three-legged basket at his elbow and carved it against his chest.

Soup was served—with vermicelli letters of the alphabet floating in it. These were last straws to the little Séguin's table manners.

"Maman, Yvonne's got more letters than me."

"Maman, Hélène keeps taking my letters out with her spoon."

"Children! Children! Quiet, quiet!" said Madame Séguin gently. "No, don't do it."

Hélène seized Yvonne's plate and pulled it towards her.

"Stop," said M. Séguin, who was like a rat, with spectacles all misted over with soup steam. "Hélène, leave the table. Go to Marie." Exit Hélène, with her apron over her head.

Soup was followed by chestnuts and Brussels sprouts. All the time the Russian priest, who wore a pale blue tie with a buttoned frock coat and a moustache fierce as a Gogol novel, kept up a flow of conversation with Mademoiselle Ambatielos. She looked very young. She was stout, with a high firm bust decorated with a spray of artificial roses. She never ceased touching the roses or her blouse or hair, or looking at her hands—with a smile trembling on her mouth and her blue eyes wide and staring. She seemed half intoxicated with her fresh young body.

"I saw you this morning when you didn't see me," said the priest.

"You didn't."

"I did."

"He didn't, did he, Madame?"

Madame Séguin smiled, and carried away the chestnuts, bringing back a dish of pears.

"I hope you will come into the salon after dinner," she said to me. "We always chat a little—we are such a family party." I smiled, wondering why pears should follow chestnuts.

"I must apologise for baby," she went on. "He is so nervous. But he spends his day in a room at the other end of the apartment to you. You will not be troubled. Only think of it! He passes whole days banging his little head against the floor and walls. The doctors cannot understand it at all."

M. Séguin pushed back his chair, said grace. I followed desperately into the salon. "I expect you have been admiring my mats," said Madame Séguin, with more animation than she had hitherto shown. "People always imagine they are the product of my industry. But, alas, no! They are all made by my friend, Madame Kummer, who has the pension on the first floor."

VIOLET

"I met a young virgin
Who sadly did moan"

There is a very unctuous and irritating English proverb to the effect that "Every cloud has a silver lining." What comfort can it be to one steeped to the eyebrows in clouds to ponder over their linings, and what an unpleasant picture-postcard seal it sets upon one's tragedy—turning it into a little ha'penny monstrosity with a moon in the left-hand corner like a vainglorious threepenny bit! Nevertheless, like most unctuous and irritating things, it is true. The lining woke me after my first night at the Pension Séguin and showed me over the feather bolster a room bright with sunlight as if every golden-haired baby in Heaven were pelting the earth with buttercup posies. "What a charming fancy!" I thought. "How much prettier than the proverb! It sounds like a day in the country with Katharine Tynan."

And I saw a little picture of myself and Katharine Tynan being handed glasses of milk by a red-faced woman with an immensely fat apron, while we discussed the direct truth of proverbs as opposed to the fallacy of playful babies. But in such a case imaginary I was ranged on the side of the proverbs. "There's a lot of sound sense in 'em," said that coarse being. "I admire the way they put their collective foot down upon the female attempt to embroider everything. 'The pitcher that goes too often to the well gets broken.' Also gut. Not even a loophole for a set of verses to a broken pitcher. No possible chance of the well being one of those symbolic founts to which all hearts in the form of pitchers are carried. The only proverb I disapprove of," went on this impossible creature, pulling a spring onion from the garden bed and chewing on it, "is the one about a bird in the hand. I naturally prefer birds in bushes." "But," said Katharine Tynan, tender and brooding, as she lifted a little green fly from her milk glass, "but if you were Saint Francis, the bird would not mind being in your hand. It would prefer the white nest of your fingers to any bush."

I jumped out of bed and ran over to the window and opened it wide and leaned out. Down below in the avenue a wind shook and swung the trees; the scent of leaves was on the lifting air. The houses lining the avenue were small and white. Charming, chaste-looking little houses, showing glimpses of lace and knots of ribbon, for all the world like country children in a row, about to play "Nuts and May." I began to imagine an adorable little creature named Yvette who lived in one and all of these houses... She spends her morning in a white lace boudoir cap, worked with daisies, sipping chocolate from a Sèvres cup with one hand, while a faithful attendant polishes the little pink nails of the other. She spends the afternoon in her tiny white and gold boudoir, curled up, a Persian kitten on her lap, while her ardent, beautiful lover leans over the back of the sofa, kissing and kissing again that thrice fascinating dimple on her left shoulder... When one of the balcony windows opened, and a stout servant swaggered out with her arms full of rugs and carpet strips. With a gesture expressing fury and disgust she flung them over the railing, disappeared, re-appeared again with a long-handled cane broom and fell upon the wretched rugs and carpets. Bang! Whack! Whack! Bang! Their feeble, pitiful jigging inflamed her to ever greater effort. Clouds of dust flew up round her, and when one little rug escaped and flopped down to the avenue below, like a fish, she leaned over the balcony, shaking her fist and the broom at it.

Lured by the noise, an old gentleman came to a window opposite and cast an eye of approval upon the industrious girl and yawned in the face of the lovely day. There was an air of detachment and deliberation about the way he carefully felt over the muscles of his arms and legs, pressed his throat, coughed, and shot a jet of spittle out of the window. Nobody seemed more surprised at this last feat than he. He seemed to regard it as a small triumph in its way, buttoning his immense stomach into a white piqué waistcoat with every appearance of satisfaction. Away flew my charming Yvette in a black and white check dress, an alpaca apron, and a market basket over her arm.

I dressed, ate a roll and drank some tepid coffee, feeling very sobered. I thought how true it was that the world was a delightful place if it were not for the people, and how more than true it was that people were not worth troubling about, and that wise men should set their affections upon nothing smaller than cities, heavenly or otherwise, and countrysides, which are always heavenly.

With these reflections, both pious and smug, I put on my hat, groped my way along the dark passage, and ran down the five flights of stairs into the Rue St. Léger. There was a garden on the opposite side of the street, through which one walked to the University and the more pretentious avenues fronting the Place du Théâtre. Although autumn was well advanced, not a leaf had fallen from the trees, the little shrubs and bushes were touched with pink and crimson, and against the blue sky the trees stood sheathed in gold. On stone benches nursemaids in white cloaks and stiff white caps chattered and wagged their heads like a company of cockatoos, and, up and down, in the sun, some genteel babies bowled hoops with a delicate air. What peculiar pleasure it is to wander through a strange city and amuse oneself as a child does, playing a solitary game!

"Pardon, Madame, mais voulez-vous…" and then the voice faltered and cried my name as though I had been given up for lost times without number; as though I had been drowned in foreign seas, and burnt in American hotel fires, and buried in a hundred lonely graves. "What on earth are you doing here?" Before me, not a day changed, not a hairpin altered, stood Violet Burton. I was flattered beyond measure at this enthusiasm, and pressed her cold, strong hand, and said "Extraordinary!"

"But what are you here for?"

"…Nerves."

"Oh, impossible, I really can't believe that."

"It is perfectly true," I said, my enthusiasm waning. There is nothing more annoying to a woman than to be suspected of nerves of iron.

"Well, you certainly don't look it," said she, scrutinising me, with that direct English frankness that makes one feel as though sitting in the glare of a window at breakfast-time.

"What are you here for?" I said, smiling graciously to soften the glare. At that she turned and looked across the lawns, and fidgetted with her umbrella like a provincial actress about to make a confession.

"I"—in a quiet affected voice—"I came here to forget… But," facing me again, and smiling energetically, "don't let's talk about that. Not yet. I can't explain. Not until I know you all over again." Very solemnly—"Not until I am sure you are to be trusted."

"Oh, don't trust me, Violet!" I cried. "I'm not to be trusted. I wouldn't if I were you." She frowned and stared.

"What a terrible thing to say. You can't be in earnest."

"Yes, I am. There's nothing I adore talking about so much as another person's secret." To my surprise, she came to my side and put her arm through mine.

"Thank you," she said, gratefully. "I think it's awfully good of you to take me into your confidence like that. Awfully. And even if it were true…but no, it can't be true, otherwise you wouldn't have told me. I mean it can't be psychologically true of the same nature to be frank and dishonourable at the same time. Can it? But then…I don't know. I suppose it is possible. Don't you find that the Russian novelists have made an upheaval of all your conclusions?" We walked, bras dessus bras dessous, down the sunny path.

"Let's sit down," said Violet. "There's a fountain quite near this bench. I often come here. You can hear it all the time." The faint noise of the water sounded like a half-forgotten tune, half sly, half laughing.

"Isn't it wonderful!" breathed Violet. "Like weeping in the night."

"Oh, Violet," said I, terrified at this turn. "Wonderful things don't weep in the night. They sleep like tops and know nothing more till again it is day."

She put her arm over the back of the bench and crossed her legs.

"Why do you persist in denying your emotions? Why are you ashamed of them?" she demanded.

"I'm not. But I keep them tucked away, and only produce them very occasionally, like special little pots of jam, when the people whom I love come to tea."

"There you are again! Emotions and jam! Now, I'm absolutely different. I live on mine. Sometimes I wish I didn't—but then again I would rather suffer through them—suffer intensely, I mean; go down into the depths with them, for the sake of that wonderful upward swing on to the pinnacles of happiness." She edged nearer to me.

"I wish I could think where I get my nature from," she went on. "Father and mother are absolutely different. I mean—they're quite normal—quite commonplace." I shook my head and raised my eyebrows. "But it is no use fighting it. It has beaten me. Absolutely—once and for all." A pause, inadequately filled by the sly, laughing water. "Now," said Violet, impressively, "you know what I meant when I said I came here to forget."

"But I assure you I don't, Violet. How can you expect me to be so subtle? I quite understand that you don't wish to tell me until you know me better. Quite!"

She opened her eyes and her mouth.

"I have told you! I mean—not straight out. Not in so many words. But then—how could I? But when I told you of my emotional nature, and that I had been in the depths and swept up to the pinnacles...surely, surely you realised that I was telling you, symbolically. What else can you have thought?"

No young girl ever performs such gymnastic feats by herself. Yet in my experience I had always imagined that the depths followed the pinnacles. I ventured to suggest so.

"They do," said Violet, gloomily. "You see them, if you look, before and after."

"Like the people in Shelley's Skylark," said I.

Violet looked vague, and I repented. But I did not know how to sympathise, and I had no idea of the relative sizes.

"It was in the summer," said Violet. "I had been most frightfully depressed. I don't know what it was. For one thing I felt as though I could not make up my mind to anything. I felt so terribly useless — that I had no place in the scheme of things—and worst of all, nobody who understood me... It may have been what I was reading at the time...but I don't think...not entirely. Still one never knows. Does one? And then I met...Mr. Farr, at a dance—"

"Oh, call him by his Christian name, Violet. You can't go on telling me about Mr. Farr and you...on the heights."

"Why on earth not? Very well—I met—Arthur. I think I must have been mad that evening. For one thing there had been a bother about going. Mother didn't want me to, because she said there wouldn't be anybody to see me home. And I was frightfully keen. I must have had a presentiment, I think. Do you believe in presentiments?... I don't know, we can't be certain, can we? Anyhow, I went. And he was there." She turned a deep scarlet and bit her lip. Oh, I really began to like Violet Burton—to like her very much indeed.

"Go on," I said.

"We danced together seven times and we talked the whole time. The music was very slow, —we talked of everything. You know...about books and theatres and all that sort of thing at first, and then—about our souls."

"...What?"

"I said—our souls. He understood me absolutely. And after the seventh dance... No, I must tell you the first thing he ever said to me. He said, 'Do you believe in Pan?' Quite quietly. Just like that. And then he said, 'I knew you did.' Wasn't that extra-or-din-ary! After the seventh dance we sat out on the landing. And...shall I go on?"

"Yes, go on."

"He said, 'I think I must be mad. I want to kiss you,'—and—I let him."

"Do go on."

"I simply can't tell you what I felt like. Fancy! I'd never kissed out of the family before. I mean—of course—never a man. And then he said: 'I must tell you—I am engaged.'"

"Well?"

"What else is there? Of course I simply rushed upstairs and tumbled everything over in the dressing-room and found my coat and went home. And next morning I made Mother let me come here. I thought," said Violet, "I thought I would have died of shame."

"Is that all?" I cried. "You can't mean to say that's all?"

"What else could there be? What on earth did you expect. How extraordinary you are—staring at me like that!"

And in the long pause I heard again the little fountain, half sly, half laughing—at me, I thought, not at Violet.

"Third storey—to the left, Madame," said the cashier, handing me a pink ticket. "One moment—I will ring for the elevator." Her black satin skirt swished across the scarlet and gold hall, and she stood among the artificial palms, her white neck and powdered face topped with masses of gleaming orange hair—like an over-ripe fungus bursting from a thick, black stem. She rang and rang. "A thousand pardons, Madame. It is disgraceful. A new attendant. He leaves this week." With her fingers on the bell she peered into the cage as though she expected to see him, lying on the floor, like a dead bird. "It is disgraceful." There appeared from nowhere a tiny figure disguised in a peaked cap and dirty white cotton gloves. "Here you are?" she scolded. "Where have you been? What have you been doing?" For answer the figure hid its face behind one of the white cotton gloves and sneezed twice. "Ugh! Disgusting! Take Madame to the third storey!" The midget stepped aside, bowed, entered after me and clashed the gates to. We ascended, very slowly, to an accompaniment of sneezes and prolonged, half whistling sniffs. I asked the top of the patent-leather cap: "Have you a cold?" "It is the air, Madame," replied the creature, speaking through its nose with a restrained air of great relish, "one is never dry here. Third floor—if you please," sneezing over my ten-centime tip.

I walked along a tiled corridor decorated with advertisements for lingerie and bust improvers—was allotted a tiny cabin and a blue print chemise and told to undress and find the Warm Room as soon as possible. Through the matchboard walls and from the corridor sounded cries and laughter and snatches of conversation.

"Are you ready?"

"Are you coming out now?"

"Wait till you see me!"

"Berthe—Berthe!"

"One moment! One moment! Immediately!"

I undressed quickly and carelessly, feeling like one of a troupe of little schoolgirls let loose in a swimming-bath.

The Warm Room was not large. It had terra cotta painted walls with a fringe of peacocks, and a glass roof, through which one could see the sky, pale and unreal as a photographer's background screen. Some round tables strewn with shabby fashion journals, a marble basin in the centre of the room, filled with yellow lilies, and on the long, towel enveloped chairs, a number of ladies, apparently languid as the flowers... I lay back with a cloth over my head, and the air, smelling of jungles and circuses and damp washing made me begin to dream... Yes, it might have been very fascinating to have married an explorer...and lived in a jungle, as long as he didn't shoot anything or take anything captive. I detest performing beasts. Oh...those circuses at home...the tent in the paddock and the children swarming over the fence to stare at the waggons and at the clown making up, with his glass stuck on the waggon wheel—and the steam organ playing the Honeysuckle and the Bee much too fast...over and over. I know what this air reminds me of—a game of follow my leader among the clothes hung out to dry...

The door opened. Two tall blonde women in red and white check gowns came in and took the chairs opposite mine. One of them carried a box of mandarins wrapped in silver paper and the other a manicure set. They were very stout, with gay, bold faces, and quantities of exquisite whipped fair hair.

Before sitting down they glanced round the room, looked the other women up and down, turned to each other, grimaced, whispered something, and one of them said, offering the box, "Have a mandarin?" At that they started laughing—they lay back and shook, and each time they caught sight of each other broke out afresh.

"Ah, that was too good," cried one, wiping her eyes very carefully, just at the corners. "You and I, coming in here, quite serious, you know, very correct—and looking round the room—and—and as a result of our careful inspection—I offer you a mandarin. No, it's too funny. I must remember that. It's good enough for a music hall. Have a mandarin?"

"But I cannot imagine," said the other, "why women look so hideous in Turkish baths—like beef-steaks in chemises. Is it the women—or is it the air? Look at that one, for instance—the skinny one, reading a book and sweating at the moustache—and those two over in the corner, discussing whether or not they ought to tell their non-existent babies how babies come—and... Heavens! Look at this one coming in. Take the box, dear. Have all the mandarins."

The newcomer was a short stout little woman with flat, white feet, and a black mackintosh cap over her hair. She walked up and down the room, swinging her arms, in affected unconcern, glancing contemptuously at the laughing women, and rang the bell for the attendant. It was answered immediately by Berthe, half naked and sprinkled with soapsuds. "Well, what is it, Madame? I've no time..."

"Please bring me a hand towel," said the Mackintosh Cap, in German.

"Pardon? I do not understand. Do you speak French?"

"Non," said the Mackintosh Cap.

"Ber-the!" shrieked one of the blonde women, "have a mandarin. Oh, mon Dieu, I shall die of laughing."

The Mackintosh Cap went through a pantomime of finding herself wet and rubbing herself dry. "V ersteben Sie?"

"Mais non, Madame," said Berthe, watching with round eyes that snapped with laughter, and she left the Mackintosh Cap, winked at the blonde women, came over, felt them as though they had been a pair of prize poulury, said "You are doing very well," and disappeared again.

The Mackintosh Cap sat down on the edge of a chair, snatched a fashion journal, smacked over the crackling pages and pretended to read, while the blonde women leaned back eating the mandarins and throwing the peelings into the lily basin. A scent of fruit, fresh and penetrating, hung on the air. I looked round at the other women. Yes, they were hideous, lying back, red and moist, with dull eyes and lank hair, the only little energy they had vented in shocked prudery at the behaviour of the two blondes. Suddenly I discovered Mackintosh Cap staring at me over the top of her fashion journal, so intently that I took flight and went into the hot room. But in vain! Mackintosh Cap followed after and planted herself in front of me.

"I know," she said, confident and confiding, "that you can speak German. I saw it in your face just now. Wasn't that a scandal about the attendant refusing me a towel? I shall speak to the management about that, and I shall get my husband to write them a letter this evening. Things always come better from a man, don't they? No," she said, rubbing her yellowish arms, "I've never been in such a scandalous place—and four francs fifty to pay! Naturally, I shall not give a tip. You wouldn't, would you? Not after that scandal about a hand towel... I've a great mind to complain about those women as well. Those two that keep on laughing and eating. Do you know who they are?" She shook her head. "They're not respectable women—you can tell at a glance. At least I can, any married woman can. They're nothing but a couple of street women. I've never been so insulted in my life. Laughing at me, mind you! The great big fat pigs like that! And I haven't sweated at all properly, just because of them. I got so angry that the sweat turned in instead of out; it does in excitement, you know, sometimes, and now instead of losing my cold I wouldn't be surprised if I brought on a fever."

I walked round the hot room in misery pursued by the Mackintosh Cap until the two blonde women came in, and seeing her, burst into another fit of laughter. To my rage and disgust Mackintosh Cap sidled up to me, smiled meaningly, and drew down her mouth.

"I don't care," she said, in her hideous German voice. "I shouldn't lower myself by paying any attention to a couple of street women. If my husband knew he'd never get over it. Dreadfully particular he is. We've been married six years. We come from Pfalzburg. It's a nice town. Four children I have living, and it was really to get over the shock of the fifth that we came here. The fifth," she whispered, padding after me, "was born, a fine healthy child, and it never breathed! Well, after nine months, a woman can't help being disappointed, can she?"

I moved towards the vapour room. "Are you going in there?" she said. "I wouldn't if I were you. Those two have gone in. They may think you want to strike up an acquaintance with them. You never know women like that." At that moment they came out, wrapping themselves in the rough gowns, and passing Mackintosh Cap like disdainful queens. "Are you going to take your chemise off in the vapour room?" asked she. "Don't mind me, you know. Woman is woman, and besides, if you'd rather, I won't look at you. I know—I used to be like that. I wouldn't mind betting," she went on savagely, "those filthy women had a good look at each other. Pooh! women like that. You can't shock them. And don't they look dreadful? Bold, and all that false hair. That manicure box one of them had was fitted up with gold. Well, I don't suppose it was real, but I think it was disgusting to bring it. One might at least cut one's nails in private, don't you think? I cannot see," she said, "what men see in such women. No, a husband and children and a home to look after, that's what a woman needs. That's what my husband says. Fancy one of these hussies peeling potatoes or choosing the meat! Are you going already?"

I flew to find Berthe, and all the time I was soaped and smacked and sprayed and thrown in a cold water tank I could not get out of my mind the ugly, wretched figure of the little German with a good husband and four children, railing against the two fresh beauties who had never peeled potatoes nor chosen the right meat. In the ante-room I saw them once again. They were dressed in blue. One was pinning on a bunch of violets, the other buttoning a pair of ivory suède gloves. In their charming feathered hats and furs they stood talking. "Yes, there they are," said a voice at my elbow.

And there was Mackintosh Cap, transformed, in a blue and white check blouse and crochet collar, with the little waist and large hips of the German woman and a terrible bird nest, which Pfalzburg doubtless called Reise-but, on her head. "How do you suppose they can afford clothes like that? The horrible, low creatures. No, they're enough to make a young girl think twice." And as the two walked out of the ante-room, Mackintosh Cap stared after them, her sallow face all mouth and eyes, like the face of a hungry child before a forbidden table.

SOMETHING CHILDISH BUT VERY NATURAL

Whether he had forgotten what it felt like, or his head had really grown bigger since the summer before, Henry could not decide. But his straw hat hurt him: it pinched his forehead and started a dull ache in the two bones just over the temples. So he chose a corner seat in a third-class "smoker," took off his hat and put it in the rack with his large black cardboard portfolio and his Aunt B's Christmas-present gloves. The carriage smelt horribly of wet india-rubber and soot. There were ten minutes to spare before the train went, so Henry decided to go and have a look at the book-stall. Sunlight darted through the glass roof of the station in long beams of blue and gold; a little boy ran up and down carrying a tray of primroses; there was something about the people—about the women especially—something idle and yet eager. The most thrilling day of the year, the first real day of Spring had unclosed its warm delicious beauty even to London eyes. It had put a spangle in every colour and a new tone in every voice, and city folks walked as though they carried real live bodies under their clothes with real live hearts pumping the stiff blood through.

Henry was a great fellow for books. He did not read many nor did he possess above half-a-dozen. He looked at all in the Charing Cross Road during lunch-time and at any odd time in London; the quantity with which he was on nodding terms was amazing. By his clean neat handling of them and by his nice choice of phrase when discussing them with one or another bookseller you would have thought that he had taken his pap with a tome propped before his nurse's bosom. But you would have been quite wrong. That was only Henry's way with everything he touched or said. That afternoon it was an anthology of English poetry, and he turned over the pages until a title struck his eye—Something Childish but very Natural!

Had I but two little wings,
And were a little feathery bird,
To you I'd fly, my dear,
But thoughts like these are idle things,
And I stay here.

But in my sleep to you I fly,
I'm always with you in my sleep,
The world is all one's own,
But then one wakes and where am I?
All, all alone.

Sleep stays not though a monarch bids,
So I love to wake at break of day,
For though my sleep be gone,
Yet while' tis dark one shuts one's lids,
And so, dreams on.

He could not have done with the little poem. It was not the words so much as the whole air of it that charmed him! He might have written it lying in bed, very early in the morning, and watching the sun dance on the ceiling. "It is stilly like that," thought Henry. "I am sure he wrote it when he was half-awake some time, for it's got a smile of a dream on it." He stared at the poem and then looked away and repeated it by heart, missed a word in the third verse and looked again, and again until he became conscious of shouting and shuffling, and he looked up to see the train moving slowly.

"God's thunder!" Henry dashed forward. A man with a flag and a whistle had his hand on a door. He clutched Henry somehow... Henry was inside with the door slammed, in a carriage that wasn't a "smoker," that had not a trace of his straw hat or the black portfolio or his Aunt B's Christmas-present gloves. Instead, in the opposite corner, close against the wall, there sat a girl. Henry did not dare to look at her, but he felt certain she was staring at him. "She must think I'm mad," he thought, "dashing into a train without even a hat, and in the evening, too." He felt so funny. He didn't know how to sit or sprawl. He put his hands in his pockets and tried to appear quite indifferent and frown at a large photograph of Bolton Abbey. But feeling her eyes on him he gave her just the tiniest glance.

Quick she looked away out of the window, and then Henry, careful of her slightest movement, went on looking. She sat pressed against the window, her cheek and shoulder half hidden by a long wave of marigold-coloured hair. One little hand in a grey cotton glove held a leather case on her lap with the initials E. M. on it. The other hand she had slipped through the window-strap, and Henry noticed a silver bangle on the wrist with a Swiss cow-bell and a silver shoe and a fish. She wore a green coat and a hat with a wreath round it. All this Henry saw while the title of the new poem persisted in his brain—Something Childish but very Natural. "I suppose she goes to some school in London," thought Henry. "She might be in an office. Oh, no, she is too young. Besides she'd have her hair up if she was. It isn't even down her back." He could not keep his eyes off that beautiful waving hair.

"My eyes are like two drunken bees...' Now, I wonder if I read that or made it up?"

That moment the girl turned round and, catching his glance, she blushed. She bent her head to hide the red colour that flew in her cheeks, and Henry, terribly embarrassed, blushed too. "I shall have to speak—have to—have to!" He started putting up his hand to raise the hat that wasn't there. He thought that funny; it gave him confidence.

"I'm—I'm most awfully sorry," he said, smiling at the girl's hat. "But I can't go on sitting in the same carriage with you and not explaining why I dashed in like that, without my hat even. I'm sure I gave you a fright, and just now I was staring at you—but that's only an awful fault of mine; I'm a terrible starer! If you'd like me to explain—how I got in here—not about the staring, of course,"—he gave a little laugh—"I will."

For a minute she said nothing, then in a low, shy voice—"It doesn't matter."

The train had flung behind the roofs and chimneys. They were swinging into the country, past little black woods and fading fields and pools of water shining under an apricot evening sky. Henry's heart began to thump and beat to the beat of the train. He couldn't leave it like that. She sat so quiet, hidden in her fallen hair. He felt that it was absolutely necessary that she should look up and understand him—understand him at least. He leant forward and clasped his hands round his knees.

"You see I'd just put all my things—a portfolio—into a third-class 'smoker' and was having a look at the book-stall," he explained.

As he told the story she raised her head. He saw her grey eyes under the shadow of her hat and her eyebrows like two gold feathers. Her lips were faintly parted. Almost unconsciously he seemed to absorb the fact that she was wearing a bunch of primroses and that her throat was white—the shape of her face wonderfully delicate against all that burning hair.

"How beautiful she is! How simply beautiful she is!" sang Henry's heart, and swelled with the words, bigger and bigger and trembling like a marvellous bubble—so that he was afraid to breathe for fear of breaking it.

"I hope there was nothing valuable in the portfolio," said she, very grave.

"Oh, only some silly drawings that I was taking back from the office," answered Henry, airily. "And—I was rather glad to lose my hat. It had been hurting me all day."

"Yes," she said, "it's left a mark," and she nearly smiled.

Why on earth should those words have made Henry feel so free suddenly and so happy and so madly excited? What was happening between them? They said nothing, but to Henry their silence was alive and warm. It covered him from his head to his feet in a trembling wave. Her marvellous words, "It's made a mark," had in some mysterious fashion established a bond between them. They could not be utter strangers to each other if she spoke so simply and so naturally. And now she was really smiling. The smile danced in her eyes, crept over her cheeks to her lips and stayed there. He leant back. The words flew from him.—"Isn't life wonderful!"

At that moment the train dashed into a tunnel. He heard her voice raised against the noise. She leant forward.

"I don't think so. But then I've been a fatalist for a long time now"—a pause—"months."

They were shattering through the dark. "Why?" called Henry.

"Oh…"

Then she shrugged, and smiled and shook her head, meaning she could not speak against the noise. He nodded and leant back. They came out of the tunnel into a sprinkle of lights and houses. He waited for her to explain. But she got up and buttoned her coat and put her hands to her hat, swaying a little. "I get out here," she said. That seemed quite impossible to Henry.

The train slowed down and the lights outside grew brighter. She moved towards his end of the carriage.

"Look here!" he stammered. "Shan't I see you again?" He got up, too, and leant against the rack with one hand. "I must see you again." The train was stopping.

She said breathlessly, "I come down from London every evening."

"You—you—you do—really?" His eagerness frightened her. He was quick to curb it. Shall we or shall we not shake hands? raced through his brain. One hand was on the door-handle, handle, the other held the little bag. The train stopped. Without another word or glance she was gone.

Then came Saturday—a half day at the office—and Sunday between. By Monday evening Henry was quite exhausted. He was at the station far too early, with a pack of silly thoughts at his heels as it were driving him up and down. "She didn't say she came by this train!" "And supposing I go up and she cuts me." "There may be somebody with her." "Why do you suppose she's ever thought of you again?" "What are you going to say if you do see her?" He even prayed, "Lord if it be Thy will, let us meet."

But nothing helped. White smoke floated against the roof of the station—dissolved and came again in swaying wreaths. Of a sudden, as he watched it, so delicate and so silent, moving with such mysterious grace above the crowd and the scuffle, he grew calm. He felt very tired—he only wanted to sit down and shut his eyes—she was not coming—a forlorn relief breathed in the words. And then he saw her quite near to him walking towards the train with the same little leather case in her hand. Henry waited. He knew, somehow, that she had seen him, but he did not move until she came close to him and said in her low, shy voice—"Did you get them again?"

"Oh, yes, thank you, I got them again," and with a funny half gesture he showed her the portfolio and the gloves. They walked side by side to the train and into an empty carriage. They sat down opposite to each other, smiling timidly but not speaking, while the train moved slowly, and slowly gathered speed and smoothness. Henry spoke first.

"It's so silly," he said, "not knowing your name." She put back a big piece of hair that had fallen on her shoulder, and he saw how her hand in the grey glove was shaking. Then he noticed that she was sitting very stiffly with her knees pressed together—and he was, too—both of them trying not to tremble so. She said "My name is Edna."

"And mine is Henry."

In the pause they took possession of each other's names and turned them over and put them away, a shade less frightened after that.

"I want to ask you something else now," said Henry. He looked at Edna, his head a little on one side. "How old are you?"

"Over sixteen," she said, "and you?"

"I'm nearly eighteen..."

"Isn't it hot?" she said suddenly, and pulled off her grey gloves and put her hands to her cheeks and kept them there. Their eyes were not frightened—they looked at each other with a sort of desperate calmness. If only their bodies would not tremble so stupidly! Still half hidden by her hair, Edna said:

"Have you ever been in love before?"

"No, never! Have you?"

"Oh, never in all my life." She shook her head. "I never even thought it possible."

His next words came in a rush. "Whatever have you been doing since last Friday evening? Whatever did you do all Saturday and all Sunday and today?"

But she did not answer—only shook her head and smiled and said, "No, you tell me."

"I?" cried Henry—and then he found he couldn't tell her either. He couldn't climb back to those mountains of days, and he had to shake his head, too.

"But it's been agony," he said, smiling brilliantly—"agony." At that she took away her hands and started laughing, and Henry joined her. They laughed until they were tired.

"It's so—so extraordinary," she said. "So suddenly, you know, and I feel as if I'd known you for years."

"So do I…" said Henry. "I believe it must be the Spring. I believe I've swallowed a butterfly—and it's fanning its wings just here." He put his hand on his heart.

"And the really extraordinary thing is," said Edna, "that I had made up my mind that I didn't care for—men at all. I mean all the girls at College—"

"Were you at College?"

She nodded. "A training college, learning to be a secretary." She sounded scornful.

"I'm in an office," said Henry. "An architect's office—such a funny little place up one hundred and thirty stairs. We ought to be building nests instead of houses, I always think.

"Do you like it?"

"No, of course I don't. I don't want to do anything, do you?"

"No, I hate it… And," she said, "my mother is a Hungarian—I believe that makes me hate it even more."

That seemed to Henry quite natural. "It would," he said.

"Mother and I are exactly alike. I haven't a thing in common with my father; he's just…a little man in the City—but mother has got wild blood in her and she's given it to me. She hates our life just as much as I do." She paused and frowned. "All the same, we don't get on a bit together—that's funny—isn't it? But I'm absolutely alone at home."

Henry was listening—in a way he was listening, but there was something else he wanted to ask her. He said, very shyly, "Would you—would you take off your hat?"

She looked startled. "Take off my hat?"

"Yes—it's your hair. I'd give anything to see your hair properly."

She protested. "It isn't really…"

"Oh, it is," cried Henry, and then, as she took off the hat and gave her head a little toss, "Oh, Edna! it's the loveliest thing in the world."

"Do you like it?" she said, smiling and very pleased. She pulled it round her shoulders like a cape of gold. "People generally laugh at it. It's such an absurd colour." But Henry would not believe that. She leaned her elbows on her knees and cupped her chin in her hands. "That's how I often sit when I'm angry and then I feel it burning me up… Silly?"

"No, no, not a bit," said Henry. "I knew you did. It's your sort of weapon against all the dull horrid things."

"However did you know that? Yes, that's just it. But however did you know?"

"Just knew," smiled Henry. "My God!" he cried, "what fools people are! All the little pollies that you know and that I know. Just look at you and me. Here we are—that's all there is to be said. I know about you and you know about me—we've just found each other—quite simply—just by being natural. That's all life is—something childish and very natural. Isn't it?"

"Yes—yes," she said eagerly. "That's what I've always thought."

"It's people that make things so—silly. As long as you can keep away from them you're safe and you're happy."

"Oh, I've thought that for a long time."

"Then you're just like me," said Henry. The wonder of that was so great that he almost wanted to cry. Instead he said very solemnly: "I believe we're the only two people alive who think as we do. In fact, I'm sure of it. Nobody understands me. I feel as though I were living in a world of strange beings—do you?"

"Always."

"We'll be in that loathsome tunnel again in a minute," said Henry. "Edna! can I—just touch your hair?"

She drew back quickly. "Oh, no, please don't," and as they were going into the dark she moved a little away from him.

"Edna! I've bought the tickets. The man at the concert hall didn't seem at all surprised that I had the money. Meet me outside the gallery doors at three, and wear that cream blouse and the corals—will you? I love you. I don't like sending these letters to the shop. I always feel those people with 'Letters received' in their window keep a kettle in their back parlour that would steam open an elephant's ear of an envelope. But it really doesn't matter, does it, darling? Can you get away on Sunday? Pretend you are going to spend the day with one of the girls from the office, and let's meet at some little place and walk or find a field where we can watch the daisies uncurling. I do love you, Edna. But Sundays without you are simply impossible. Don't get run over before Saturday, and don't eat anything out of a tin or drink anything from a public fountain. That's all, darling."

"My dearest, yes, I'll be there on Saturday—and I've arranged about Sunday, too. That is one great blessing. I'm quite free at home. I have just come in from the garden. It's such a lovely evening. Oh, Henry, I could sit and cry, I love you so tonight. Silly—isn't it? I either feel so happy I can hardly stop laughing or else so sad I can hardly stop crying and both for the same reason. But we are so young to have found each other, aren't we? I am sending you a violet. It is quite warm. I wish you were here now, just for a minute even. Good-night, darling. I am Edna."

"Safe," said Edna, "safe! And excellent places, aren't they, Henry?"

She stood up to take off her coat and Henry made a movement to help her. "No—no—it's off." She tucked it under the seat. She sat down beside him. "Oh, Henry, what have you got there? Flowers?"

"Only two tiny little roses." He laid them in her lap.

"Did you get my letter all right?" asked Edna, unpinning the paper.

"Yes," he said, "and the violet is growing beautifully. You should see my room. I planted a little piece of it in every corner and one on my pillow and one in the pocket of my pyjama jacket."

She shook her hair at him. "Henry, give me the programme."

"Here it is—you can read it with me. I'll hold it for you."

"No, let me have it."

"Well, then, I'll read it for you."

"No, you can have it after."

"Edna," he whispered.

"Oh, please don't," she pleaded. "Not here—the people."

Why did he want to touch her so much and why did she mind? Whenever he was with her he wanted to hold her hand or take her arm when they walked together, or lean against her—not hard—just lean lightly so that his shoulder should touch her shoulder—and she wouldn't even have that. All the time that he was away from her he was hungry, he craved the nearness of her. There seemed to be comfort and warmth breathing from Edna that he needed to keep him calm. Yes, that was it. He couldn't get calm with her because she wouldn't let him touch her. But she loved him. He knew that. Why did she feel so curiously about it? Every time he tried to or even asked for her hand she shrank back and looked at him with pleading frightened eyes as though he wanted to hurt her. They could say anything to each other. And there wasn't any question of their belonging to each other. And yet he couldn't touch her. Why, he couldn't even help her off with her coat. Her voice dropped into his thoughts.

"Henry!" He leaned to listen, setting his lips. "I want to explain something to you. I will—I will—I promise—after the concert."

"All right." He was still hurt.

"You're not sad, are you?" he said.

He shook his head.

"Yes, you are, Henry."

"No, really not." He looked at the roses lying in her hands.

"Well, are you happy?"

"Yes. Here comes the orchestra."

It was twilight when they came out of the hall. A blue net of light hung over the streets and houses, and pink clouds floated in a pale sky. As they walked away from the hall Henry felt they were very little and alone. For the first time since he had known Edna his heart was heavy.

"Henry!" She stopped suddenly and stared at him. "Henry, I'm not coming to the station with you. Don't—don't wait for me. Please, please leave me."

"My God!" cried Henry, and started, "what's the matter—Edna—darling—Edna, what have I done?"

"Oh, nothing—go away," and she turned and ran across the street into a square and leaned up against the square railings—and hid her face in her hands.

"Edna—Edna—my little love—you're crying. Edna, my baby girl!"

She leaned her arms along the railings and sobbed distractedly.

"Edna—stop—it's all my fault. I'm a fool—I'm a thundering idiot. I've spoiled your afternoon. I've tortured you with my idiotic mad bloody clumsiness. That's it. Isn't it, Edna? For God's sake."

"Oh," she sobbed, "I do hate hurting you so. Every time you ask me to let—let you hold my hand or—or kiss me I could kill myself for not doing it—for not letting you. I don't know why I don't even." She said wildly. "It's not that I'm frightened of you—it's not that—it's only a feeling, Henry, that I can't understand myself even. Give me your handkerchief, darling." He pulled it from his pocket. "All through the concert I've been haunted by this, and every time we meet I know it's bound to come up. Somehow I feel if once we did that—you know—held each other's hands and kissed it would be all changed—and I feel we wouldn't be free like we are—we'd be doing something secret. We wouldn't be children any more silly, isn't it? I'd feel awkward with you, Henry, and I'd feel shy, and I do so feel that just because you and I are you and I, we don't need that sort of thing." She turned and looked at him, pressing her hands to her cheeks in the way he knew so well, and behind her as in a dream he saw the sky and half a white moon and the trees of the square with their unbroken buds. He kept twisting, twisting up in his hands the concert programme. "Henry! You do understand me—don't you?"

"Yes, I think I do. But you're not going to be frightened any more, are you?" He tried to smile. "We'll forget, Edna. I'll never mention it again. We'll bury the bogy in this square—now—you and I—won't we?"

"But," she said, searching his face—"will it make you love me less?"

"Oh, no," he said. "Nothing could—nothing on earth could do that."

London became their play-ground. On Saturday afternoons they explored. They found their own shops where they bought cigarettes and sweets for Edna—and their own tea-shop with their own table—their own streets—and one night when Edna was supposed to be at a lecture at the Polytechnic they found their own village. It was the name that made them go there. "There's white geese in that name," said Henry, telling it to Edna. "And a river and little low houses with old men sitting outside them—old sea captains with wooden legs winding up their watches, and there are little shops with lamps in the windows."

It was too late for them to see the geese or the old men, but the river was there and the houses and even the shops with lamps. In one a woman sat working a sewing-machine on the counter. They heard the whirring hum and they saw her big shadow filling the shop. "Too full for a single customer," said Henry. "It is a perfect place."

The houses were small and covered with creepers and ivy. Some of them had worn wooden steps leading up to the doors. You had to go down a little flight of steps to enter some of the others; and just across the road—to be seen from every window—was the river, with a walk beside it and some high poplar trees.

"This is the place for us to live in," said Henry. "There's a house to let, too. I wonder if it would wait if we asked it. I'm sure it would."

"Yes, I would like to live there," said Edna.

They crossed the road and she leaned against the trunk of a tree and looked up at the empty house, with a dreamy smile.

"There is a little garden at the back, dear," said Henry, "a lawn with one tree on it and some daisy bushes round the wall. At night the stars shine in the tree like tiny candles. And inside there are two rooms downstairs and a big room with folding doors upstairs and above that an attic. And there are eight stairs to the kitchen—very dark, Edna. You are rather frightened of them, you know. 'Henry, dear, would you mind bringing the lamp? I just want to make sure that Euphemia has raked out the fire before we go to bed.'"

"Yes," said Edna. "Our bedroom is at the very top—that room with the two square windows. When it is quiet we can hear the river flowing and the sound of the poplar trees far, far away, rustling and flowing in our dreams, darling."

"You're not cold—are you?" he said, suddenly.

"No—no, only happy."

"The room with the folding doors is yours." Henry laughed. "It's a mixture—it isn't a room at all. It's full of your toys and there's a big blue chair in it where you sit curled up in front of the fire with the flames in your curls—because though we're married you refuse to put your hair up and only tuck it inside your coat for the church service. And there's a rug on the floor for me to lie on, because I'm so lazy. Euphemia—that's our servant—only comes in the day. After she's gone we go down to the kitchen and sit on the table and eat an apple, or perhaps we make some tea, just for the sake of hearing the kettle sing. That's not joking. If you listen to a kettle right through it's like an early morning in Spring."

"Yes, I know," she said. "All the different kinds of birds."

A little cat came through the railings of the empty house and into the road. Edna called it and bent down and held out her hands—"Kitty! Kitty!" The little cat ran to her and rubbed against her knees.

"If we're going for a walk just take the cat and put it inside the front door," said Henry, still pretending. "I've got the key."

They walked across the road and Edna stood stroking the cat in her arms while Henry went up the steps and pretended to open the door.

He came down again quickly. "Let's go away at once. It's going to turn into a dream."

The night was dark and warm. They did not want to go home. "What I feel so certain of is," said Henry, "that we ought to be living there, now. We oughtn't to wait for things. What's age? You're as old as you'll ever be and so am I. You know," he said, "I have a feeling often and often that it's dangerous to wait for things—that if you wait for things they only go further and further away."

"But, Henry,—money! You see we haven't any money."

"Oh, well,—perhaps if I disguised myself as an old man we could get a job as caretakers in some large house—that would be rather fun. I'd make up a terrific history of the house if anyone came to look over it and you could dress up and be the ghost moaning and wringing your hands in the deserted picture gallery, to frighten them off. Don't you ever feel that money is more or less accidental—that if one really wants things it's either there or it doesn't matter?"

She did not answer that—she looked up at the sky and said, "Oh dear, I don't want to go home."

"Exactly—that's the whole trouble—and we oughtn't to go home. We ought to be going back to the house and find an odd saucer to give the cat the dregs of the milk-jug in. I'm not really laughing—I'm not even happy. I'm lonely for you, Edna—I would give anything to lie down and cry" and he added limply, "with my head in your lap and your darling cheek in my hair."

"But, Henry," she said, coming closer, "you have faith, haven't you? I mean you are absolutely certain that we shall have a house like that and everything we want—aren't you?"

"Not enough—that's not enough. I want to be sitting on those very stairs and taking off these very boots this very minute. Don't you? Is faith enough for you?"

"If only we weren't so young" she said miserably. "And yet," she sighed, "I'm sure I don't feel very young—I feel twenty at least."

Henry lay on his back in the little wood. When he moved the dead leaves rustled beneath him, and above his head the new leaves quivered like fountains of green water steeped in sunlight. Somewhere out of sight Edna was gathering primroses. He had been so full of dreams that morning that he could not keep pace with her delight in the flowers. "Yes, love, you go and come back for me. I'm too lazy." She had thrown off her hat and knelt down beside him, and by and by her voice and her footsteps had grown fainter.

Now the wood was silent except for the leaves, but he knew that she was not far away and he moved so that the tips of his fingers touched her pink jacket. Ever since waking he had felt so strangely that he was not really awake at all, but just dreaming. The time before, Edna was a dream and now he and she were dreaming together and somewhere in some dark place another dream waited for him. "No, that can't be true because I can't ever imagine the world without us. I feel that we two together mean something that's got to be there just as naturally as trees or birds or clouds." He tried to remember what it had felt like without Edna, but he could not get back to those days. They were hidden by her; Edna, with the marigold hair and strange, dreamy smile filled him up to the brim. He breathed her; he ate and drank her. He walked about with a shining ring of Edna keeping the world away or touching whatever it lighted on with its own beauty. "Long after you have stopped laughing," he told her, "I can hear your laugh running up and down my veins—and yet—are we a dream?" And suddenly he saw himself and Edna as two very small children walking through the streets, looking through windows, buying things and playing with them, talking to each other, smiling—he saw even their gestures and the way they stood, so often, quite still, face to face—and then he rolled over and pressed his face in the leaves—faint with longing. He wanted to kiss Edna, and to put his arms round her and press her to him and feel her cheek hot against his kiss and kiss her until he'd no breath left and so stifle the dream.

"No, I can't go on being hungry like this," said Henry, and jumped up and began to run in the direction she had gone. She had wandered a long way. Down in a green hollow he saw her kneeling, and when she saw him she waved and said—"Oh, Henry—such beauties! I've never seen such beauties. Come and look." By the time he had reached her he would have cut off his hand rather than spoil her happiness. How strange Edna was that day! All the time she talked to Henry her eyes laughed; they were sweet and mocking. Two little spots of colour like strawberries glowed on her cheeks and "I wish I could feel tired," she kept saying. "I want to walk over the whole world until I die. Henry—come along. Walk faster—Henry! If I start flying suddenly, you'll promise to catch hold of my feet, won't you? Otherwise I'll never come down." And "Oh," she cried, "I am so happy. I'm so frightfully happy!" They came to a weird place, covered with heather. It was early afternoon and the sun streamed down upon the purple.

"Let's rest here a little," said Edna, and she waded into the heather and lay down.

"Oh, Henry, it's so lovely. I can't see anything except the little bells and the sky."

Henry knelt down by her and took some primroses out of her basket and made a long chain to go round her throat. "I could almost fall asleep," said Edna. She crept over to his knees and lay hidden in her hair just beside him.

"It's like being under the sea, isn't it, dearest, so sweet and so still?"

"Yes," said Henry, in a strange husky voice.

"Now I'll make you one of violets." But Edna sat up. "Let's go in," she said.

They came back to the road and walked a long way. Edna said, "No, I couldn't walk over the world—I'm tired now." She trailed on the grass edge of the road. "You and I are tired, Henry! How much further is it?"

"I don't know—not very far," said Henry, peering into the distance. Then they walked in silence.

"Oh," she said at last, "it really is too far, Henry, I'm tired and I'm hungry. Carry my silly basket of primroses." He took them without looking at her.

At last they came to a village and a cottage with a notice "Teas Provided."

"This is the place," said Henry. "I've often been here. You sit on the little bench and I'll go and order the tea." She sat down on the bench, in the pretty garden all white and yellow with spring flowers. A woman came to the door and leaned against it watching them eat. Henry was very nice to her, but Edna did not say a word. "You haven't been here for a long spell," said the woman.

"No—the garden's looking wonderful."

"Fair," said she. "Is the young lady your sister?" Henry nodded Yes, and took some jam.

"There's a likeness," said the woman. She came down into the garden and picked a head of white jonquils and handed it to Edna. "I suppose you don't happen to know anyone who wants a cottage," said she. "My sister's taken ill and she left me hers. I want to let it."

"For a long time?" asked Henry, politely.

"Oh," said the woman vaguely, "that depends."

Said Henry, "Well—I might know of somebody—could we go and look at it?"

"Yes, it's just a step down the road, the little one with the apple trees in front—I'll fetch you the key."

While she was away Henry turned to Edna and said, "Will you come?" She nodded.

They walked down the road and in through the gate and up the grassy path between the pink and white trees. It was a tiny place—two rooms downstairs and two rooms upstairs. Edna leaned out of the top window, and Henry stood at the doorway. "Do you like it?" he asked.

"Yes," she called, and then made a place for him at the window. "Come and look. It's so sweet."

He came and leant out of the window. Below them were the apple trees tossing in a faint wind that blew a long piece of Edna's hair across his eyes. They did not move. It was evening—the pale green sky was sprinkled with stars. "Look!" she said—"stars, Henry."

"There will be a moon in two T's," said Henry.

She did not seem to move and yet she was leaning against Henry's shoulder; he put his arm round her—"Are all those trees down there—apple?" she asked in a shaky voice.

"No, darling," said Henry. "Some of them are full of angels and some of them are full of sugar almonds—but evening light is awfully deceptive." She sighed. "Henry—we mustn't stay here any longer."

He let her go and she stood up in the dusky room and touched her hair. "What has been the matter with you all day?" she said—and then did not wait for an answer but ran to him and put her arms round his neck, and pressed his head into the hollow of her shoulder. "Oh," she breathed, "I do love you. Hold me, Henry." He put his arms round her, and she leaned against him and looked into his eyes.

"Hasn't it been terrible, all today?" said Edna. "I knew what was the matter and I've tried every way I could to tell you that I wanted you to kiss me—that I'd quite got over the feeling."

"You're perfect, perfect, perfect," said Henry.

"The thing is," said Henry, "how am I going to wait until evening?" He took his watch out of his pocket, went into the cottage and popped it into a china jar on the mantelpiece. He'd looked at it seven times in one hour, and now he couldn't remember what time it was. Well, he'd look once again. Half-past four. Her train arrived at seven. He'd have to start for the station at half-past six. Two hours more to wait. He went through the cottage again—downstairs and upstairs. "It looks lovely," he said. He went into the garden and picked a round bunch of white pinks and put them in a vase on the little table by Edna's bed. "I don't believe this," thought Henry. "I don't believe this for a minute. It's too much. She'll be here in two hours and we'll walk home, and then I'll take that white jug off the kitchen table and go across to Mrs. Biddie's and get the milk, and then come back, and when I come back she'll have lighted the lamp in the kitchen and I'll look through the window and see her moving about in the pool of lamplight. And then we shall have supper, and after supper (Bags I washing up!) I shall put some wood on the fire and we'll sit on the hearth-rug and watch it burning. There won't be a sound except the wood and perhaps the wind will creep round the house once And then we shall change our candles and she will go up first with her shadow on the wall beside her, and she will call out, Good-night, Henry—and I shall answer—Good-night, Edna. And then I shall dash upstairs and jump into bed and watch the tiny bar of light from her room brush my door, and the moment it disappears will shut my eyes and sleep until morning. Then we'll have all tomorrow and tomorrow and tomorrow night. Is she thinking all this, too? Edna, come quickly!"

Had I two little wings,
And were a little feathery bird,
To you I'd fly, my dear—

"No, no, dearest Because the waiting is a sort of Heaven, too, darling. If you can understand that. Did you ever know a cottage could stand on tip-toe. This one is doing it now."

He was downstairs and sat on the doorstep with his hands clasped round his knees. That night when they found the village—and Edna said, "Haven't you faith, Henry?" "I hadn't then. Now I have," he said, "I feel just like God."

He leaned his head against the lintel. He could hardly keep his eyes open, not that he was sleepy, but for some reason and a long time passed.

Henry thought he saw a big white moth flying down the road. It perched on the gate. No, it wasn't a moth. It was a little girl in a pinafore. What a nice little girl, and he smiled in his sleep, and she smiled, too, and turned in her toes as she walked. "But she can't be living here," thought Henry. "Because this is ours. Here she comes."

When she was quite close to him she took her hand from under her pinafore and gave him a telegram and smiled and went away. There's a funny present! thought Henry, staring at it. "Perhaps it's only a make-believe one, and it's got one of those snakes inside it that fly up at you." He laughed gently in the dream and opened it very carefully. "It's just a folded paper." He took it out and spread it open.

The garden became full of shadows—they span a web of darkness over the cottage and the trees and Henry and the telegram. But Henry did not move.

AN INDISCREET JOURNEY

She is like St. Anne. Yes, the concierge is the image of St. Anne, with that black cloth over her head, the wisps of grey hair hanging, and the tiny smoking lamp in her hand. Really very beautiful, I thought, smiling at St. Anne, who said severely: "Six o'clock. You have only just got time. There is a bowl of milk on the writing table." I jumped out of my pyjamas and into a basin of cold water like any English lady in any French novel. The concierge, persuaded that I was on my way to prison cells and death by bayonets, opened the shutters and the cold clear light came through. A little steamer hooted on the river; a cart with two horses at a gallop flung past. The rapid swirling water; the tall black trees on the far side, grouped together like negroes conversing. Sinister, very, I thought, as I buttoned on my age-old Burberry. (That Burberry was very significant. It did not belong to me. I had borrowed it from a friend. My eye lighted upon it hanging in her little dark hall. The very thing! The perfect and adequate disguise—an old Burberry. Lions have been faced in a Burberry. Ladies have been rescued from open boats in mountainous seas wrapped in nothing else. An old Burberry seems to me the sign and the token of the undisputed venerable traveller, I decided, leaving my purple peg-top with the real seal collar and cuffs in exchange.)

"You will never get there," said the concierge, watching me turn up the collar. "Never! Never!" I ran down the echoing stairs—strange they sounded, like a piano flicked by a sleepy housemaid—and on to the Quai. "Why so fast, *ma mignonne?*" said a lovely little boy in coloured socks, dancing in front of the electric lotus buds that curve over the entrance to the Métro. Alas! there was not even time to blow him a kiss. When I arrived at the big station I had only four minutes to spare, and the platform entrance was crowded and packed with soldiers, their yellow papers in one hand and big untidy bundles. The Commissaire of Police stood on one side, a Nameless Official on the other. Will he let me pass? Will he? He was an old man with a fat swollen face covered with big warts. Horn-rimmed spectacles squatted on his nose. Trembling, I made an effort. I conjured up my sweetest early-morning smile and handed it with the papers. But the delicate thing fluttered against the horn spectacles and fell. Nevertheless, he let me pass, and I ran, ran in and out among the soldiers and up the high steps into the yellow-painted carriage.

"Does one go direct to X?" I asked the collector who dug at my ticket with a pair of forceps and handed it back again. "No, Mademoiselle, you must change at X.Y.Z."

"At—?"

"X.Y.Z."

Again I had not heard. "At what time do we arrive there if you please?"

"One o'clock." But that was no good to me. I hadn't a watch. Oh, well—later.

Ah! the train had begun to move. The train was on my side. It swung out of the station, and soon we were passing the vegetable gardens, passing the tall blind houses to let, passing the servants beating carpets. Up already and walking in the fields, rosy from the rivers and the red-fringed pools, the sun lighted upon the swinging train and stroked my muff and told me to take off that Burberry. I was not alone in the carriage. An old woman sat opposite, her skirt turned back over her knees, a bonnet of black lace on her head. In her fat hands, adorned with a wedding and two mourning rings, she held a letter. Slowly, slowly she sipped a sentence, and then looked up and out of the window, her lips trembling a little, and then another sentence, and again the old face turned to the light, tasting it... Two soldiers leaned out of the window, their heads nearly touching—one of them was whistling, the other had his coat fastened with some rusty safety-pins. And now there were soldiers everywhere working on the railway line, leaning against trucks or standing hands on hips, eyes fixed on the train as though they expected at least one camera at every window. And now we were passing big wooden sheds like rigged-up dancing halls or seaside pavilions, each flying a flag. In and out of them walked the Red Cross men; the wounded sat against the walls sunning themselves. At all the bridges, the crossings, the stations, a petit soldat, all boots and bayonet. Forlorn and desolate he looked,— like a little comic picture waiting for the joke to be written underneath. Is there really such a thing as war? Are all these laughing voices really going to the war? These dark woods lighted so mysteriously by the white stems of the birch and the ash—these watery fields with the big birds flying over—these rivers green and blue in the light—have battles been fought in places like these?

What beautiful cemeteries we are passing! They flash gay in the sun. They seem to be full of cornflowers and poppies and daisies. How can there be so many flowers at this time of the year? But they are not flowers at all. They are bunches of ribbons tied on to the soldiers' graves I glanced up and caught the old woman's eye. She smiled and folded the letter. "It is from my son—the first we have had since October. I am taking it to my daughter-in-law."

"...?"

"Yes, very good," said the old woman, shaking down her skirt and putting her arm through the handle of her basket. "He wants me to send him some handkerchieves and a piece of stout string."

What is the name of the station where I have to change? Perhaps I shall never know. I got up and leaned my arms across the window rail, my feet crossed. One cheek burned as in infancy on the way to the sea-side. When the war is over I shall have a barge and drift along these rivers with a white cat and a pot of mignonette to bear me company.

Down the side of the hill filed the troops, winking red and blue in the light. Far away, but plainly to be seen, some more flew by on bicycles. But really, ma France adorée, this uniform is ridiculous. Your soldiers are stamped upon your bosom like bright irreverent transfers.

The train slowed down, stopped... Everybody was getting out except me. A big boy, his sabots tied to his back with a piece of string, the inside of his tin wine cup stained a lovely impossible pink, looked very friendly. Does one change here perhaps for X? Another whose képi had come out of a wet paper cracker swung my suit-case to earth. What darlings soldiers are! "*Merci bien, Monsieur, vous êtes tout à fait aimable*..." "Not this way," said a bayonet. "Nor this," said another. So I followed the crowd. "Your passport, Mademoiselle..." "We, Sir Edward Grey..." I ran through the muddy square and into the buffet.

A green room with a stove jutting out and tables on each side. On the counter, beautiful with coloured bottles, a woman leans, her breasts in her folded arms. Through an open door I can see a kitchen, and the cook in a white coat breaking eggs into a bowl and tossing the shells into a corner. The blue and red coats of the men who are eating hang upon the walls. Their short swords and belts are piled upon chairs. Heavens! what a noise. The sunny air seemed all broken up and trembling with it. A little boy, very pale, swung from table to table, taking the orders, and poured me out a glass of purple coffee. Ssssb, came from the eggs. They were in a pan. The woman rushed from behind the counter and began to help the boy. Toute de suite, tout' suite! she chirruped to the loud impatient voices. There came a clatter of plates and the poppop of corks being drawn.

Suddenly in the doorway I saw someone with a pail of fish—brown speckled fish, like the fish one sees in a glass case, swimming through forests of beautiful pressed sea-weed. He was an old man in a tattered jacket, standing humbly, waiting for someone to attend to him. A thin beard fell over his chest, his eyes under the tufted eyebrows were bent on the pail he carried. He looked as though he had escaped from some holy picture, and was entreating the soldiers' pardon for being there at all...

But what could I have done? I could not arrive at X with two fishes hanging on a straw; and I am sure it is a penal offence in France to throw fish out of railway-carriage windows, I thought, miserably climbing into a smaller, shabbier train. Perhaps I might have taken them to—ah, mon Dieu—I had forgotten the name of my uncle and aunt again! Buffard, Buffon—what was it? Again I read the unfamiliar letter in the familiar handwriting.

"My dear niece

"Now that the weather is more settled, your uncle and I would be charmed if you would pay us a little visit. Telegraph me when you are coming. I shall meet you outside the station if I am free. Otherwise our good friend, Madame Grinçon, who lives in the little toll-house by the bridge, juste en face de la gare, will conduct you to our home. Je vous embrasse bien tendrement, Julie Boiffard."

A visiting card was enclosed: M. Paul Boiffard.

Boiffard—of course that was the name. Ma tante Julie et mon oncle Paul—suddenly they were there with me, more real, more solid than any relations I had ever known. I saw tante Julie bridling, with the soup-tureen in her hands, and oncle Paul sitting at the table, with a red and white napkin tied round his neck. Boiffard—Boiffard—I must remember the name. Supposing the Commissaire Militaire should ask me who the relations were I was going to and I muddled the name—Oh, how fatal! Buffard—no, Boiffard. And then for the first time, folding Aunt Julie's letter, I saw scrawled in a corner of the empty back page: Venez vite, vite. Strange impulsive woman! My heart began to beat...

"Ah, we are not far off now," said the lady opposite. "You are going to X, Mademoiselle?"

"*Oui*, Madame."

"I also... You have been there before?"

"No, Madame. This is the first time."

"Really, it is a strange time for a visit."

I smiled faintly, and tried to keep my eyes off her hat. She was quite an ordinary little woman, but she wore a black velvet toque, with an incredibly surprised looking sea-gull camped on the very top of it. Its round eyes, fixed on me so inquiringly, were almost too much to bear. I had a dreadful impulse to shoo it away, or to lean forward and inform her of its presence...

"*Excusez-moi*, madame, but perhaps you have not remarked there is an *espèce de sea-gull couché sur votre chapeau*."

Could the bird be there on purpose? I must not laugh... I must not laugh. Had she ever looked at herself in a glass with that bird on her head?

"It is very difficult to get into X at present, to pass the station," she said, and she shook her head with the sea-gull at me. "Ah, such an affair. One must sign one's name and state one's business."

"Really, is it as bad as all that?"

"But naturally. You see the whole place is in the hands of the military, and"—she shrugged—"they have to be strict. Many people do not get beyond the station at all. They arrive. They are put in the waitingroom, and there they remain."

Did I or did I not detect in her voice a strange, insulting relish?

"I suppose such strictness is absolutely necessary," I said coldly, stroking my muff.

"Necessary," she cried. "I should think so. Why, mademoiselle, you cannot imagine what it would be like otherwise! You know what women are like about soldiers"—she raised a final hand—"mad, completely mad. But—" and she gave a little laugh of triumph—"they could not get into X. *Mon Dieu*, no! There is no question about that."

"I don't suppose they even try," said I.

"Don't you?" said the sea-gull.

Madame said nothing for a moment. "Of course the authorities are very hard on the men. It means instant imprisonment, and then—off to the firing-line without a word."

"What are you going to X for?" said the sea-gull. "What on earth are you doing here?"

"Are you making a long stay in X, mademoiselle?"

She had won, she had won. I was terrified. A lamp-post swam past the train with the fatal name upon it. I could hardly breathe—the train had stopped. I smiled gaily at Madame and danced down the steps to the platform...

It was a hot little room completely furnished with two colonels seated at two tables. They were large grey-whiskered men with a touch of burnt red on their cheeks. Sumptuous and omnipotent they looked. One smoked what ladies love to call a heavy Egyptian cigarette, with a long creamy ash, the other toyed with a gilded pen. Their heads rolled on their tight collars, like big over-ripe fruits. I had a terrible feeling, as I handed my passport and ticket, that a soldier would step forward and tell me to kneel. I would have knelt without question.

"What's this?" said God I., querulously. He did not like my passport at all. The very sight of it seemed to annoy him. He waved a dissenting hand at it, with a "*Non, je ne peux pas manger ça*" air.

"But it won't do. It won't do at all, you know. Look,—read for yourself," and he glanced with extreme distaste at my photograph, and then with even greater distaste his pebble eyes looked at me.

"Of course the photograph is deplorable," I said, scarcely breathing with terror, "but it has been viséd and viséd."

He raised his big bulk and went over to God II.

"Courage!" I said to my muff and held it firmly, "Courage!"

God II. held up a finger to me, and I produced Aunt Julie's letter and her card. But he did not seem to feel the slightest interest in her. He stamped my passport idly, scribbled a word on my ticket, and I was on the platform again.

"That way—you pass out that way."

Terribly pale, with a faint smile on his lips, his hand at salute, stood the little corporal. I gave no sign, I am sure I gave no sign. He stepped behind me.

"And then follow me as though you do not see me," I heard him half whisper, half sing.

How fast he went, through the slippery mud towards a bridge. He had a postman's bag on his back, a paper parcel and the Matin in his hand. We seemed to dodge through a maze of policemen, and I could not keep up at all with the little corporal who began to whistle. From the toll-house "our good friend, Madame Grinçon," her hands wrapped in a shawl, watched our coming, and against the toll-house there leaned a tiny faded cab. *Montez vite, vite!* said the little corporal, hurling my suit-case, the postman's bag, the paper parcel and the *Matin* on to the floor.

"A-ie! A-ie! Do not be so mad. Do not ride yourself. You will be seen," wailed "our good friend, Madame Grinçon."

"Ah, *je m'en f...*" said the little corporal.

The driver jerked into activity. He lashed the bony horse and away we flew, both doors, which were the complete sides of the cab, flapping and banging

"Bon jour, mon amie."

"Bon jour, mon ami."

And then we swooped down and clutched at the banging doors. They would not keep shut. They were fools of doors.

"Lean back, let me do it!" I cried.

"Policemen are as thick as violets everywhere."

At the barracks the horse reared up and stopped. A crowd of laughing faces blotted the window.

"*Prends ça, mon vieux,*" said the little corporal, handing the paper parcel.

"It's all right," called someone.

We waved, we were off again. By a river, down a strange white street, with little houses on either side, gay in the late sunlight.

"Jump out as soon as he stops again. The door will be open. Run straight inside. I will follow. The man is already paid. I know you will like the house. It is quite white. And the room is white, too, and the people are—"

"White as snow."

We looked at each other. We began to laugh. "Now," said the little corporal.

Out I flew and in at the door. There stood, presumably, my aunt Julie. There in the background hovered, I supposed, my uncle Paul.

"Bon jour, madame!"

"Bon jour, monsieur!"

"It is all right, you are safe," said my aunt Julie. Heavens, how I loved her! And she opened the door of the white room and shut it upon us. Down went the suit-case, the postman's bag, the Matin. I threw my passport up into the air, and the little corporal caught it.

What an extraordinary thing. We had been there to lunch and to dinner each day; but now in the dusk and alone I could not find it. I clop-clopped in my borrowed sabots through the greasy mud, right to the end of the village, and there was not a sign of it. I could not even remember what it looked like, or if there was a name painted on the outside, or any bottles or tables showing at the window. Already the village houses were sealed for the night behind big wooden shutters. Strange and mysterious they looked in the ragged drifting light and thin rain, like a company of beggars perched on the hill-side, their bosoms full of rich unlawful gold. There was nobody about but the soldiers. A group of wounded stood under a lamp-post, petting a mangy, shivering dog. Up the street came four big boys singing:

Dodo, mon homme, fais vit' dodo...

and swung off down the hill to their sheds behind the railway station. They seemed to take the last breath of the day with them. I began to walk slowly back.

"It must have been one of these houses. I remember it stood far back from the road—and there were no steps, not even a porch—one seemed to walk right through the window."

And then quite suddenly the waiting-boy came out of just such a place. He saw me and grinned cheerfully, and began to whistle through his teeth.

"Bon soir, mon petit."

"Bon soir, madame." And he followed me up the café to our special table, right at the far end by the window, and marked by a bunch of violets that I had left in a glass there yesterday.

"You are two?" asked the waiting-boy, flicking the table with a red and white cloth. His long swinging steps echoed over the bare floor. He disappeared into the kitchen and came back to light the lamp that hung from the ceiling under a spreading shade, like a haymaker's hat. Warm light shone on the empty place that was really a barn, set out with dilapidated tables and chairs. Into the middle of the room a black stove jutted. At one side of it there was a table with a row of bottles on it, behind which Madame sat and took the money and made entries in a red book. Opposite her desk a door led into the kitchen. The walls were covered with a creamy paper patterned all over with green and swollen trees—hundreds and hundreds of trees reared their mushroom heads to the ceiling. I began to wonder who had chosen the paper and why. Did Madame think it was beautiful, or that it was a gay and lovely thing to eat one's dinner at all seasons in the middle of a forest... On either side of the clock there hung a picture: one, a young gentleman in black tights wooing a pear-shaped lady in yellow over the back of a garden seat, Premier Rencontre; two, the black and yellow in amorous confusion, Triomphe d'Amour.

The clock ticked to a soothing lilt, *C'est ça, c'est ça*. In the kitchen the waiting-boy was washing up. I heard the ghostly chatter of the dishes.

And years passed. Perhaps the war is long since over—there is no village outside at all—the streets are quiet under the grass. I have an idea this is the sort of thing one will do on the very last day of all—sit in an empty café and listen to a clock ticking until—.

Madame came through the kitchen door, nodded to me and took her seat behind the table, her plump hands folded on the red book. Ping went the door. A handful of soldiers came in, took off their coats and began to play cards, chaffing and poking fun at the pretty waiting-boy, who threw up his little round head, rubbed his thick fringe out of his eyes and cheeked them back in his broken voice. Sometimes his voice boomed up from his throat, deep and harsh, and then in the middle of a sentence it broke and scattered in a funny squeaking. He seemed to enjoy it himself. You would not have been surprised if he had walked into the kitchen on his hands and brought back your dinner turning a catherine-wheel.

Ping went the door again. Two more men came in. They sat at the table nearest Madame, and she leaned to them with a birdlike movement, her head on one side. Oh, they had a grievance! The Lieutenant was a fool—nosing about—springing out at them—and they'd only been sewing on buttons. Yes, that was all—sewing on buttons, and up comes this young spark. "Now then, what are you up to?" They mimicked the idiotic voice. Madame drew down her mouth, nodding sympathy. The waiting-boy served them with glasses. He took a bottle of some orangecoloured stuff and put it on the table-edge. A shout from the card-players made him turn sharply, and crash! over went the bottle, spilling on the table, the floor—smash! to tinkling atoms. An amazed silence. Through it the drip-drip of the wine from the table on to the floor. It looked very strange dropping so slowly, as though the table were crying. Then there came a roar from the card-players. "You'll catch it, my lad! That's the style! Now you've done it!... Sept, huit, neuf." They started playing again. The waiting-boy never said a word. He stood, his head bent, his hands spread out, and then he knelt and gathered up the glass, piece by piece, and soaked the wine up with a cloth. Only when Madame cried cheerfully, "You wait until be finds out," did he raise his head.

"He can't say anything, if I pay for it," he muttered, his face jerking, and he marched off into the kitchen with the soaking cloth.

"*Il pleure de colére*," said Madame delightedly, patting her hair with her plump hands.

The café slowly filled. It grew very warm. Blue smoke mounted from the tables and hung about the haymaker's hat in misty wreaths. There was a suffocating smell of onion soup and boots and damp cloth. In the din the door sounded again. It opened to let in a weed of a fellow, who stood with his back against it, one hand shading his eyes.

"Hullo! you've got the bandage off?"

"How does it feel, *mon vieux*?"

"Let's have a look at them."

But he made no reply. He shrugged and walked unsteadily to a table, sat down and leant against the wall. Slowly his hand fell. In his white face his eyes showed, pink as a rabbit's. They brimmed and spilled, brimmed and spilled. He dragged a white cloth out of his pocket and wiped them.

"It's the smoke," said someone. "It's the smoke tickles them up for you."

His comrades watched him a bit, watched his eyes fill again, again brim over. The water ran down his face, off his chin on to the table. He rubbed the place with his coat-sleeve, and then, as though forgetful, went on rubbing, rubbing with his hand across the table, staring in front of him. And then he started shaking his head to the movement of his hand. He gave a loud strange groan and dragged out the cloth again.

"*Huit, neuf, dix*," said the card-players.

"*P'tit*, some more bread."

"Two coffees."

"*Un Picon!*"

The waiting-boy, quite recovered, but with scarlet cheeks, ran to and fro. A tremendous quarrel flared up among the card-players, raged for two minutes, and died in flickering laughter. "Ooof!" groaned the man with the eyes, rocking and mopping. But nobody paid any attention to him except Madame. She made a little grimace at her two soldiers.

"*Mais vous savez, c'est un peu dégoûtant, ça,*" she said severely.

"Ah, *oui*, Madame," answered the soldiers, watching her bent head and pretty hands, as she arranged for the hundredth time a frill of lace on her lifted bosom.

"*V'là monsieur!*" cawed the waiting-boy over his shoulder to me. For some silly reason I pretended not to hear, and I leaned over the table smelling the violets, until the little corporal's hand closed over mine.

"Shall we have *un peu de charcuterie* to begin with?" he asked tenderly.

"In England," said the blue-eyed soldier, "you drink whiskey with your meals. *N'est-ce pas*, mademoiselle? A little glass of whiskey neat before eating. Whiskey and soda with your bifteks, and after, more whiskey with hot water and lemon."

"Is it true, that?" asked his great friend who sat opposite, a big red-faced chap with a black beard and large moist eyes and hair that looked as though it had been cut with a sewingmachine.

"Well, not quite true," said I.

"*Si, si,*" cried the blue-eyed soldier. "I ought to know. I'm in business. English travellers come to my place, and it's always the same thing."

"Bah, I can't stand whiskey," said the little corporal. "It's too disgusting the morning after. Do you remember, ma fille, the whiskey in that little bar at Montmartre?"

"*Souvenir tendre,*" sighed Blackbeard, putting two fingers in the breast of his coat and letting his head fall. He was very drunk.

"But I know something that you've never tasted," said the blue-eyed soldier pointing a finger at me; "something really good."

Cluck he went with his tongue. "*É-patant*! And the curious thing is that you'd hardly know it from whiskey except that it's"—he felt with his hand for the word—"finer, sweeter perhaps, not so sharp, and it leaves you feeling gay as a rabbit next morning."

"What is it called?"

"Mirabelle!" He rolled the word round his mouth, under his tongue. "Ah-ha, that's the stuff."

"I could eat another mushroom," said Blackbeard. "I would like another mushroom very much. I am sure I could eat another mushroom if Mademoiselle gave it to me out of her hand."

"You ought to try it," said the blue-eyed soldier, leaning both hands on the table and speaking so seriously that I began to wonder how much more sober he was than Blackbeard. "You ought to try it, and tonight. I would like you to tell me if you don't think it's like whiskey."

"Perhaps they've got it here," said the little corporal, and he called the waiting-boy. "P'tit!"

"*Non*, monsieur," said the boy, who never stopped smiling. He served us with dessert plates painted with blue parrots and horned beetles.

"What is the name for this in English?" said Blackbeard, pointing. I told him "Parrot."

"Ah, *mon Dieu!*... Pair-rot..." He put his arms round his plate. "I love you, *ma petite* pair-rot. You are sweet, you are blonde, you are English. You do not know the difference between whiskey and mirabelle."

The little corporal and I looked at each other, laughing. He squeezed up his eyes when he laughed, so that you saw nothing but the long curly lashes.

"Well, I know a place where they do keep it," said the blue-eyed soldier. "Café des Amis. We'll go there—I'll pay—I'll pay for the whole lot of us." His gesture embraced thousands of pounds.

But with a loud whirring noise the clock on the wall struck half-past eight; and no soldier is allowed in a café after eight o'clock at night.

"It is fast," said the blue-eyed soldier. The little corporal's watch said the same. So did the immense turnip that Blackbeard produced, and carefully deposited on the head of one of the horned beetles.

"Ah, well, we'll take the risk," said the blue-eyed soldier, and he thrust his arms into his immense cardboard coat. "It's worth it," he said. "It's worth it. You just wait."

Outside, stars shone between wispy clouds, and the moon fluttered like a candle flame over a pointed spire. The shadows of the dark plume-like trees waved on the white houses. Not a soul to be seen. No sound to be heard but the Hsh! Hsh! of a far-away train, like a big beast shuffling in its sleep.

"You are cold," whispered the little corporal. "You are cold, ma fille."

"No, really not."

"But you are trembling."

"Yes, but I'm not cold."

"What are the women like in England?" asked Blackbeard. "After the war is over I shall go to England. I shall find a little English woman and marry her—and her pair-rot." He gave a loud choking laugh.

"Fool!" said the blue-eyed soldier, shaking him; and he leant over to me. "It is only after the second glass that you really taste it," he whispered. "The second little glass and then—ah!—then you know."

Café des Amis gleamed in the moonlight. We glanced quickly up and down the road. We ran up the four wooden steps, and opened the ringing glass door into a low room lighted with a hanging lamp, where about ten people were dining. They were seated on two benches at a narrow table.

"Soldiers!" screamed a woman, leaping up from behind a white soup-tureen—a scrag of a woman in a black shawl. "Soldiers! At this hour! Look at that clock, look at it." And she pointed to the clock with the dripping ladle.

"It's fast," said the blue-eyed soldier. It's fast, madame. And don't make so much noise, I beg of you. We will drink and we will go."

"Will you?" she cried, running round the table and planting herself in front of us. "That's just what you won't do. Coming into an honest woman's house this hour of the night—making a scene—getting the police after you. Ah, no! Ah, no! It's a disgrace, that's what it is."

"Sh!" said the little corporal, holding up his hand. Dead silence. In the silence we heard steps passing.

"The police," whispered Blackbeard, winking at a pretty girl with rings in her ears, who smiled back at him, saucy. "Sh!"

The faces lifted, listening. "How beautiful they are!" I thought. "They are like a family party having supper in the New Testament…" The steps died away.

"Serve you very well right if you had been caught," scolded the angry woman. "I'm sorry on your account that the police didn't come. You deserve it—you deserve it."

"A little glass of mirabelle and we will go," persisted the blue-eyed soldier.

Still scolding and muttering she took four glasses from the cupboard and a big bottle.

"But you're not going to drink in here. Don't you believe it." The little corporal ran into the kitchen. "Not there! Not there!"

Idiot!" she cried. "Can't you see there's a window there, and a wall opposite where the police come every evening to…"

"Sh!" Another scare.

"You are mad and you will end in prison,—all four of you," said the woman. She flounced out of the room. We tiptoed after her into a dark smelling scullery, full of pans of greasy water, of salad leaves and meat-bones.

"There now," she said, putting down the glasses. "Drink and go!"

"Ah, at last!" The blue-eyed soldier's happy voice trickled through the dark. "What do you think? Isn't it just as I said? Hasn't it got a taste of excellent, *excellent* whiskey?"

SPRING PICTURES

I

It is raining. Big soft drops splash on the people's hands and cheeks; immense warm drops like melted stars. "Here are roses! Here are lilies! Here are violets!" caws the old hag in the gutter. But the lilies, bunched together in a frill of green, look more like faded cauliflowers. Up and down she drags the creaking barrow. A bad, sickly smell comes from it. Nobody wants to buy. You must walk in the middle of the road, for there is no room on the pavement. Every single shop brims over; every shop shows a tattered frill of soiled lace and dirty ribbon to charm and entice you. There are tables set out with toy cannons and soldiers and Zeppelins and photograph frames complete with ogling beauties. There are immense baskets of yellow straw hats piled up like pyramids of pastry, and strings of coloured boots and shoes so small that nobody could wear them. One shop is full of little squares of mackintosh, blue ones for girls and pink ones for boys with Bébé printed in the middle of each...

"Here are lilies! Here are roses! Here are pretty violets!" warbles the old hag, bumping into another barrow. But this barrow is still. It is heaped with lettuces. Its owner, a fat old woman, sprawls across, fast asleep, her nose in the lettuce roots... Who is ever going to buy anything here...? The sellers are women. They sit on little canvas stools, dreamy and vacant looking. Now and again one of them gets up and takes a feather duster, like a smoky torch, and flicks it over a thing or two and then sits down again. Even the old man in tangerine spectacles with a balloon of a belly, who turns the revolving stand of 'comic' postcards round and round cannot decide...

Suddenly, from the empty shop at the corner a piano strikes up, and a violin and flute join in. The windows of the shop are scrawled over—New Songs. First Floor. Entrance Free. But the windows of the first floor being open, nobody bothers to go up. They hang about grinning as the harsh voices float out into the warm rainy air. At the doorway there stands a lean man in a pair of burst carpet slippers. He has stuck a feather through the broken rim of his hat; with what an air he wears it! The feather is magnificent. It is gold epaulettes, frogged coat, white kid gloves, gilded cane. He swaggers under it and the voice rolls off his chest, rich and ample.

"Come up! Come up! Here are the new songs! Each singer is an artiste of European reputation. The orchestra is famous and second to none. You can stay as long as you like. It is the chance of a lifetime, and once missed never to return!" But nobody moves. Why should they? They know all about those girls—those famous artistes. One is dressed in cream cashmere and one in blue. Both have dark crimped hair and a pink rose pinned over the ear... They know all about the pianist's button boots—the left foot—the pedal foot—burst over the bunion on his big toe. The violinist's bitten nails, the long, far too long cuffs of the flute player—all these things are as old as the new songs.

For a long time the music goes on and the proud voice thunders. Then somebody calls down the stairs and the showman, still with his grand air, disappears. The voices cease. The piano, the violin and the flute dribble into quiet. Only the lace curtain gives a wavy sign of life from the first floor.

It is raining still; it is getting dusky... Here are roses! Here are lilies! Who will buy my violets?...

II

Hope! You misery—you sentimental, faded female! Break your last string and have done with it. I shall go mad with your endless thrumming; my heart throbs to it and every little pulse beats in time. It is morning. I lie in the empty bed—the huge bed big as a field and as cold and unsheltered. Through the shutters the sunlight comes up from the river and flows over the ceiling in trembling waves. I hear from outside a hammer tapping, and far below in the house a door swings open and shuts. Is this my room? Are those my clothes folded over an armchair? Under the pillow, sign and symbol of a lonely woman, ticks my watch. The bell jangles. Ah! At last! I leap out of bed and run to the door. Play faster—faster—Hope!

"Your milk, Mademoiselle," says the concierge, gazing at me severely.

"Ah, thank you," I cry, gaily swinging the milk bottle. "No letters for me?"

"Nothing, mademoiselle."

"But the postman—he has called already?"

"A long half-hour ago, mademoiselle."

Shut the door. Stand in the little passage a moment. Listen—listen for her hated twanging. Coax her—court her—implore her to play just once that charming little thing for one string only. In vain.

III

Across the river, on the narrow stone path that fringes the bank, a woman is walking. She came down the steps from the Quay, walking slowly, one hand on her hip. It is a beautiful evening; the sky is the colour of lilac and the river of violet leaves. There are big bright trees along the path full of trembling light, and the boats, dancing up and down, send heavy curls of foam rippling almost to her feet. Now she has stopped. Now she has turned suddenly. She is leaning up against a tree, her hands over her face; she is crying. And now she is walking up and down wringing her hands. Again she leans against the tree, her back against it, her head raised and her hands clasped as though she leaned against someone dear. Round her shoulders she wears a little grey shawl; she covers her face with the ends of it and rocks to and fro.

But one cannot cry for ever, so at last she becomes serious and quiet, patting her hair into place, smoothing her apron. She walks a step or two. No, too soon, too soon! Again her arms fly up—she runs back—again she is blotted against the tall tree. Squares of gold light show in the houses; the street lamps gleam through the new leaves; yellow fans of light follow the dancing boats. For a moment she is a blur against the tree, white, grey and black, melting into the stones and the shadows. And then she is gone.

LATE AT NIGHT

(Virginia is seated by the fire. Her outdoor things are thrown on a chair; her boots are faintly steaming in the fender.)

Virginia (laying the letter down): I don't like this letter at all—not at all. I wonder if he means it to be so snubbing—or if it's just his way. (Reads). "Many thanks for the socks. As I have had five pairs sent me lately, I am sure you will be pleased to hear I gave yours to a friend in my company." No; it can't be my fancy. He must have meant it; it is a dreadful snub.

Oh, I wish I hadn't sent him that letter telling him to take care of himself. I'd give anything to have that letter back. I wrote it on a Sunday evening, too—that was so fatal. I never ought to write letters on Sunday evenings—I always let myself go so. I can't think why Sunday evenings always have such a funny effect on me. I simply yearn to have someone to write to—or to love. Yes, that's it; they make me feel sad and full of love. Funny, isn't it!

I must start going to church again; it's fatal sitting in front of the fire and thinking. There are the hymns, too; one can let oneself go so safely in the hymns. (She croons) "And then for those our Dearest and our Best"—(but her eye lights on the next sentence in the letter). "It was most kind of you to have knitted them yourself." Really! Really, that is too much! Men are abominably arrogant! He actually imagines that I knitted them myself. Why, I hardly know him; I've only spoken to him a few times. Why on earth should I knit him socks? He must think I am far gone to throw myself at his head like that. For it certainly is throwing oneself at a man's head to knit him socks—if he's almost a stranger. Buying him an odd pair is a different matter altogether. No; I shan't write to him again— that's definite. And, besides, what would be the use? I might get really keen on him and he'd never care a straw for me. Men don't.

I wonder why it is that after a certain point I always seem to repel people. Funny, isn't it! They like me at first; they think me uncommon, or original; but then immediately I want to show them—even give them a hint—that I like them, they seem to get frightened and begin to disappear. I suppose I shall get embittered about it later on. Perhaps they know somehow that I've got so much to give. Perhaps it's that that frightens them. Oh, I feel I've got such boundless, boundless love to give to somebody—I would care for somebody so utterly and so completely—watch over them—keep everything horrible away—and make them feel that if ever they wanted anything done I lived to do it. If only I felt that somebody wanted me, that I was of use to somebody, I should become a different person. Yes; that is the secret of life for me—to feel loved, to feel wanted, to know that somebody leaned on me for everything absolutely—for ever. And I am strong, and far, far richer than most women. I am sure that most women don't have this tremendous yearning to—express themselves. I suppose that's it—to come into flower, almost. I'm all folded and shut away in the dark, and nobody cares. I suppose that is why I feel this tremendous tenderness for plants and sick animals and birds—it's one way of getting rid of this wealth, this burden of love. And then, of course, they are so helpless—that's another thing. But I have a feeling that if a man were really in love with you he'd be just as helpless, too. Yes, I am sure that men are very helpless...

I don't know why, I feel inclined to cry tonight. Certainly not because of this letter; it isn't half important enough. But I keep wondering if things will ever change or if I shall go on like this until I am old—just wanting and wanting. I'm not as young as I was even now. I've got lines, and my skin isn't a bit what it used to be. I never was really pretty, not in the ordinary way, but I did have lovely skin and lovely hair—and I walked well. I only caught sight of myself in a glass today—stooping and shuffling along... I looked dowdy and elderly. Well, no; perhaps not quite as bad as that; I always exaggerate about myself. But I'm faddy about things now—that's a sign of age, I'm sure. The wind—I can't bear being blown about in the wind now; and I hate having wet feet. I never used to care about those things—I used almost to revel in them—they made me feel so one with Nature in a way. But now I get cross and I want to cry and I yearn for something to make me forget. I suppose that's why women take to drink. Funny, isn't it!

The fire is going out. I'll burn this letter. What's it to me? Pooh! I don't care. What is it to me? The five other women can send him socks! And I don't suppose he was a bit what I imagined. I can just hear him saying, "It was most kind of you, to have knitted them yourself." He has a fascinating voice. I think it was his voice that attracted me to him—and his hands; they looked so strong—they were such man's hands. Oh, well, don't sentimentalise over it; burn it!... No, I can't now—the fire's gone out. I'll go to bed. I wonder if he really meant to be snubbing. Oh, I am tired. Often when I go to bed now I want to pull the clothes over my head—and just cry. Funny, isn't it!

TWO TUPPENNY ONES, PLEASE

Lady: Yes, there is, dear; there's plenty of room. If the lady next to me would move her seat and sit opposite... Would you mind? So that my friend may sit next to me... Thank you so much! Yes, dear, both the cars on war work; I'm getting quite used to buses. Of course, if we go to the theatre, I phone Cynthia. She's still got one car. Her chauffeur's been called up... Ages ago... Killed by now, I think. I can't quite remember. I don't like her new man at all. I don't mind taking any reasonable risk, but he's so obstinate—he charges everything he sees. Heaven alone knows what would happen if he rushed into something that wouldn't swerve aside. But the poor creature's got a withered arm, and something the matter with one of his feet, I believe she told me. I suppose that's what makes him so careless. I mean—well!... Don't you know!...

Friend...?

Lady. Yes, she's sold it. My dear, it was far too small. There were only ten bedrooms, you know. There were only ten bedrooms in that house. Extraordinary! One wouldn't believe it from the outside—would one? And with the governesses and the nurses—and so on. All the menservants had to sleep out... You know what that means.

Friend...!!

Conductor. Fares, please. Pass your fares along.

Lady. How much is it? Tuppence, isn't it? Two tuppenny ones, please. Don't bother—I've got some coppers, somewhere or other.

Friend...!

Lady. No, it's all right. I've got some—if only I can find them.

Conductor. Parse your fares, please.

Friend...!

Lady. Really? So I did. I remember now. Yes, I paid coming. Very well, I'll let you, just this once. War time, my dear.

Conductor. "Ow far do you want ter go?

Lady. To the Boltons.

Conductor. Another 'a'penny each.

Lady. No—oh, no! I only paid tuppence coming. Are you quite sure?

Conductor (savagely). Read it on the board for yourself.

Lady. Oh, very well. Here's another penny. (To friend): "Isn't it extraordinary how disobliging these men are? After all, he's paid to do his job. But they are nearly all alike. I've heard these motor buses affect the spine after a time. I suppose that's it... You've heard about Teddie—haven't you?"

Friend...

Lady. He's got his... He's got his... Now what is it? Whatever can it be? How ridiculous of me!

Friend...?

Lady. Oh, no! He's been a Major for ages.

Friend...?

Lady. Colonel? Oh, no, my dear, it's something much higher than that. Not his company—he's had his company a long time. Not his battalion...

Friend...?

Lady. Regiment! Yes, I believe it is his regiment. But what I was going to say is he's been made a... Oh, how silly I am! What's higher than a Brigadier-General? Yes, I believe that's it. Chief of Staff. Of course, Mrs. T.'s frightfully gratified.

Friend...

Lady. Oh, my dear, everybody goes over the top nowadays. Whatever his position may be. And Teddy is such a sport, I really don't see how... Too dreadful—isn't it!

Friend...?

Lady. Didn't you know? She's at the War Office, and doing very well. I believe she got a rise the other day. She's something to do with notifying the deaths, or finding the missing. I don't know exactly what it is. At any rate, she says it is too depressing for words, and she has to read the most heartrending letters from parents, and so on. Happily, they're a very cheery little group in her room—all officers' wives, and they make their own tea, and get cakes in turn from Stewart's. She has one afternoon a week off, when she shops or has her hair waved. Last time she and I went to see Yvette's Spring Show.

Friend...?

Lady. No, not really. I'm getting frightfully sick of these coat-frocks, aren't you? I mean, as I was saying to her, what is the use of paying an enormous price for having one made by Yvette, when you can't really tell the difference, in the long run, between it and one of those cheap ready-made ones. Of course, one has the satisfaction for oneself of knowing that the material is good, and so on—but it looks nothing. No; I advised her to get a good coat and skirt. For, after all, a good coat and skirt always tells. Doesn't it?

Friend...!

Lady. Yes, I didn't tell her that—but that's what I had in mind. She's much too fat for those coat-frocks. She goes out far too much at the hips. I half ordered a rather lovely indefinite blue one for myself, trimmed with the new lobster red... I've lost my good Kate, you know.

Friend...!

Lady. Yes, isn't it annoying! Just when I got her more or less trained. But she went off her head, like they all do nowadays, and decided that she wanted to go into munitions. I told her when she gave notice that she would go on the strict understanding that if she got a job (which I think is highly improbable), she was not to come back and disturb the other servants.

Conductor (savagely). Another penny each, if you're going on.

Lady. Oh, we're there. How extraordinary! I never should have noticed...

Friend...?

Lady. Tuesday? Bridge on Tuesday? No, dear, I'm afraid I can't manage Tuesday. I trot out the wounded every Tuesday you know. I let cook take them to the Zoo, or some place like that—don't you know. Wednesday—I'm perfectly free on Wednesday.

Conductor. It'll be Wednesday before you get off the bus if you don't 'urry up.

Lady. That's quite enough, my man.

Friend...!!

THE BLACK CAP

(A lady and her husband are seated at breakfast. He is quite calm, reading the newspaper and eating; but she is strangely excited, dressed for travelling, and only pretending to eat.)

She. Oh, if you should want your flannel shirts, they are on the right-hand bottom shelf of the linen press.

He (at a board meeting of the Meat Export Company). No.

She. You didn't hear what I said. I said if you should want your flannel shirts, they are on the right-hand bottom shelf of the linen press.

He (positively). I quite agree!

She. It does seem rather extraordinary that on the very morning that I am going away you cannot leave the newspaper alone for five minutes.

He (mildly). My dear woman, I don't want you to go. In fact, I have asked you not to go. I can't for the life of me see...

She. You know perfectly well that I am only going because I absolutely must. I've been putting it off and putting it off, and the dentist said last time...

He. Good! Good! Don't let's go over the ground again. We've thrashed it out pretty thoroughly, haven't we?

Servant. Cab's here, m'm.

She. Please put my luggage in.

Servant. Very good, m'm.

(She gives a tremendous sigh.)

He. You haven't got too much time if you want to catch that train.

She. I know. I'm going. (In a changed tone.) Darling, don't let us part like this. It makes me feel so wretched. Why is it that you always seem to take a positive delight in spoiling my enjoyment?

He. I don't think going to the dentist is so positively enjoyable.

She. Oh, you know that's not what I mean. You're only saying that to hurt me. You know you are begging the question.

He (laughing). And you are losing your train. You'll be back on Thursday evening, won't you?

She (in a low, desperate voice). Yes, on Thursday evening. Good-bye, then. (Comes over to him, and takes his head in her hands.) Is there anything really the matter? Do at least look at me. Don't you—care—at—all?

He. My darling girl! This is like an exit on the cinema.

She (letting her hands fall). Very well. Good-bye. (Gives a quick tragic glance round the dining-room and goes.)

(On the way to the station.)

She. How strange life is! I didn't think I should feel like this at all. All the glamour seems to have gone, somehow. Oh, I'd give anything for the cab to turn round and go back. The most curious thing is that I feel if he really had made me believe he loved me it would have been much easier to have left him. But that's absurd. How strong the hay smells. It's going to be a very hot day. I shall never see these fields again. Never! never! But in another way I am glad that it happened like this; it puts me so finally, absolutely in the right for ever! He doesn't want a woman at all. A woman has no meaning for him. He's not the type of man to care deeply for anybody except himself. I've become the person who remembers to take the links out of his shirts before they go to the wash—that is all! And that's not enough for me. I'm young—I'm too proud. I'm not the type of woman to vegetate in the country and rave over "our" own lettuces...

What you have been trying to do, ever since you married me is to make me submit, to turn me into your shadow, to rely on me so utterly that you'd only to glance up to find the right time printed on me somehow, as if I were a clock. You have never been curious about me; you never wanted to explore my soul. No; you wanted me to settle down to your peaceful existence. Oh! how your blindness has outraged me—how I hate you for it! I am glad—thankful—thankful to have left you! I'm not a green girl; I am not conceited, but I do know my powers. It's not for nothing that I've always longed for riches and passion and freedom, and felt that they were mine by right. (She leans against the buttoned back of the cab and murmurs.) "You are a Queen. Let mine be the joy of giving you your kingdom." (She smiles at her little royal hands.) I wish my heart didn't beat so hard. It really hurts me. It tires me so and excites me so. It's like someone in a dreadful hurry beating against a door... This cab is only crawling along; we shall never be at the station at this rate. Hurry! Hurry! My love, I am coming as quickly as ever I can. Yes, I am suffering just like you. It's dreadful, isn't it unbearable—this last half-hour without each other... Oh, God! the horse has begun to walk again. Why doesn't he beat the great strong brute of a thing... Our wonderful life! We shall travel all over the world together. The whole world shall be ours because of our love. Oh, be patient! I am coming as fast as I possibly can... Ah, now it's downhill; now we really are going faster. (An old man attempts to cross the road.) Get out of my way, you old fool! He deserves to be run over... Dearest—dearest; I am nearly there. Only be patient!

(At the station.)

Put it in a first-class smoker... There's plenty of time after all. A full ten minutes before the train goes. No wonder he's not here. I mustn't appear to be looking for him. But I must say I'm disappointed. I never dreamed of being the first to arrive. I thought he would have been here and engaged a carriage and bought papers and flowers... How curious! I absolutely saw in my mind a paper of pink carnations... He knows how fond I am of carnations. But pink ones are not my favourites. I prefer dark red or pale yellow. He really will be late if he doesn't come now. The guard has begun to shut the doors. Whatever can have happened? Something dreadful. Perhaps at the last moment he has shot himself... I could not bear the thought of ruining your life... But you are not ruining my life. Ah, where are you? I shall have to get into the carriage... Who is this? That's not him! It can't be—yes, it is. What on earth has he got on his head? A black cap. But how awful! He's utterly changed. What can he be wearing a black cap for? I wouldn't have known him. How absurd he looks coming towards me, smiling, in that appalling cap!

He. My darling, I shall never forgive myself. But the most absurd, tragic-comic thing happened. (They get into the carriage.) I lost my hat. It simply disappeared. I had half the hotel looking for it. Not a sign! So finally, in despair, I had to borrow this from another man who was staying there. (The train moves off.) You're not angry. (Tries to take her in his arms.)

She. Don't! We're not even out of the station yet.

He (ardently). Great God! What do I care if the whole world were to see us? (Tries to take her in his arms.) My wonder! My joy!

She. Please don't! I hate being kissed in trains.

He (profoundly hurt). Oh, very well. You are angry. It's serious. You can't get over the fact that I was late. But if you only knew the agony I suffered...

She. How can you think I could be so small-minded? I am not angry at all.

He. Then why won't you let me kiss you?

She (laughing hysterically). You look so different somehow—almost a stranger.

He (jumps up and looks at himself in the glass anxiously, and fatuously, she decides). But it's all right, isn't it?

She. Oh, quite all right; perfectly all right. Oh, oh, oh! (She begins to laugh and cry with rage.)

(They arrive).

She (while he gets a cab). I must get over this. It's an obsession. It's incredible that anything should change a man so. I must tell him. Surely it's quite simple to say: Don't you think now that you are in the city you had better buy yourself a hat? But that will make him realise how frightful the cap has been. And the extraordinary thing is that he doesn't realise it himself. I mean if he has looked at himself in the glass, and doesn't think that cap too ridiculous, how different our points of view must be... How deeply different! I mean, if I had seen him in the street I would have said I could not possibly love a man who wore a cap like that. I couldn't even have got to know him. He isn't my style at all. (She looks round.) Everybody is smiling at it. Well, I don't wonder! The way it makes his ears stick out, and the way it makes him have no back to his head at all.

He. The cab is ready, my darling. (They get in.)

He (tries to take her hand). The miracle that we two should be driving together, so simply, like this.

(She arranges her veil.)

He (tries to take her hand, very ardent). I'll engage one room, my love.

She. Oh, no! Of course you must take two.

He. But don't you think it would be wiser not to create suspicion?

She. I must have my own room. (To herself.) You can hang your cap behind your own door! (She begins to laugh hysterically.)

He. Ah! thank God! My queen is her happy self again!

(At the hotel.)

Manager. Yes, Sir, I quite understand. I think I've got the very thing for you, Sir. Kindly step this way. (He takes them into a small sitting-room, with a bedroom leading out of it.) This would suit you nicely, wouldn't it? And if you liked, we could make you up a bed on the sofa.

He. Oh, admirable! Admirable!

(The Manager goes).

She (furious). But I told you I wanted a room to myself. What a trick to play upon me! I told you I did not want to share a room. How dare you treat me like this? (She mimics.) Admirable! Admirable! I shall never forgive you for that!

He (overcome). Oh, God, what is happening! I don't understand—I'm in the dark. Why have you suddenly, on this day of days, ceased to love me? What have I done? Tell me!

She (sinks on the sofa). I'm very tired. If you do love me, please leave me alone. I—I only want to be alone for a little.

He (tenderly). Very well. I shall try to understand. I do begin to understand. I'll go out for half-an-hour, and then, my love, you may feel calmer. (He looks round, distracted.)

She. What is it?

He. My heart—you are sitting on my cap. (She gives a positive scream and moves into the bedroom. He goes. She waits a moment, and then puts down her veil, and takes up her suitcase.)

(In the taxi.)

She. Yes, Waterloo. (She leans back.) Ah, I've escaped—I've escaped! I shall just be in time to catch the afternoon train home. Oh, it's like a dream—I'll be home before supper. I'll tell him that the city was too hot or the dentist away. What does it matter? I've a right to my own home... It will be wonderful driving up from the station; the fields will smell so delicious. There is cold fowl for supper left over from yesterday, and orange jelly... I have been mad, but now I am sane again. Oh, my husband!

A SUBURBAN FAIRY TALE

Mr. and Mrs. B. sat at breakfast in the cosy red dining-room of their "snug little crib just under half-an-hour's run from the City."

There was a good fire in the grate—for the dining-room was the living-room as well—the two windows overlooking the cold empty garden patch were closed, and the air smelled agreeably of bacon and eggs, toast and coffee. Now that this rationing business was really over Mr. B. made a point of a thoroughly good tuck-in before facing the very real perils of the day. He didn't mind who knew it—he was a true Englishman about his breakfast—he had to have it; he'd cave in without it, and if you told him that these Continental chaps could get through half the morning's work he did on a roll and a cup of coffee—you simply didn't know what you were talking about.

Mr. B. was a stout youngish man who hadn't been able—worse luck—to chuck his job and join the Army; he'd tried for four years to get another chap to take his place but it was no go. He sat at the head of the table reading the Daily Mail. Mrs. B. was a youngish plump little body, rather like a pigeon. She sat opposite, preening herself behind the coffee set and keeping an eye of warning love on little B. who perched between them, swathed in a napkin and tapping the top of a soft-boiled egg.

Alas! Little B. was not at all the child that such parents had every right to expect. He was no fat little trot, no dumpling, no firm little pudding. He was under-sized for his age, with legs like macaroni, tiny claws, soft, soft hair that felt like mouse fur, and big wide-open eyes. For some strange reason everything in life seemed the wrong size for Little B.—too big and too violent. Everything knocked him over, took the wind out of his feeble sails and left him gasping and frightened. Mr. and Mrs. B. were quite powerless to prevent this; they could only pick him up after the mischief was done—and try to set him going again. And Mrs. B. loved him as only weak children are loved—and when Mr. B. thought what a marvellous little chap he was too—thought of the spunk of the little man, he—well he—by George—he...

"Why aren't there two kinds of eggs?" said Little B. "Why aren't there little eggs for children and big eggs like what this one is for grown-ups?"

"Scotch hares," said Mr. B. "Fine Scotch hares for 5s. 3d. How about getting one, old girl?"

"It would be a nice change, wouldn't it?" said Mrs. B. "Jugged."

And they looked across at each other and there floated between them the Scotch hare in its rich gravy with stuffing balls and a white pot of red-currant jelly accompanying it.

"We might have had it for the week-end," said Mrs. B. "But the butcher has promised me a nice little sirloin and it seems a pity"... Yes, it did and yet... Dear me, it was very difficult to decide. The hare would have been such a change—on the other hand, could you beat a really nice little sirloin?

"There's hare soup, too," said Mr. B. drumming his fingers on the table. "Best soup in the world!"

"O-Oh!" cried Little B. so suddenly and sharply that it gave them quite a start—"Look at the whole lot of sparrows flown on to our lawn"—he waved his spoon. "Look at them," he cried. "Look!" And while he spoke, even though the windows were closed, they heard a loud shrill cheeping and chirping from the garden.

"Get on with your breakfast like a good boy, do," said his mother, and his father said, "You stick to the egg, old man, and look sharp about it."

"But look at them—look at them all hopping," he cried. "They don't keep still not for a minute. Do you think they're hungry, father?"

Cheek-a-cheep-cheep-cheek! cried the sparrows.

"Best postpone it perhaps till next week," said Mr. B., "and trust to luck they're still to be had then."

"Yes, perhaps that would be wiser," said Mrs. B.

Mr. B. picked another plum out of his paper.

"Have you bought any of those controlled dates yet?"

"I managed to get two pounds yesterday," said Mrs. B.

"Well a date pudding's a good thing," said Mr. B. And they looked across at each other and there floated between them a dark round pudding covered with creamy sauce. "It would be a nice change, wouldn't it?" said Mrs. B.

Outside on the grey frozen grass the funny eager sparrows hopped and fluttered. They were never for a moment still. They cried, flapped their ungainly wings. Little B., his egg finished, got down, took his bread and marmalade to eat at the window.

"Do let us give them some crumbs," he said. "Do open the window, father, and throw them something. Father, please!"

"Oh, don't nag, child," said Mrs. B., and his father said—"Can't go opening windows, old man. You'd get your head bitten off."

"But they're hungry," cried Little B., and the sparrows' little voices were like ringing of little knives being sharpened. Cheek-a-cheep-cheep-cheek! they cried.

Little B. dropped his bread and marmalade inside the china flower pot in front of the window. He slipped behind the thick curtains to see better, and Mr. and Mrs. B. went on reading about what you could get now without coupons—no more ration books after May—a glut of cheese—a glut of it—whole cheeses revolved in the air between them like celestial bodies.

Suddenly as Little B. watched the sparrows on the grey frozen grass, they grew, they changed, still flapping and squeaking. They turned into tiny little boys, in brown coats, dancing, jigging outside, up and down outside the window squeaking, "Want something to eat, want something to eat!" Little B. held with both hands to the curtain. "Father," he whispered, "Father! They're not sparrows. They're little boys. Listen, Father!" But Mr. and Mrs. B. would not hear. He tried again. "Mother," he whispered. "Look at the little boys. They're not sparrows, Mother!" But nobody noticed his nonsense.

"All this talk about famine," cried Mr. B., "all a Fake, all a Blind."

With white shining faces, their arms flapping in the big coats, the little boys danced. "Want something to eat—want something to eat."

"Father," muttered Little B. "Listen, Father! Mother, listen, please!"

"Really!" said Mrs. B. "The noise those birds are making! I've never heard such a thing."

"Fetch me my shoes, old man," said Mr. B.

Cheek-a-cheep-cheep-cheek! said the sparrows.

Now where had that child got to? "Come and finish your nice cocoa, my pet," said Mrs. B.

Mr. B. lifted the heavy cloth and whispered, "Come on, Rover," but no little dog was there.

"He's behind the curtain," said Mrs. B.

"He never went out of the room," said Mr. B.

Mrs. B. went over to the window, and Mr. B. followed. And they looked out. There on the grey frozen grass, with a white white face, the little boy's thin arms flapping like wings, in front of them all, the smallest, tiniest was Little B. Mr. and Mrs. B. heard his voice above all the voices, "Want something to eat, want something to eat."

Somehow, somehow, they opened the window. "You shall! All of you. Come in at once. Old man! Little man!"

But it was too late. The little boys were changed into sparrows again, and away they flew—out of sight—out of call.

CARNATION

On those hot days Eve—curious Eve—always carried a flower. She snuffed it and snuffed it, twirled it in her fingers, laid it against her cheek, held it to her lips, tickled Katie's neck with it, and ended, finally, by pulling it to pieces and eating it, petal by petal.

"Roses are delicious, my dear Katie," she would say, standing in the dim cloak room, with a strange decoration of flowery hats on the hat pegs behind her—"but carnations are simply divine! They taste like—like—ah well!" And away her little thin laugh flew, fluttering among those huge, strange flower heads on the wall behind her. (But how cruel her little thin laugh was! It had a long sharp beak and claws and two bead eyes, thought fanciful Katie.)

Today it was a carnation. She brought a carnation to the French class, a deep, deep red one, that looked as though it had been dipped in wine and left in the dark to dry. She held it on the desk before her, half shut her eyes and smiled.

"Isn't it a darling?" said she. But—

"Un peu de silence, s'il vous plaît," came from M. Hugo. Oh, bother! It was too hot! Frightfully hot! Grilling simply!

The two square windows of the French Room were open at the bottom and the dark blinds drawn half way down. Although no air came in, the blind cord swung out and back and the blind lifted. But really there was not a breath from the dazzle outside.

Even the girls, in the dusky room, in their pale blouses, with stiff butterfly-bow hair ribbons perched on their hair, seemed to give off a warm, weak light, and M. Hugo's white waistcoat gleamed like the belly of a shark.

Some of the girls were very red in the face and some were white. Vera Holland had pinned up her black curls à la japonaise with a penholder and a pink pencil; she looked charming. Francie Owen pushed her sleeves nearly up to the shoulders, and then she inked the little blue vein in her elbow, shut her arm together, and then looked to see the mark it made; she had a passion for inking herself; she always had a face drawn on her thumb nail, with black, forked hair. Sylvia Mann took off her collar and tie, took them off simply, and laid them on the desk beside her, as calm as if she were going to wash her hair in her bedroom at home. She had a nerve! Jennie Edwards tore a leaf out of her notebook and wrote "Shall we ask old Hugo-Wugo to give us a thrippenny vanilla on the way home!!!" and passed it across to Connie Baker, who turned absolutely purple and nearly burst out crying. All of them lolled and gaped, staring at the round clock, which seemed to have grown paler, too; the hands scarcely crawled.

"Un peu de silence, s'il vous plaît," came from M. Hugo. He held up a puffy hand. "Ladies, as it is so 'ot we will take no more notes today, but I will read you," and he paused and smiled a broad, gentle smile, "a little French poetry."

"Go—od God!" moaned Francie Owen.

M. Hugo's smile deepened. "Well, Mees Owen, you need not attend. You can paint yourself. You can 'ave my red ink as well as your black one."

How well they knew the little blue book with red edges that he tugged out of his coat tail pocket! It had a green silk marker embroidered in forget-me-nots. They often giggled at it when he handed the book round. Poor old Hugo-Wugo! He adored reading poetry. He would begin, softly and calmly, and then gradually his voice would swell and vibrate and gather itself together, then it would be pleading and imploring and entreating, and then rising, rising triumphant, until it burst into light, as it were, and then—gradually again, it ebbed, it grew soft and warm and calm and died down into nothingness.

The great difficulty was, of course, if you felt at all feeble, not to get the most awful fit of the giggles. Not because it was funny, really, but because it made you feel uncomfortable, queer, silly, and somehow ashamed for old Hugo-Wugo. But—oh dear—if he was going to inflict it on them in this heat...!

"Courage, my pet," said Eve, kissing the languid carnation.

He began, and most of the girls fell forward, over the desks, their heads on their arms, dead at the first shot. Only Eve and Katie sat upright and still. Katie did not know enough French to understand, but Eve sat listening, her eyebrows raised, her eyes half veiled, and a smile that was like the shadow of her cruel little laugh, like the wing shadows of that cruel little laugh fluttering over her lips. She made a warm, white cup of her fingers—the carnation inside. Oh, the scent! It floated across to Katie. It was too much. Katie turned away to the dazzling light outside the window.

Down below, she knew, there was a cobbled courtyard with stable buildings round it. That was why the French Room always smelled faintly of ammonia. It wasn't unpleasant; it was even part of the French language for Katie—something sharp and vivid and—and—biting!

Now she could hear a man clatter over the cobbles and the jing-jang of the pails he carried. And now Hoo-hor-her! Hoo-hor-her! as he worked the pump, and a great gush of water followed. Now he was flinging the water over something, over the wheels of a carriage, perhaps. And she saw the wheel, propped up, clear of the ground, spinning round, flashing scarlet and black, with great drops glancing off it. And all the while he worked the man kept up a high bold whistling, that skimmed over the noise of the water as a bird skims over the sea. He went away—he came back again leading a cluttering horse.

Hoo-hor-her! Hoo-hor-her! came from the pump. Now he dashed the water over the horse's legs and then swooped down and began brushing.

She saw him simply—in a faded shirt, his sleeves rolled up, his chest bare, all splashed with water—and as he whistled, loud and free, and as he moved, swooping and bending, Hugo-Wugo's voice began to warm, to deepen, to gather together, to swing, to rise—somehow or other to keep time with the man outside (Oh, the scent of Eve's carnation!) until they became one great rushing, rising, triumphant thing, bursting into light, and then—

The whole room broke into pieces.

"Thank you, ladies," cried M. Hugo, bobbing at his high desk, over the wreckage.

And "Keep it, dearest," said Eve. "Souvenir tendre," and she popped the carnation down the front of Katie's blouse.

SEE-SAW

Spring. As the people leave the road for the grass their eyes become fixed and dreamy like the eyes of people wading in the warm sea. There are no daisies yet, but the sweet smell of the grass rises, rises in tiny waves the deeper they go. The trees are in full leaf. As far as one can see there are fans, hoops, tall rich plumes of various green. A light wind shakes them, blowing them together, blowing them free again; in the blue sky floats a cluster of tiny white clouds like a brood of ducklings. The people wander over the grass—the old ones inclined to puff and waddle after their long winter snooze; the young ones suddenly linking hands and making for that screen of trees in the hollow or the shelter of that clump of dark gorse tipped with yellow—walking very fast, almost running, as though they had heard some lovely little creature caught in the thicket crying to them to be saved.

On the top of a small green mound there is a very favourite bench. It has a young chestnut growing beside it, shaped like a mushroom. Below the earth has crumbled, fallen away, leaving three or four clayey hollows—caves—caverns—and in one of them two little people had set up house with a minute pickaxe, an empty match box, a blunted nail and a shovel for furniture. He had red hair cut in a deep fringe, light blue eyes, a faded pink smock and brown button shoes. Her flowery curls were caught up with a yellow ribbon and she wore two dresses—her this week's underneath and her last week's on top. This gave her rather a bulky air.

"If you don't get me no sticks for my fire," said she, "there won't be no dinner." She wrinkled her nose and looked at him severely. "You seem to forget I've got a fire to make." He took it very easy, balancing on his toes—"Well—where's I to find any sticks?"

"Oh," said she—flinging up her hands—"anywhere of course—" And then she whispered just loud enough for him to hear, "they needn't be real ones—you know."

"Ooh," he breathed. And then he shouted in a loud distinct tone: "Well I'll just go an' get a few sticks."

He came back in a moment with an armful.

"Is that a whole pennorth?" said she, holding out her skirts for them.

"Well," said he, "I don't know, because I had them give to me by a man that was moving."

"Perhaps they're bits of what was broke," said she. "When we moved, two of the pictures was broken and my Daddy lit the fire with them, and my Mummy said—she said—" a tiny pause— "soldier's manners!"

"What's that?" said he.

"Good gracious!" She made great eyes at him. "Don't you know?"

"No," said he. "What does it mean?"

She screwed up a bit of her skirt, scrunched it, then looked away—"Oh, don't bother me, child," said she.

He didn't care. He took the pickaxe and hacked a little piece out of the kitchen floor.

"Got a newspaper?"

He plucked one out of the air and handed it to her. Ziz, ziz, ziz! She tore it into three pieces—knelt down and laid the sticks over. "Matches, please." The real box was a triumph, and the blunted nails. But funny—Zip, zip, zip, it wouldn't light. They looked at each other in consternation.

"Try the other side," said she. Zip. "Ah! that's better." There was a great glow—and they sat down on the floor and began to make the pie.

To the bench beside the chestnut came two fat old babies and plumped themselves down.

She wore a bonnet trimmed with lilac and tied with lilac velvet strings; a black satin coat and a lace tie—and each of her hands, squeezed into black kid gloves, showed a morsel of purplish flesh. The skin of his swollen old face was tight and glazed—and he sat down clasping his huge soft belly as though careful not to jolt or alarm it.

"Very hot," said he, and he gave a low, strange trumpeting cry with which she was evidently familiar, for she gave no sign. She looked into the lovely distance and quivered:

"Nellie cut her finger last night."

"Oh, did she?" said the old snorter. Then—"How did she do that?"

"At dinner," was the reply, "with a knife."

They both looked ahead of them—panting—then, "Badly?"

The weak worn old voice, the old voice that reminded one somehow of a piece of faintly smelling dark lace, said, "Not very badly."

Again he gave that low strange cry. He took off his hat, wiped the rim and put it on again.

The voice beside him said with a spiteful touch: "I think it was carelessness"—and he replied, blowing out his cheeks: "Bound to be!"

But then a little bird flew on to a branch of the young chestnut above them—and shook over the old heads a great jet of song.

He took off his hat, heaved himself up, and beat in its direction in the tree. Away it flew.

"Don't want bird muck falling on us," said he, lowering his belly carefully—carefully again.

The fire was made.

"Put your hand in the oven," said she, "an' see if it's hot."

He put his hand in, but drew it out again with a squeak, and danced up and down. "It's ever so hot," said he.

This seemed to please her very much. She too got up and went over to him, and touched him with a finger.

"Do you like playing with me?" And he said, in his small solid way, "Yes, I do." At that she flung away from him and cried, "I'll never be done if you keep on bothering me with these questions."

As she poked the fire he said: "Our dog's had kittens."

"Kittens!" She sat back on her heels—"Can a dog have kittens?"

"Of course they can," said he. "Little ones, you know."

"But cats have kittens," cried she. "Dogs don't, dogs have—" she stopped, stared—looked for the word—couldn't find it—it was gone. "They have—"

"Kittens," cried he. "Our dog's been an' had two."

She stamped her foot at him. She was pink with exasperation. "It's not kittens," she wailed, "it's—"

"It is—it is—it is—" he shouted, waving the shovel.

She threw her top dress over her head, and began to cry. "It's not—it's—it's…"

Suddenly, without a moment's warning, he lifted his pinafore and made water.

At the sound she emerged.

"Look what you've been an' done," said she, too appalled to cry any more. "You've put out my fire."

"Ah, never mind. Let's move. You can take the pickaxe and the match box."

They moved to the next cave. "It's much nicer here," said he.

"Off you go," said she, "and get me some sticks for my fire."

The two old babies above began to rumble, and obedient to the sign they got up without a word and waddled away.

THIS FLOWER

"But I tell you, my lord fool, out of this nettle danger, we pluck this flower, safety."

As she lay there, looking up at the ceiling, she had her moment—yes, she had her moment! And it was not connected with anything she had thought or felt before, not even with those words the doctor had scarcely ceased speaking. It was single, glowing, perfect; it was like—a pearl, too flawless to match with another... Could she describe what happened? Impossible. It was as though, even if she had not been conscious (and she certainly had not been conscious all the time) that she was fighting against the stream of life—the stream of life indeed!—she had suddenly ceased to struggle. Oh, more than that! She had yielded, yielded absolutely, down to every minutest pulse and nerve, and she had fallen into the bright bosom of the stream and it had borne her... She was part of her room—part of the great bouquet of southern anemones, of the white net curtains that blew in stiff against the light breeze, of the mirrors, the white silky rugs; she was part of the high, shaking, quivering clamour, broken with little bells and crying voices that went streaming by outside,—part of the leaves and the light.

Over. She sat up. The doctor had reappeared. This strange little figure with his stethoscope still strung round his neck—for she had asked him to examine her heart—squeezing and kneading his freshly washed hands, had told her...

It was the first time she had ever seen him. Roy, unable, of course, to miss the smallest dramatic opportunity, had obtained his rather shady Bloomsbury address from the man in whom he always confided everything, who, although he'd never met her, knew "all about them."

"My darling," Roy had said, "we'd better have an absolutely unknown man just in case it's—well, what we don't either of us want it to be. One can't be too careful in affairs of this sort. Doctors do talk. It's all damned rot to say they don't." Then, "Not that I care a straw who on earth knows. Not that I wouldn't—if you'd have me—blazon it on the skies, or take the front page of the Daily Mirror and have our two names on it, in a heart, you know—pierced by an arrow."

Nevertheless, of course, his love of mystery and intrigue, his passion for "keeping our secret beautifully" (his phrase!) had won the day, and off he'd gone in a taxi to fetch this rather sodden-looking little man.

She heard her untroubled voice saying, "Do you mind not mentioning anything of this to Mr. King? If you'd tell him that I'm a little run down and that my heart wants a rest. For I've been complaining about my heart."

Roy had been really too right about the kind of man the doctor was. He gave her a strange, quick, leering look, and taking off the stethoscope with shaking fingers he folded it into his bag that looked somehow like a broken old canvas shoe.

"Don't you worry, my dear," he said huskily. "I'll see you through."

Odious little toad to have asked a favour of! She sprang to her feet, and picking up her purple cloth jacket, went over to the mirror. There was a soft knock at the door, and Roy—he really did look pale, smiling his half-smile—came in and asked the doctor what he had to say.

"Well," said the doctor, taking up his hat, holding it against his chest and beating a tattoo on it, "all I've got to say is that Mrs.—h'm—Madam wants a bit of a rest. She's a bit run down. Her heart's a bit strained. Nothing else wrong."

In the street a barrel-organ struck up something gay, laughing, mocking, gushing, with little trills, shakes, jumbles of notes.

That's all I got to say, to say,   That's all I got to say,

it mocked. It sounded so near she wouldn't have been surprised if the doctor were turning the handle.

She saw Roy's smile deepen; his eyes took fire. He gave a little "Ah!" of relief and happiness. And just for one moment he allowed himself to gaze at her without caring a jot whether the doctor saw or not, drinking her up with that gaze she knew so well, as she stood tying the pale ribbons of her camisole and drawing on the little purple cloth jacket. He jerked back to the doctor, "She shall go away. She shall go away to the sea at once," said he, and then, terribly anxious, "What about her food?" At that, buttoning her jacket in the long mirror, she couldn't help laughing at him.

"That's all very well," he protested, laughing back delightedly at her and at the doctor. "But if I didn't manage her food, doctor, she'd never eat anything but caviare sandwiches and—and white grapes. About wine—oughtn't she to have wine?"

Wine would do her no harm.

"Champagne," pleaded Roy. How he was enjoying himself!

"Oh, as much champagne as she likes," said the doctor, "and a brandy and soda with her lunch if she fancies it."

Roy loved that; it tickled him immensely.

"Do you hear that?" he asked solemnly, blinking and sucking in his cheeks to keep from laughing. "Do you fancy a brandy and soda?"

And, in the distance, faint and exhausted, the barrel-organ:

A brandy and so-da,   A brandy and soda, please!   A brandy and soda, please!

The doctor seemed to hear that, too. He shook hands with her and Roy went with him into the passage to settle his fee.

She heard the front door close and then—rapid, rapid steps along the passage. This time he simply burst into her room, and she was in his arms, crushed up small while he kissed her with warm quick kisses, murmuring between them, "My darling, my beauty, my delight. You're mine, you're safe." And then three soft groans. "Oh! Oh! Oh! the relief!" Still keeping his arms round her he leant his head against her shoulder as though exhausted. "If you knew how frightened I've been," he murmured. "I thought we were in for it this time. I really did. And it would have been so—fatal—so fatal!"

"Two purl—two plain—woolinfrontoftheneedle—and knit two together." Like an old song, like a song that she had sung so often that only to breathe was to sing it, she murmured the knitting pattern. Another vest was nearly finished for the mission parcel.

"It's your vests, Mrs. Bean, that are so acceptable. Look at these poor little mites without a shred!" And the churchwoman showed her a photograph of repulsive little black objects with bellies shaped like lemons...

"Two purl—two plain." Down dropped the knitting on to her lap; she gave a great long sigh, stared in front of her for a moment and then picked the knitting up and began again. What did she think about when she sighed like that? Nothing. It was a habit. She was always sighing. On the stairs, particularly, as she went up and down, she stopped, holding her dress up with one hand, the other hand on the bannister, staring at the steps—sighing.

"Woolinfrontoftheneedle..." She sat at the dining-room window facing the street. It was a bitter autumn day; the wind ran in the street like a thin dog; the houses opposite looked as though they had been cut out with a pair of ugly steel scissors and pasted on to the grey paper sky. There was not a soul to be seen.

"Knit two together!" The clock struck three. Only three? It seemed dusk already; dusk came floating into the room, heavy, powdery dusk settling on the furniture, filming over the mirror. Now the kitchen clock struck three—two minutes late—for this was the clock to go by and not the kitchen clock. She was alone in the house. Dollicas was out shopping; she had been gone since a quarter to two. Really, she got slower and slower! What did she do with the time? One cannot spend more than a certain time buying a chicken... And oh, that habit of hers of dropping the stove-rings when she made up the fire! And she set her lips, as she had set her lips for the past thirty-five years, at that habit of Dollicas'.

There came a faint noise from the street, a noise of horses' hooves. She leaned further out to see. Good gracious! It was a funeral. First the glass coach, rolling along briskly with the gleaming, varnished coffin inside (but no wreaths), with three men in front and two standing at the back, then some carriages, some with black horses, some with brown. The dust came bowling up the road, half hiding the procession. She scanned the houses opposite to see which had the blinds down. What horrible looking men, too! laughing and joking. One leaned over to one side and blew his nose with his black glove—horrible! She gathered up the knitting, hiding her hands in it. Dollicas surely would have known... There, they were passing... It was the other end...

What was this? What was happening? What could it mean? Help, God! Her old heart leaped like a fish and then fell as the glass coach drew up outside her door, as the outside men scrambled down from the front, swung off the back, and the tallest of them, with a glance of surprise at the windows, came quickly, stealthily, up the garden path.

"No!" she groaned. But yes, the blow fell, and for the moment it struck her down. She gasped, a great cold shiver went through her, and stayed in her hands and knees. She saw the man withdraw a step and again—that puzzled glance at the blinds—then—

"No!" she groaned, and stumbling, catching hold of things, she managed to get to the door before the blow fell again. She opened it, her chin trembled, her teeth clacked; somehow or other she brought out, "The wrong house!"

Oh! he was shocked. As she stepped back she saw behind him the black hats clustered at the gate. "The wrong' ouse!" he muttered. She could only nod. She was shutting the door again when he fished out of the tail of his coat a black, brass-bound notebook and swiftly opened it. "No. 20 Shuttleworth Crescent?"

"S—street! Crescent round the corner." Her hand lifted to point, but shook and fell.

He was taking off his hat as she shut the door and leaned against it, whimpering in the dusky hall, "Go away! Go away!"

Clockety-clock-clock. Cluk! Cluk! Clockety-clock-cluk! sounded from outside, and then a faint Cluk! Cluk! and then silence. They were gone. They were out of sight. But still she stayed leaning against the door, staring into the hall, staring at the hall-stand that was like a great lobster with hat-pegs for feelers. But she thought of nothing; she did not even think of what had happened. It was as if she had fallen into a cave whose walls were darkness...

She came to herself with a deep inward shock, hearing the gate bang and quick, short steps crunching the gravel; it was Dollicas hurrying round to the back door. Dollicas must not find her there; and wavering, wavering like a candle-flame, back she went into the dining-room to her seat by the window.

Dollicas was in the kitchen. Klang! went one of the iron rings into the fender. Then her voice, "I'm just putting on the teakettle'm." Since they had been alone she had got into the way of shouting from one room to another. The old woman coughed to steady herself. "Please bring in the lamp," she cried.

"The lamp!" Dollicas came across the passage and stood in the doorway. "Why, it's only just on four' m."

"Never mind," said Mrs. Bean dully.

"Bring it in!" And a moment later the elderly maid appeared, carrying the gentle lamp in both hands. Her broad soft face had the look it always had when she carried anything, as though she walked in her sleep. She set it down on the table, lowered the wick, raised it, and then lowered it again. Then she straightened up and looked across at her mistress.

"Why, 'm, whatever's that you're treading on?"

It was the mission vest.

"T't! T't!" As Dollicas picked it up she thought, "The old lady has been asleep. She's not awake yet." Indeed the old lady looked glazed and dazed, and when she took up the knitting she drew out a needle of stitches and began to unwind what she had done.

"Don't forget the mace," she said. Her voice sounded thin and dry. She was thinking of the chicken for that night's supper. And Dollicas understood and answered, "It's a lovely young bird!" as she pulled down the blind before going back to her kitchen...

Children are unaccountable little creatures. Why should a small boy like Dicky, good as gold as a rule, sensitive, affectionate, obedient, and marvellously sensible for his age, have moods when, without the slightest warning, he suddenly went "mad dog," as his sisters called it, and there was no doing anything with him?

"Dicky, come here! Come here, sir, at once! Do you hear your mother calling you? Dicky!"

But Dicky wouldn't come. Oh, he heard right enough. A clear, ringing little laugh was his only reply. And away he flew; hiding, running through the uncut hay on the lawn, dashing past the woodshed, making a rush for the kitchen garden, and there dodging, peering at his mother from behind the mossy apple trunks, and leaping up and down like a wild Indian.

It had begun at tea-time. While Dicky's mother and Mrs. Spears, who was spending the afternoon with her, were quietly sitting over their sewing in the drawing-room, this, according to the servant girl, was what had happened at the children's tea. They were eating their first bread and butter as nicely and quietly as you please, and the servant girl had just poured out the milk and water, when Dicky had suddenly seized the bread plate, put it upside down on his head, and clutched the bread knife.

"Look at me!" he shouted.

His startled sisters looked, and before the servant girl could get there, the bread plate wobbled, slid, flew to the floor, and broke into shivers. At this awful point the little girls lifted up their voices and shrieked their loudest.

"Mother, come and look what he's done!"

"Dicky's broke a great big plate!"

"Come and stop him, mother!"

You can imagine how mother came flying. But she was too late. Dicky had leapt out of his chair, run through the French windows on to the verandah, and, well—there she stood—popping her thimble on and off, helpless. What could she do? She couldn't chase after the child. She couldn't stalk Dicky among the apples and damsons. That would be too undignified. It was more than annoying, it was exasperating. Especially as Mrs. Spears, Mrs. Spears of all people, whose two boys were so exemplary, was waiting for her in the drawing-room.

"Very well, Dicky," she cried, "I shall have to think of some way of punishing you."

"I don't care," sounded the high little voice, and again there came that ringing laugh. The child was quite beside himself...

"Oh, Mrs. Spears, I don't know how to apologise for leaving you by yourself like this."

"It's quite all right, Mrs. Bendall," said Mrs. Spears, in her soft, sugary voice, and raising her eyebrows in the way she had. She seemed to smile to herself as she stroked the gathers. "These little things will happen from time to time. I only hope it was nothing serious."

"It was Dicky," said Mrs. Bendall, looking rather helplessly for her only fine needle. And she explained the whole affair to Mrs. Spears.

"And the worst of it is, I don't know how to cure him. Nothing when he's in that mood seems to have the slightest effect on him."

Mrs. Spears opened her pale eyes. "Not even a whipping?" said she.

But Mrs. Bendall, threading her needle, pursed up her lips. "We never have whipped the children," she said. "The girls never seem to have needed it. And Dicky is such a baby, and the only boy. Somehow..."

"Oh, my dear," said Mrs. Spears, and she laid her sewing down. "I don't wonder Dicky has these little outbreaks. You don't mind my saying so? But I'm sure you make a great mistake in trying to bring up children without whipping them. Nothing really takes its place. And I speak from experience, my dear. I used to try gentler measures"—Mrs. Spears drew in her breath with a little hissing sound—"soaping the boys' tongues, for instance, with yellow soap, or making them stand on the table for the whole of Saturday afternoon. But no, believe me," said Mrs. Spears, "there is nothing, there is nothing like handing them over to their father."

Mrs. Bendall in her heart of hearts was dreadfully shocked to hear of that yellow soap. But Mrs. Spears seemed to take it so much for granted, that she did too.

"Their father," she said. "Then you don't whip them yourself?"

"Never." Mrs. Spears seemed quite shocked at the idea. "I don't think it's the mother's place to whip the children. It's the duty of the father. And, besides, he impresses them so much more."

"Yes, I can imagine that," said Mrs. Bendall, faintly.

"Now my two boys," Mrs. Spears smiled kindly, encouragingly, at Mrs. Bendall, "would behave just like Dicky if they were not afraid to. As it is..."

"Oh, your boys are perfect little models," cried Mrs. Bendall.

They were. Quieter, better-behaved little boys, in the presence of grown-ups, could not be found. In fact, Mrs. Spears' callers often made the remark that you never would have known that there was a child in the house. There wasn't—very often.

In the front hall, under a large picture of fat, cheery old monks fishing by the riverside, there was a thick, dark horsewhip that had belonged to Mr. Spears' father. And for some reason the boys preferred to play out of sight of this, behind the dog-kennel or in the tool-house, or round about the dustbin.

"It's such a mistake," sighed Mrs. Spears; breathing softly, as she folded her work, "to be weak with children when they are little. It's such a sad mistake, and one so easy to make. It's so unfair to the child. That is what one has to remember. Now Dicky's little escapade this afternoon seemed to me as though he'd done it on purpose. It was the child's way of showing you that he needed a whipping."

"Do you really think so?" Mrs. Bendall was a weak little thing, and this impressed her very much.

"I do; I feel sure of it. And a sharp reminder now and then," cried Mrs. Spears in quite a professional manner, "administered by the father, will save you so much trouble in the future. Believe me, my dear." She put her dry, cold hand over Mrs. Bendall's.

"I shall speak to Edward the moment he comes in," said Dicky's mother firmly.

The children had gone to bed before the garden gate banged, and Dicky's father staggered up the steep concrete steps carrying his bicycle. It had been a bad day at the office. He was hot, dusty, tired out.

But by this time Mrs. Bendall had become quite excited over the new plan, and she opened the door to him herself.

"Oh, Edward, I'm so thankful you have come home," she cried.

"Why, what's happened?" Edward lowered the bicycle and took off his hat. A red angry pucker showed where the brim had pressed. "What's up?"

"Come—come into the drawing-room," said Mrs. Bendall, speaking very fast. "I simply can't tell you how naughty Dicky has been. You have no idea—you can't have at the office all day—how a child of that age can behave. He's been simply dreadful. I have no control over him—none. I've tried everything, Edward, but it's all no use. The only thing to do," she finished breathlessly, "is to whip him—is for you to whip him, Edward."

In the corner of the drawing-room there was a what-not, and on the top shelf stood a brown china bear with a painted tongue. It seemed in the shadow to be grinning at Dicky's father, to be saying, "Hooray, this is what you've come home to!"

"But why on earth should I start whipping him?" said Edward, staring at the bear. "We've never done it before."

"Because," said his wife, "don't you see, it's the only thing to do. I can't control the child..." Her words flew from her lips. They beat round him, beat round his tired head. "We can't possibly afford a nurse. The servant girl has more than enough to do. And his naughtiness is beyond words. You don't understand, Edward; you can't, you're at the office all day."

The bear poked out his tongue. The scolding voice went on. Edward sank into a chair.

"What am I to beat him with?" he said weakly.

"Your slipper, of course," said his wife. And she knelt down to untie his dusty shoes.

"Oh, Edward," she wailed, "you've still got your cycling clips on in the drawing-room. No, really—"

"Here, that's enough," Edward nearly pushed her away. "Give me that slipper." He went up the stairs. He felt like a man in a dark net. And now he wanted to beat Dicky. Yes, damn it, he wanted to beat something. My God, what a life! The dust was still in his hot eyes, his arms felt heavy.

He pushed open the door of Dicky's slip of a room. Dicky was standing in the middle of the floor in his night-shirt. At the sight of him Edward's heart gave a warm throb of rage.

"Well, Dicky, you know what I've come for," said Edward.

Dicky made no reply.

"I've come to give you a whipping."

No answer.

"Lift up your nightshirt."

At that Dicky looked up. He flushed a deep pink. "Must I?" he whispered.

"Come on, now. Be quick about it," said Edward, and, grasping the slipper, he gave Dicky three hard slaps.

"There, that'll teach you to behave properly to your mother."

Dicky stood there, hanging his head.

"Look sharp and get into bed," said his father.

Still he did not move. But a shaking voice said, "I've not done my teeth yet, Daddy."

"Eh, what's that?"

Dicky looked up. His lips were quivering, but his eyes were dry. He hadn't made a sound or shed a tear. Only he swallowed and said, huskily, "I haven't done my teeth, Daddy."

But at the sight of that little face Edward turned, and, not knowing what he was doing, he bolted from the room, down the stairs, and out into the garden. Good God! What had he done? He strode along and hid in the shadow of the pear tree by the hedge. Whipped Dicky—whipped his little man with a slipper—and what the devil for? He didn't even know. Suddenly he barged into his room— and there was the little chap in his nightshirt. Dicky's father groaned and held on to the hedge. And he didn't cry. Never a tear. If only he'd cried or got angry. But that "Daddy"! And again he heard the quivering whisper. Forgiving like that without a word. But he'd never forgive himself—never. Coward! Fool! Brute! And suddenly he remembered the time when Dicky had fallen off his knee and sprained his wrist while they were playing together. He hadn't cried then, either. And that was the little hero he had just whipped.

Something's got to be done about this, thought Edward. He strode back to the house, up the stairs, into Dicky's room. The little boy was lying in bed. In the half light his dark head, with the square fringe, showed plain against the pale pillow. He was lying quite still, and even now he wasn't crying. Edward shut the door and leaned against it. What he wanted to do was to kneel down by Dicky's bed and cry himself and beg to be forgiven. But, of course, one can't do that sort of thing. He felt awkward, and his heart was wrung.

"Not asleep yet, Dicky?" he said lightly.

"No, Daddy."

Edward came over and sat on his boy's bed, and Dicky looked at him through his long lashes.

"Nothing the matter, little chap, is there?" said Edward, half whispering.

"No-o, Daddy," came from Dicky.

Edward put out his hand, and carefully he took Dicky's hot little paw.

"You—you mustn't think any more of what happened just now, little man," he said huskily. "See? That's all over now. That's forgotten. That's never going to happen again. See?"

"Yes, Daddy."

"So the thing to do now is to buck up, little chap," said Edward, "and to smile." And he tried himself an extraordinary trembling apology for a smile. "To forget all about it—to—eh? Little man... Old boy..."

Dicky lay as before. This was terrible. Dicky's father sprang up and went over to the window. It was nearly dark in the garden. The servant girl had run out, and she was snatching, twitching some white clothes off the bushes and piling them over her arm. But in the boundless sky the evening star shone, and a big gum tree, black against the pale glow, moved its long leaves softly. All this he saw, while he felt in his trouser pocket for his money. Bringing it out, he chose a new sixpence and went back to Dicky.

"Here you are, little chap. Buy yourself something," said Edward softly, laying the sixpence on Dicky's pillow.

But could even that—could even a whole sixpence—blot out what had been?

POISON

The post was very late. When we came back from our walk after lunch it still had not arrived.

"Pas encore, Madame," sang Annette, scurrying back to her cooking.

We carried our parcels into the dining-room. The table was laid. As always, the sight of the table laid for two—for two people only—and yet so finished, so perfect, there was no possible room for a third, gave me a queer, quick thrill as though I'd been struck by that silver lightning that quivered over the white cloth, the brilliant glasses, the shallow bowl of freezias.

"Blow the old postman! Whatever can have happened to him?" said Beatrice. "Put those things down, dearest."

"Where would you like them...?"

She raised her head; she smiled her sweet, teasing smile.

"Anywhere—Silly."

But I knew only too well that there was no such place for her, and I would have stood holding the squat liqueur bottle and the sweets for months, for years, rather than risk giving another tiny shock to her exquisite sense of order.

"Here—I'll take them." She plumped them down on the table with her long gloves and a basket of figs. "The Luncheon Table. Short story by—by—" She took my arm. "Let's go on to the terrace—" and I felt her shiver. "Ça sent," she said faintly, "de la cuisine..."

I had noticed lately—we had been living in the south for two months—that when she wished to speak of food, or the climate, or, playfully, of her love for me, she always dropped into French.

We perched on the balustrade under the awning. Beatrice leaned over gazing down—down to the white road with its guard of cactus spears. The beauty of her ear, just her ear, the marvel of it was so great that I could have turned from regarding it to all that sweep of glittering sea below and stammered: "You know—her ear! She has ears that are simply the most..."

She was dressed in white, with pearls round her throat and lilies-of-the-valley tucked into her belt. On the third finger of her left hand she wore one pearl ring—no wedding ring.

"Why should I, mon ami? Why should we pretend? Who could possibly care?"

And of course I agreed, though privately, in the depths of my heart, I would have given my soul to have stood beside her in a large, yes, a large, fashionable church, crammed with people, with old reverend clergymen, with The Voice that breathed o'er Eden, with palms and the smell of scent, knowing there was a red carpet and confetti outside, and somewhere, a wedding-cake and champagne and a satin shoe to throw after the carriage—if I could have slipped our wedding-ring on to her finger.

Not because I cared for such horrible shows, but because I felt it might possibly perhaps lessen this ghastly feeling of absolute freedom, her absolute freedom, of course.

Oh, God! What torture happiness was—what anguish! I looked up at the villa, at the windows of our room hidden so mysteriously behind the green straw blinds. Was it possible that she ever came moving through the green light and smiling that secret smile, that languid, brilliant smile that was just for me? She put her arm round my neck; the other hand softly, terribly, brushed back my hair.

"Who are you?" Who was she? She was—Woman.

... On the first warm evening in Spring, when lights shone like pearls through the lilac air and voices murmured in the fresh-flowering gardens, it was she who sang in the tall house with the tulle curtains. As one drove in the moonlight through the foreign city hers was the shadow that fell across the quivering gold of the shutters. When the lamp was lighted, in the new-born stillness her steps passed your door. And she looked out into the autumn twilight, pale in her furs, as the automobile swept by...

In fact, to put it shortly, I was twenty-four at the time. And when she lay on her back, with the pearls slipped under her chin, and sighed "I'm thirsty, dearest. Donne-moi un orange," I would gladly, willingly, have dived for an orange into the jaws of a crocodile—if crocodiles ate oranges.

"Had I two little feathery wings   And were a little feathery bird..."

sang Beatrice.

I seized her hand. "You wouldn't fly away?"

"Not far. Not further than the bottom of the road."

"Why on earth there?"

She quoted: "He cometh not, she said..."

"Who? The silly old postman? But you're not expecting a letter."

"No, but it's maddening all the same. Ah!" Suddenly she laughed and leaned against me. "There he is—look—like a blue beetle."

And we pressed our cheeks together and watched the blue beetle beginning to climb.

"Dearest," breathed Beatrice. And the word seemed to linger in the air, to throb in the air like the note of a violin.

"What is it?"

"I don't know," she laughed softly. "A wave of—a wave of affection, I suppose."

I put my arm round her. "Then you wouldn't fly away?"

And she said rapidly and softly: "No! No! Not for worlds. Not really. I love this place. I've loved being here. I could stay here for years, I believe. I've never been so happy as I have these last two months, and you've been so perfect to me, dearest, in every way."

This was such bliss—it was so extraordinary, so unprecedented, to hear her talk like this that I had to try to laugh it off.

"Don't! You sound as if you were saying good-bye."

"Oh, nonsense, nonsense. You mustn't say such things even in fun!" She slid her little hand under my white jacket and clutched my shoulder. "You've been happy, haven't you?"

"Happy? Happy? Oh, God—if you knew what I feel at this moment... Happy! My Wonder! My Joy!"

I dropped off the balustrade and embraced her, lifting her in my arms. And while I held her lifted I pressed my face in her breast and muttered: "You are mine?" And for the first time in all the desperate months I'd known her, even counting the last month of—surely—Heaven—I believed her absolutely when she answered:

"Yes, I am yours."

The creak of the gate and the postman's steps on the gravel drew us apart. I was dizzy for the moment. I simply stood there, smiling, I felt, rather stupidly. Beatrice walked over to the cane chairs.

"You go—go for the letters," said she.

I—well—I almost reeled away. But I was too late. Annette came running. "Pas de lettres" said she.

My reckless smile in reply as she handed me the paper must have surprised her. I was wild with joy. I threw the paper up into the air and sang out:

"No letters, darling!" as I came over to where the beloved woman was lying in the long chair.

For a moment she did not reply. Then she said slowly as she tore off the newspaper wrapper: "The world forgetting, by the world forgot."

There are times when a cigarette is just the very one thing that will carry you over the moment. It is more than a confederate, even; it is a secret, perfect little friend who knows all about it and understands absolutely. While you smoke you look down at it—smile or frown, as the occasion demands; you inhale deeply and expel the smoke in a slow fan. This was one of those moments. I walked over to the magnolia and breathed my fill of it. Then I came back and leaned over her shoulder. But quickly she tossed the paper away on to the stone.

"There's nothing in it," said she. "Nothing. There's only some poison trial. Either some man did or didn't murder his wife, and twenty thousand people have sat in court every day and two million words have been wired all over the world after each proceeding."

"Silly world!" said I, flinging into another chair. I wanted to forget the paper, to return, but cautiously, of course, to that moment before the postman came. But when she answered I knew from her voice the moment was over for now. Never mind. I was content to wait—five hundred years, if need be—now that I knew.

"Not so very silly," said Beatrice. "After all it isn't only morbid curiosity on the part of the twenty thousand."

"What is it, darling?" Heavens knows I didn't care.

"Guilt!" she cried. "Guilt! Didn't you realise that? They're fascinated like sick people are fascinated by anything—any scrap of news about their own case. The man in the dock may be innocent enough, but the people in court are nearly all of them poisoners. Haven't you ever thought"—she was pale with excitement—"of the amount of poisoning that goes on? It's the exception to find married people who don't poison each other—married people and lovers. Oh," she cried, "the number of cups of tea, glasses of wine, cups of coffee that are just tainted. The number I've had myself, and drunk, either knowing or not knowing—and risked it. The only reason why so many couples"—she laughed—"survive, is because the one is frightened of giving the other the fatal dose. That dose takes nerve! But it's bound to come sooner or later. There's no going back once the first little dose has been given. It's the beginning of the end, really—don't you agree? Don't you see what I mean?"

She didn't wait for me to answer. She unpinned the lilies-of-the-valley and lay back, drawing them across her eyes.

"Both my husbands poisoned me," said Beatrice. "My first husband gave me a huge dose almost immediately, but my second was really an artist in his way. Just a tiny pinch, now and again, cleverly disguised—Oh, so cleverly!—until one morning I woke up and in every single particle of me, to the ends of my fingers and toes, there was a tiny grain. I was just in time..."

I hated to hear her mention her husbands so calmly, especially today. It hurt. I was going to speak, but suddenly she cried mournfully:

"Why! Why should it have happened to me? What have I done? Why have I been all my life singled out by... It's a conspiracy."

I tried to tell her it was because she was too perfect for this horrible world—too exquisite, too fine. It frightened people. I made a little joke.

"But I—I haven't tried to poison you."

Beatrice gave a queer small laugh and bit the end of a lily stem.

"You!" said she. "You wouldn't hurt a fly!"

Strange. That hurt, though. Most horribly.

Just then Annette ran out with our apéritifs. Beatrice leaned forward and took a glass from the tray and handed it to me. I noticed the gleam of the pearl on what I called her pearl finger. How could I be hurt at what she said?

"And you," I said, taking the glass, "you've never poisoned anybody."

That gave me an idea; I tried to explain.

"You—you do just the opposite. What is the name for one like you who, instead of poisoning people, fills them—everybody, the postman, the man who drives us, our boatman, the flower-seller, me— with new life, with something of her own radiance, her beauty, her—"

Dreamily she smiled; dreamily she looked at me.

"What are you thinking of—my lovely darling?"

"I was wondering," she said, "whether, after lunch, you'd go down to the post-office and ask for the afternoon letters. Would you mind, dearest? Not that I'm expecting one—but—I just thought, perhaps—it's silly not to have the letters if they're there. Isn't it? Silly to wait till tomorrow." She twirled the stem of the glass in her fingers. Her beautiful head was bent. But I lifted my glass and drank, sipped rather—sipped slowly, deliberately, looking at that dark head and thinking of— postmen and blue beetles and farewells that were not farewells and...

Good God! Was it fancy? No, it wasn't fancy. The drink tasted chill, bitter, queer.

"Y'are very snug in here," piped old Mr. Woodifield, and he peered out of the great, green-leather armchair by his friend the boss's desk as a baby peers out of its pram. His talk was over; it was time for him to be off. But he did not want to go. Since he had retired, since his…stroke, the wife and the girls kept him boxed up in the house every day of the week except Tuesday. On Tuesday he was dressed and brushed and allowed to cut back to the City for the day. Though what he did there the wife and girls couldn't imagine. Made a nuisance of himself to his friends, they supposed.… Well, perhaps so. All the same, we cling to our last pleasures as the tree clings to its last leaves. So there sat old Woodifield, smoking a cigar and staring almost greedily at the boss, who rolled in his office chair, stout, rosy, five years older than he, and still going strong, still at the helm. It did one good to see him.

Wistfully, admiringly, the old voice added, "It's snug in here, upon my word!"

"Yes, it's comfortable enough," agreed the boss, and he flipped the *Financial Times* with a paper-knife. As a matter of fact he was proud of his room; he liked to have it admired, especially by old Woodifield. It gave him a feeling of deep, solid satisfaction to be planted there in the midst of it in full view of that frail old figure in the muffler.

"I've had it done up lately," he explained, as he had explained for the past—how many?—weeks. "New carpet," and he pointed to the bright red carpet with a pattern of large white rings. "New furniture," and he nodded towards the massive bookcase and the table with legs like twisted treacle. "Electric heating!" He waved almost exultantly towards the five transparent, pearly sausages glowing so softly in the tilted copper pan.

But he did not draw old Woodifield's attention to the photograph over the table of a grave-looking boy in uniform standing in one of those spectral photographers' parks with photographers' storm-clouds behind him. It was not new. It had been there for over six years.

"There was something I wanted to tell you," said old Woodifield, and his eyes grew dim remembering. "Now what was it? I had it in my mind when I started out this morning." His hands began to tremble, and patches of red showed above his beard.

Poor old chap, he's on his last pins, thought the boss. And, feeling kindly, he winked at the old man, and said jokingly, "I tell you what. I've got a little drop of something here that'll do you good before you go out into the cold again. It's beautiful stuff. It wouldn't hurt a child." He took a key off his watch-chain, unlocked a cupboard below his desk, and drew forth a dark, squat bottle. "That's the medicine," said he. "And the man from whom I got it told me on the strict Q.T. it came from the cellars at Windor Castle."

Old Woodifield's mouth fell open at the sight. He couldn't have looked more surprised if the boss had produced a rabbit.

"It's whisky, ain't it?" he piped feebly.

The boss turned the bottle and lovingly showed him the label. Whisky it was.

"D'you know," said he, peering up at the boss wonderingly, "they won't let me touch it at home." And he looked as though he was going to cry.

"Ah, that's where we know a bit more than the ladies," cried the boss, swooping across for two tumblers that stood on the table with the water-bottle, and pouring a generous finger into each. "Drink it down. It'll do you good. And don't put any water with it. It's sacrilege to tamper with stuff like this. Ah!" He tossed off his, pulled out his handkerchief, hastily wiped his moustaches, and cocked an eye at old Woodifield, who was rolling his in his chaps.

The old man swallowed, was silent a moment, and then said faintly, "It's nutty!"

But it warmed him; it crept into his chill old brain—he remembered.

"That was it," he said, heaving himself out of his chair. "I thought you'd like to know. The girls were in Belgium last week having a look at poor Reggie's grave, and they happened to come across your boy's. They're quite near each other, it seems."

Old Woodifield paused, but the boss made no reply. Only a quiver in his eyelids showed that he heard.

"The girls were delighted with the way the place is kept," piped the old voice. "Beautifully looked after. Couldn't be better if they were at home. You've not been across, have yer?"

"No, no!" For various reasons the boss had not been across.

"There's miles of it," quavered old Woodifield, "and it's all as neat as a garden. Flowers growing on all the graves. Nice broad paths." It was plain from his voice how much he liked a nice broad path.

The pause came again. Then the old man brightened wonderfully.

"D'you know what the hotel made the girls pay for a pot of jam?" he piped. "Ten francs! Robbery, I call it. It was a little pot, so Gertrude says, no bigger than a half-crown. And she hadn't taken more than a spoonful when they charged her ten francs. Gertrude brought the pot away with her to teach 'em a lesson. Quite right, too; it's trading on our feelings. They think because we're over there having a look round we're ready to pay anything. That's what it is." And he turned towards the door.

"Quite right, quite right!" cried the boss, though what was quite right he hadn't the least idea. He came round by his desk, followed the shuffling footsteps to the door, and saw the old fellow out. Woodifield was gone.

For a long moment the boss stayed, staring at nothing, while the grey-haired office messenger, watching him, dodged in and out of his cubby-hole like a dog that expects to be taken for a run. Then: "I'll see nobody for half an hour, Macey," said the boss. "Understand? Nobody at all."

"Very good, sir."

The door shut, the firm heavy steps recrossed the bright carpet, the fat body plumped down in the spring chair, and leaning forward, the boss covered his face with his hands. He wanted, he intended, he had arranged to weep.…

It had been a terrible shock to him when old Woodifield sprang that remark upon him about the boy's grave. It was exactly as though the earth had opened and he had seen the boy lying there with Woodifield's girls staring down at him. For it was strange. Although over six years had passed away, the boss never thought of the boy except as lying unchanged, unblemished in his uniform, asleep for ever. "My son!" groaned the boss. But no tears came yet. In the past, in the first few months and even years after the boy's death, he had only to say those words to be overcome by such grief that nothing short of a violent fit of weeping could relieve him. Time, he had declared then, he had told everybody, could make no difference. Other men perhaps might recover, might live their loss down, but not he. How was it possible? His boy was an only son. Ever since his birth the boss had worked at building up this business for him; it had no other meaning if it was not for the boy. Life itself had come to have no other meaning. How on earth could he have slaved, denied himself, kept going all those years without the promise for ever before him of the boy's stepping into his shoes and carrying on where he left off?

And that promise had been so near being fulfilled. The boy had been in the office learning the ropes for a year before the war. Every morning they had started off together; they had come back by the same train. And what congratulations he had received as the boy's father! No wonder; he had taken to it marvellously. As to his popularity with the staff, every man jack of them down to old Macey couldn't make enough of the boy. And he wasn't the least spoilt. No, he was just his bright natural self, with the right word for everybody, with that boyish look and his habit of saying, "Simply splendid!"

But all that was over and done with as though it never had been. The day had come when Macey had handed him the telegram that brought the whole place crashing about his head. "Deeply regret to inform you..." And he had left the office a broken man, with his life in ruins.

Six years ago, six years.... How quickly time passed! It might have happened yesterday. The boss took his hands from his face; he was puzzled. Something seemed to be wrong with him. He wasn't feeling as he wanted to feel. He decided to get up and have a look at the boy's photograph. But it wasn't a favourite photograph of his; the expression was unnatural. It was cold, even stern-looking. The boy had never looked like that.

At that moment the boss noticed that a fly had fallen into his broad inkpot, and was trying feebly but deperately to clamber out again. Help! help! said those struggling legs. But the sides of the inkpot were wet and slippery; it fell back again and began to swim. The boss took up a pen, picked the fly out of the ink, and shook it on to a piece of blotting-paper. For a fraction of a second it lay still on the dark patch that oozed round it. Then the front legs waved, took hold, and, pulling its small, sodden body up, it began the immense task of cleaning the ink from its wings. Over and under, over and under, went a leg along a wing, as the stone goes over and under the scythe. Then there was a pause, while the fly, seeming to stand on the tips of its toes, tried to expand first one wing and then the other. It succeeded at last, and, sitting down, it began, like a minute cat, to clean its face. Now one could imagine that the little front legs rubbed against each other lightly, joyfully. The horrible danger was over; it had escaped; it was ready for life again.

But just then the boss had an idea. He plunged his pen back into the ink, leaned his thick wrist on the blotting-paper, and as the fly tried its wings down came a great heavy blot. What would it make of that? What indeed! The little beggar seemed absolutely cowed, stunned, and afraid to move because of what would happen next. But then, as if painfully, it dragged itself forward. The front legs waved, caught hold, and, more slowly this time, the task began from the beginning.

He's a plucky little devil, thought the boss, and he felt a real admiration for the fly's courage. That was the way to tackle things; that was the right spirit. Never say die; it was only a question of... But the fly had again finished its laborious task, and the boss had just time to refill his pen, to shake fair and square on the new-cleaned body yet another dark drop. What about it this time? A painful moment of suspense followed. But behold, the front legs were again waving; the boss felt a rush of relief. He leaned over the fly and said to it tenderly, "You artful little b..." And he actually had the brilliant notion of breathing on it to help the drying process. All the same, there was something timid and weak about its efforts now, and the boss decided that this time should be the last, as he dipped the pen deep into the inkpot.

It was. The last blot fell on the soaked blotting-paper, and the draggled fly lay in it and did not stir. The back legs were stuck to the body; the front legs were not to be seen.

"Come on," said the boss. "Look sharp!" And he stirred it with his pen—in vain. Nothing happened or was likely to happen. The fly was dead.

The boss lifted the corpse on the end of the paper-knife and flung it into the waste-paper basket. But such a grinding feeling of wretchedness seized him that he felt positively frightened. He started forward and pressed the bell for Macey.

"Bring me some fresh blotting-paper," he said sternly,"and look sharp about it." And while the old dog padded away he fell to wondering what it was he had been thinking about before. What was it? It was... He took out his handkerchief and passed it inside his collar. For the life of him he could not remember.

A CUP OF TEA

Rosemary Fell was not exactly beautiful. No, you couldn't have called her beautiful. Pretty? Well, if you took her to pieces... But why be so cruel as to take anyone to pieces? She was young, brilliant, extremely modem, exquisitely well dressed, amazingly well read in the newest of the new books, and her parties were the most delicious mixture of the really important people and... artists—quaint creatures, discoveries of hers, some of them too terrifying for words, but others quite presentable and amusing.

Rosemary had been married two years. She had a duck of a boy. No, not Peter—Michael. And her husband absolutely adored her. They were rich, really rich, not just comfortably well off, which is odious and stuffy and sounds like one's grandparents. But if Rosemary wanted to shop she would go to Paris as you and I would go toBond Street. If she wanted to buy flowers, the car pulled up at that perfect shop in Regent Street, and Rosemary inside the shop just gazed in her dazzled, rather exotic way, and said: "I want those and those and those. Give me four bunches of those. And that jar of roses. Yes, I'll have all the roses in the jar. No, no lilac. I hate lilac. It's got no shape." The attendant bowed and put the lilac out of sight, as though this was only too true; lilac was dreadfully shapeless. "Give me those stumpy little tulips. Those red and white ones." And she was followed to the car by a thin shop-girl staggering under an immense white paper armful that looked like a baby in long clothes....

One winter afternoon she had been buying something in a little antique shop inCurzon Street. It was a shop she liked. For one thing, one usually had it to oneself. And then the man who kept it was ridiculously fond of serving her. He beamed whenever she came in. He clasped his hands; he was so gratified he could scarcely speak. Flattery, of course. All the same, there was something...

"You see, madam," he would explain in his low respectful tones, "I love my things. I would rather not part with them than sell them to someone who does not appreciate them, who has not that fine feeling which is so rare..." And, breathing deeply, he unrolled a tiny square of blue velvet and pressed it on the glass counter with his pale fingertips.

Today it was a little box. He had been keeping it for her. He had shown it to nobody as yet. An exquisite little enamel box with a glaze so fine it looked as though it had been baked in cream. On the lid a minute creature stood under a flowery tree, and a more minute creature still had her arms round his neck. Her hat, really no bigger than a geranium petal, hung from a branch; it had green ribbons. And there was a pink cloud like a watchful cherub floating above their heads. Rosemary took her hands out of her long gloves. She always took off her gloves to examine such things. Yes, she liked it very much. She loved it; it was a great duck. She must have it. And, turning the creamy box, opening and shutting it, she couldn't help noticing how charming her hands were against the blue velvet. The shopman, in some dim cavern of his mind, may have dared to think so too. For he took a pencil, leant over the counter, and his pale, bloodless fingers crept timidly towards those rosy, flashing ones, as he murmured gently: "If I may venture to point out to madam, the flowers on the little lady's bodice."

"Charming!" Rosemary admired the flowers. But what was the price? For a moment the shopman did not seem to hear. Then a murmur reached her. "Twenty-eight guineas, madam."

"Twenty-eight guineas." Rosemary gave no sign. She laid the little box down; she buttoned her gloves again. Twenty-eight guineas. Even if one is rich... She looked vague. She stared at a plump tea-kettle like a plump hen above the shopman's head, and her voice was dreamy as she answered: "Well, keep it for me—will you? I'll..."

But the shopman had already bowed as though keeping it for her was all any human being could ask. He would be willing, of course, to keep it for her for ever.

The discreet door shut with a click. She was outside on the step, gazing at the winter afternoon. Rain was falling, and with the rain it seemed the dark came too, spinning down like ashes. There was a cold bitter taste in the air, and the new-lighted lamps looked sad. Sad were the lights in the houses opposite. Dimly they burned as if regretting something. And people hurried by, hidden under their hateful umbrellas. Rosemary felt a strange pang. She pressed her muff against her breast; she wished she had the little box, too, to cling to. Of course the car was there. She'd only to cross the pavement. But still she waited. There are moments, horrible moments in life, when one emerges from shelter and looks out, and it's awful. One oughtn't to give way to them. One ought to go home and have an extra-special tea. But at the very instant of thinking that, a young girl, thin, dark, shadowy—where had she come from?—was standing at Rosemary's elbow and a voice like a sigh, almost like a sob, breathed: "Madam, may I speak to you a moment?"

"Speak to me?" Rosemary turned. She saw a little battered creature with enormous eyes, someone quite young, no older than herself, who clutched at her coat-collar with reddened hands, and shivered as though she had just come out of the water.

"M-madam, stammered the voice. Would you let me have the price of a cup of tea?"

"A cup of tea?" There was something simple, sincere in that voice; it wasn't in the least the voice of a beggar. "Then have you no money at all?" asked Rosemary.

"None, madam," came the answer.

"How extraordinary!" Rosemary peered through the dusk and the girl gazed back at her. How more than extraordinary! And suddenly it seemed to Rosemary such an adventure. It was like something out of a novel by Dostoevsky, this meeting in the dusk. Supposing she took the girl home? Supposing she did do one of those things she was always reading about or seeing on the stage, what would happen? It would be thrilling. And she heard herself saying afterwards to the amazement of her friends: "I simply took her home with me," as she stepped forward and said to that dim person beside her: "Come home to tea with me."

The girl drew back startled. She even stopped shivering for a moment. Rosemary put out a hand and touched her arm. "I mean it," she said, smiling. And she felt how simple and kind her smile was. "Why won't you? Do. Come home with me now in my car and have tea."

"You—you don't mean it, madam," said the girl, and there was pain in her voice.

"But I do," cried Rosemary. "I want you to. To please me. Come along."

The girl put her fingers to her lips and her eyes devoured Rosemary. "You're—you're not taking me to the police station?" she stammered.

"The police station!" Rosemary laughed out. "Why should I be so cruel? No, I only want to make you warm and to hear—anything you care to tell me."

Hungry people are easily led. The footman held the door of the car open, and a moment later they were skimming through the dusk.

"There!" said Rosemary. She had a feeling of triumph as she slipped her hand through the velvet strap. She could have said, "Now I've got you," as she gazed at the little captive she had netted. But of course she meant it kindly. Oh, more than kindly. She was going to prove to this girl that— wonderful things did happen in life, that—fairy godmothers were real, that—rich people had hearts, and that women were sisters. She turned impulsively, saying'. "Don't be frightened. After all, why shouldn't you come back with me? We're both women. If I'm the more fortunate, you ought to expect..."

But happily at that moment, for she didn't know how the sentence was going to end, the car stopped. The bell was rung, the door opened, and with a charming, protecting, almost embracing movement, Rosemary drew the other into the hall. Warmth, softness, light, a sweet scent, all those things so familiar to her she never even thought about them, she watched that other receive. It was fascinating. She was like the rich little girl in her nursery with all the cupboards to open, all the boxes to unpack.

"Come, come upstairs," said Rosemary, longing to begin to be generous. "Come up to my room." And, besides, she wanted to spare this poor little thing from being stared at by the servants; she decided as they mounted the stairs she would not even ring to Jeanne, but take off her things by herself. The great things were to be natural!

And "There!" cried Rosemary again, as they reached her beautiful big bedroom with the curtains drawn, the fire leaping on her wonderful lacquer furniture, her gold cushions and the primrose and blue rugs.

The girl stood just inside the door; she seemed dazed. But Rosemary didn't mind that.

"Come and sit down," she cried, dragging her big chair up to the fire, "m this comfy chair. Come and get warm. You look so dreadfully cold."

"I daren't, madam," said the girl, and she edged backwards.

"Oh, please,"—Rosemary ran forward—"you mustn't be frightened, you mustn't, really. Sit down, when I've taken off my things we shall go into the next room and have tea and be cozy. Why are you afraid?" And gently she half pushed the thin figure into its deep cradle.

But there was no answer. The girl stayed just as she had been put, with her hands by her sides and her mouth slightly open. To be quite sincere, she looked rather stupid. But Rosemary wouldn't acknowledge it. She leant over her, saying:

"Won't you take off your hat? Your pretty hair is all wet. And one is so much more comfortable without a hat, isn't one?"

There was a whisper that sounded like "Very good, madam," and the crushed hat was taken off.

"And let me help you off with your coat, too," said Rosemary.

The girl stood up. But she held on to the chair with one hand and let Rosemary pull. It was quite an effort. The other scarcely helped her at all. She seemed to stagger like a child, and the thought came and went through Rosemary's mind, that if people wanted helping they must respond a little, just a little, otherwise it became very difficult indeed. And what was she to do with the coat now? She left it on the floor, and the hat too. She was just going to take a cigarette off the mantelpiece when the girl said quickly, but so lightly and strangely: "I'm very sorry, madam, but I'm going to faint. I shall go off, madam, if I don't have something."

"Good heavens, how thoughtless I am!" Rosemary rushed to the bell.

"Tea! Tea at once! And some brandy immediately!"

The maid was gone again, but the girl almost cried out: "No, I don't want no brandy.* I never drink brandy. It's a cup of tea I want, madam." And she burst into tears.

It was a terrible and fascinating moment. Rosemary knelt beside her chair.

"Don't cry, poor little thing," she said. "Don't cry." And she gave the other her lace handkerchief. She really was touched beyond words. She put her arm round those thin, bird-like shoulders.

Now at last the other forgot to be shy, forgot everything except that they were both women, and gasped out: "I can't go on no longer like this. I can't bear it. I can't bear it. I shall do away with myself. I can't bear no more."

"You shan't have to. I'll look after you. Don't cry any more. Don't you see what a good thing it was that you met me? We'll have tea and you'll tell me everything. And I shall arrange something. I promise. Do stop crying. It's so exhausting. Please!"

The other did stop just in time for Rosemary to get up before the tea came. She had the table placed between them. She plied the poor little creature with everything, all the sandwiches, all the bread and butter, and every time her cup was empty she filled it with tea, cream and sugar. People always said sugar was so nourishing. As for herself she didn't eat; she smoked and looked away tactfully so that the other should not be shy.

And really the effect of that slight meal was marvelous. When the tea-table was carried away a new being, a light, frail creature with tangled hair, dark lips, deep, lighted eyes, lay back in the big chair in a kind of sweet languor, looking at the blaze. Rosemary lit a fresh cigarette; it was time to begin.

"And when did you have your last meal?" she asked softly.

But at that moment the door-handle turned.

"Rosemary, may I come in?" It was Philip.

"Of course."

He came in. "Oh, I'm so sorry," he said, and stopped and stared.

"It's quite all right," said Rosemary, smiling. "This is my friend, Miss _"

"Smith, madam," said the languid figure, who was strangely still and unafraid.

"Smith," said Rosemary. "We are going to have a little talk."

"Oh yes," said Philip. "Quite," and his eye caught sight of the coat and hat on the floor. He came over to the fire and turned his back to it. "It's a beastly afternoon," he said curiously, still looking at that listless figure, looking at its hands and boots, and then at Rosemary again.

"Yes, isn't it?" said Rosemary enthusiastically. "Vile."

Philip smiled his charming smile. "As a matter of fact," said he, "I wanted you to come into the library for a moment. Would you? Will Miss Smith excuse us?"

The big eyes were raised to him, but Rosemary answered for her: "Of course she will." And they went out of the room together.

"I say," said Philip, when they were alone. "Explain. Who is she? What does it all mean?"

Rosemary, laughing, leaned against the door and said: "I picked her up inCurzon Street. Really. She's a real pick-up. She asked me for the price of a cup of tea, and I brought her home withme."

"But what on earth are you going to do with her?" cried Philip.

"Be nice to her," said Rosemary quickly. "Be frightfully nice to her. Look after her. I don't know how. We haven't talked yet. But show her—treat her—make her feel—"

"My darling girl," said Philip, "you're quite mad, you know. It simply can't be done."

"I knew you'd say that," retorted Rosemary. Why not? I want to. Isn't that a reason? And besides, one's always reading about these things. I decided—"

"But," said Philip slowly, and he cut the end of a cigar, "she's so astonishingly pretty."

"Pretty?" Rosemary was so surprised that she blushed. "Do you think so? I—I hadn't thought about it."

"Good Lord!" Philip struck a match. "She's absolutely lovely. Look again, my child. I was bowled over when I came into your room just now. However... I think you're making a ghastly mistake. Sorry, darling, if I'm crude and all that. But let me know if Miss Smith is going to dine with us in time for me to look up The Milliner's Gazette."

"You absurd creature!" said Rosemary, and she went out of the library, but not back to her bedroom. She went to her writing-room and sat down at her desk. Pretty! Absolutely lovely! Bowled over! Her heart beat like a heavy bell. Pretty! Lovely! She drew her check-book towards her. But no, checks would be no use, of course. She opened a drawer and took out five pound notes, looked at them, put two back, and holding the three squeezed in her hand, she went back to her bedroom.

Half an hour later Philip was still in the library, when Rosemary came in.

"I only wanted to tell you," said she, and she leaned against the door again and looked at him with her dazzled exotic gaze, "Miss Smith won't dine with us tonight."

Philip put down the paper. "Oh, what's happened? Previous engagement?"

Rosemary came over and sat down on his knee. "She insisted on going," said she, "so I gave the poor little thing a present of money. I couldn't keep her against her will, could I?" she added softly.

Rosemary had just done her hair, darkened her eyes a little and put on her pearls. She put up her hands and touched Philip's cheeks.

"Do you like me?" said she, and her tone, sweet, husky, troubled him.

"I like you awfully," he said, and he held her tighter. "Kiss me."

There was a pause.

Then Rosemary said dreamily: "I saw a fascinating little box today. It cost twenty-eight guineas. May I have it?"

Philip jumped her on his knee. "You may, little wasteful one," said he.

But that was not really what Rosemary wanted to say.

"Philip," she whispered, and she pressed his head against her bosom, "am I pretty?"

Katherine Mansfield – A Short Biography

New Zealand in the 1880s was a politically turbulent, progressive environment. Despite the normality of masculine dominance, there was an uprising of strength of mind and independence of character amongst various middle class women who were employed by progressively minded newspapers and journals who, bolstered by their own success, formed the incubative literary environment into which Katherine Mansfield Beauchamp was born, on 14th October 1888. Prominent female and feminist writers such as Mary Taylor, Mary Colclough (who utilised the ironically derogatory pseudonym Polly Plum) and Ellen Ellis had established a formative and politicised collective female literary and critical identity which would find its first recognition as part of the now-famous Contagious Diseases Prevention Act.

Her family, based in Wellington, were socially prominent, her father being a middle-class colonial banker while she was the cousin of Countess Elizabeth von Arnim, the Australian-born British novelist. She had three sisters, two elder and one younger, and a younger brother. Harold Beauchamp, her father, would become the chairman of the Bank of New Zealand, receiving a knighthood for his services to crown and country, and her grandfather, Arthur Beauchamp, had briefly represented the parliamentary electorate of Picton in Parliament. The family moved between suburbs in Wellington, beginning in Thorndon and arriving in Karori in 1893, where Mansfield spoke of "the happiest years of [her] childhood". During this time she attended various schools in each district, displaying literary and musical talent beyond that which was expected of girls her age. It was during her time at the Wellington Girls' High School that her first published stories appeared in the High School Reporter, in 1898 and 1899. Her musical talents found their outlet in the 'cello, and in 1902 she found herself enamoured by fellow 'cellist Arnold Trowell, from whose father she received 'cello lessons, though she would find her infatuation largely unreciprocated by the young Trowell. This rejection, combined with a wider social awareness of the difference between the colonising, ex-patriot community to which she belonged and to the indigenous Māori people, led to a humanist approach to race difference and a positive portrayal of those ethnic minorities, who often found themselves portrayed in favourable light in her stories. A prime example of this can be found in How Pearl Button Was Kidnapped, the 1912 modernist story in which a child, taken into Māori culture at birth, is later alienated and affrighted by the white men who come to 'liberate' her from the Māori who had previously taken her in and looked after her.

Having moved to London in 1903 she and her sisters attended Queen's College, where she resumed her 'cello playing, expecting to take the talent to a professional level, though her contributions to the school newspaper and subsequent dedication to the same eventually led her to become editor, proving key as an indication of the path her career would take. During this period she found interest in the work of the French symbolists and Oscar Wilde, and the vivacious charisma she exhibited in her approach to life and work saw her appreciated and respected by her peers. While in London, and despite her prominent position as editor of the Queen's College paper, she did not actively pursue politics, either as a reader, writer or an activist. Most surprisingly is that, despite the women of New Zealand being granted the right to vote in 1893, she did not follow the suffragette movement in the UK, indicating a level of detachment from or apathy towards the wider social and political issues which dominated the nation at that time.

During her residence at Queen's College, she spent some time travelling in continental Europe, particularly to Belgium and Germany in between 1903 and 1906. By 1906 she had finished her stint of schooling at Queen's College and returned to her home in New Zealand in 1906, which marked the beginning of her endeavours in short stories proper. The Australian journal Native Companion published several of her works, which were to be the first of many of which she was paid, and it was this critical interest and public success which cemented her decision to become a full-time writer. These instances of publication are the first recorded examples of her using the pseudonym K. Mansfield. Despite her success here and the abundance of life upon which to comment and record, having been exposed to the hustle and bustle of London, she soon tired of the provincial New Zealand lifestyle and resolved to return to London, finally heading back two years later in 1908. Her father, though saddened by the absence of his daughter, sent her an annuity of £100 for the remainder of her life. The hustle and bustle which she so missed found itself to some extent manifest in the two, openly recorded, lesbian relationships she had on returning to London. These were quite comfortably recorded in her journals, and this period has been described as evidence of her "transgressive impetus". Nevertheless, she continued to sustain male lovers, even attempting to repress her feelings towards women at certain times. The picture of confidence which she portrayed in her journals and in society, then, was not always supported by her emotional security behind closed doors. The first of these relationships was with Maata Mahupuku, a young Māori woman whom Mansfield had met first in Wellington and then again coincidentally in London. Writing particularly candidly in 1907, she announced "I want Maata - I want her as I have had her - terribly. This is unclean I know but true". The second of these relationships, with Edith Kathleen Bendall, lasted between 1906 to 1908, and Mansfield was equally adoring, lustful and open in her journals.

Now back in London, she found herself swept up by the bohemian lifestyle which prevailed throughout much of London society, particularly its more artistic side, of the era. This, perhaps, explains the scarcity of her work during the first fifteen months there, during which she published only one story and one poem. Seeking out the Trowell family while she was there, with whom she had variably studied the 'cello and fallen somewhat in love, she found Arnold in love with another and so embarked on a passionate love affair with his brother, Garnet. She had become pregnant by Garnet by 1909, though his parents considered the relationship beneath both him and them, and so they separated shortly thereafter. Acting on something of a rebound, she hastily married George Bowden, a singing teacher some eleven years her senior. Marrying on 2nd March, she left him that evening before the marriage was consummated. A brief reunion with Garnet followed, after which her mother, Annie Beauchamp, arrived in London in 1909. Blaming the breakdown of her marriage to Bowden on the relationship between her and Bendall, Annie had her daughter quickly sent to the spa town of Bad Wörishofen in Bavaria, Germany. Upon arrival she attempted, innocuously, to lift her suitcase atop a cupboard, an action which resulted in a miscarriage. Although it is not clear whether Annie know of this miscarriage, Mansfield left Germany shortly thereafter and was left out of her mother's will.

This time in Bavaria had a significant and lasting effect on her approach to literate, both reading and writing. Having been introduced to the works of Anton Chekhov, she returned to London in January 1910 and saw over a dozen of her works published in A.R. Orage's socialist magazine and highly regarded intellectual journal, The New Age. Orage lived with Beatrice Hastings, the writer, poet and critic, and during this period she and Mansfield became lovers. Her first published collection, In a German Pension, was inspired by her time there and was well-received by a variety of literary critics, both for its literary excellence and for its negative, comical portrayal of the Germans. Later, though, she would describe the work as "immature". Of this collection, the most successful story was Frau Brechenmacher Attends a Wedding. Though the volume itself sold relatively poorly, one of the stories she submitted to the magazine 'Rhythm' garnered the attention of its editor, John Middleton Murray, though he requested something darker instead. In response to his demand, she wrote The Woman at the Stone, which was subsequently published.

By 1911, she and Murray were in a relationship, though it started rockily; she left him twice between 1911 and 1913. Part of the stress which caused this was brought about when the magazine's publisher absconded to Europe and Murray had to pick up the magazine's debts. Though Mansfield pledged the allowance she received from her father towards the magazine, it lasted only three more issues before it was discontinued in 1913. Mansfield's ill-health at this time encouraged her and Murray, induced by their friend Gilbert Cannan, to rend a cottage by his windmill in Cholesbury in Buckinghamshire. It has been suggested that she was suffering from gonorrhoea by this time, although there is little real evidence of this. They stayed here for a year before moving to Pais in January 1914, hoping that a new environment would boost their creativity. She managed only one story during her time there, Something Childish But Very Natural, before the bank called for Murray to return to London and formally declare the bankruptcy with which he had been crippled by the magazine debt. Mansfield proceeded to have a brief affair with the French writer Francis Carco, visiting in Paris in February 1915. She would later retell this in An Indiscreet Journey.

Her brother, Leslie Heron Beauchamp, died as a New Zealand soldier while fighting the first world war in France. Shocked and traumatised by the unexpected news, she began to take refuge in nostalgia for her childhood, a reminiscing about early memories which found itself manifested in her writing. In a poem she wrote shortly after his death, she describes a dream, writing

> By the remembered stream my brother stands
> Waiting for me with berries in his hands [...]
> 'These are my body. Sister, take and eat.'

The shock of the experience proved the boost to her creative which she had sought in moving to France, and she now entered her most prolific period of writing, becoming intensely aware of her own mortality as she witnessed the war unfold around her. She and Murray reconciled and their relationship duly improved, though the friendship they had forged with D.H. Lawrence and his wife Frieda von Richthofen in 1913 was deteriorating, and the two couples fell out in 1916. Following this, Mansfield endeavoured to broaden her literary connections and made acquaintance with, among others, Virginia Woolf, T.S. Eliot, Lytton Strachey and Bertrand Russell. She and Murray separated again in 1917, though he continued to visit her in her new apartment. Her networking paid off as Woolf and her publisher husband, Leonard, who had recently established Hogarth Press, approached her for a story and Mansfield offered Prelude, which she had begun in 1915. Its lack of external plot and claustrophobic attention towards a small family of New Zealanders moving home opened it up for critical criticism on publication in 1918, though it would endure this initially hostile welcome to become one of her more celebrated stories.

December 1917 saw her diagnosed with tuberculosis and, having briefly considered the idea of entering a sanatorium but rejected it in order that her writing would not be stifled, she resolved to move abroad to Europe in order to avoid the harsh British winter. Settling on Bandol, in France, she stayed at a near-deserted and cold hotel, which left her depressed. While there she wrote Je ne parle pas français, one of her darkest works and considered to be inspired at least in part by Fyodor Dostoevsky's Notes from the Underground, casting Murray in a pale, negative light. Meanwhile, she collected her second set of stories and titled it Bliss, named after one of its stories which had been published in 1918, the collection being published in 1920. Her divorce from Bowden now completed, she married Murray in April 1918. Their turbulent relationship prevailed, for they parted two weeks later, only to reunite shortly thereafter. In March 1919 Murray took the post of editor of Athenaeum, a weekly journal with a prestigious reputation. She stayed in San Remo for the winter of 1918-19, and during this time she felt strain on her relationship with Murray again, which caused him to visit her over Christmas. Despite this their relationship continued to be fraught, though his journeying to visit her inspired The Man Without a Temperament, a story about a wife in ill-health and a patient husband. This story has been called a turning-point in her writing, after which she was able to express "a new objectivity that gives the story a universal dimension". Concurrently, Bliss was met with critical acclaim, while the equally praised volume The Garden Party followed in 1922.

Mansfield focused the final years of her life seeking ever-less orthodox cures for her Tuberculosis, including the 'revolutionary' practice of the Russian physician Ivan Manoukhim, a treatment which involved a bombardment of x-rays of her spleen, causing only heat flashes and numbness in her legs. Encouraged by the inevitability of her death to explore spirituality, she endeavoured to atone for the rebellion of her earlier years. She became a resident of Georges Gurdieff's Institute for the Harmonious Development of Man in Fontainbleau, France, in 1922, where she was cared for by

Olgivanna Lazovitch Hinzenburg and later Mrs Frank Lloyd Wright. This care served only to delay the massive pulmonary haemorrhage she suffered on 9th January 1923, having run up a flight of stairs to show Murray how much better she was feeling. Murray then undertook to publish the works she had completed during these final years, resulting in two volumes of short stories, The Dove's Nest (1923) and Something Childish (1924), a collection entitled Poems, The Aloe, a compendium of her critical writing entitled Novels and Novelists and various letters and journals. Considered one of the best short story writers of her period, the excitement, drama and darkness of her life found itself manifested in her work.

Collections
In a German Pension (1911)
Bliss: and Other Stories (1920)
The Garden Party: and Other Stories (1922)
The Doves' Nest: and Other Stories (1923)
The Montana Stories (1923)
Poems (1923)
Childish (1924) published in the US as The Little Girl
The Journal of Katherine Mansfield (1927, 1954)
The Letters of Katherine Mansfield (2 vols., 1928–29)
The Aloe (1930)
Novels and Novelists (1930)
The Short Stories of Katherine Mansfield (1937)
The Scrapbook of Katherine Mansfield (1939)
The Collected Stories of Katherine Mansfield (1945, 1974)
Letters to John Middleton Murry, 1913–1922 (1951)

Short Stories
The Tiredness of Rosabel (1908)
Germans at Meat (1911 from in a German Pension)
A Birthday (1911 from in a German Pension)
A Blaze (1911 from in a German Pension)
The Woman at the Store (1912)
How Pearl Button Was Kidnapped (1912)
Millie (1913)
Something Childish But Very Natural (1914)
The Little Governess (1915)
Pictures (1917)
Feuille d'Album (1917)
A Dill Pickle (1917)
Je Ne Parle Pas Français (1917)
Prelude (1918)
A Suburban Fairy Tale (1919)
An Indiscreet Journey (1920)
Bliss (1920)
Miss Brill (1920)
Psychology (1920)
Revelations (1920)
Sun and Moon (1920)

The Wind Blows (1920)
Mr Reginald Peacock's Day (1920)
Marriage à la Mode (1921)
The Voyage (1921)
Her First Ball (1921)
Mr and Mrs Dove (1921)
Life of Ma Parker (1921)
The Daughters of the Late Colonel (1921)
The Little Girl (1912)
The Stranger (1921)
The Man Without a Temperament (1921)
At The Bay (1922)
The Fly (1922)
The Garden Party (1922)
A Cup of Tea (1922)
The Doll's House (1922)
A Married Man's Story (1923)
The Canary (1923)
The Singing Lesson
An Ideal Family
Sixpence
The Apple-Tree

www.ingramcontent.com/pod-product-compliance
Lightning Source LLC
Chambersburg PA
CBHW072228190626
46809CB00017B/1515

* 9 781783 942213 *